HEART OF STONE

NAMESAKE CHRONICLES: BOOK 1

By Rachel Marie Lang

"Heart of Stone: Namesake Chronicles, Book One"
Author: Rachel Marie Lang
Publisher: Rachel Lang Books
ISBN # 978-0-9920773-1-0
@ Copyright 2013

I would like to thank these people,
without them this book would never have got this far.

To my parents, Jim and Wendy, for encouraging me
and finding ways to make things happen.

To my brother Andrew,
for inspiring me and believing in me,
and drawing the map.

To my sister and brother, Sara and David,
for giving me tips and insight.

To my grandparents,
for supporting and believing in me.

To my dear friends,
for giving me ideas and getting excited with me.

Thank you all for everything.

Signed Rachel Lang
September 6, 2013 Orillia, Ontario

Heart of Stone

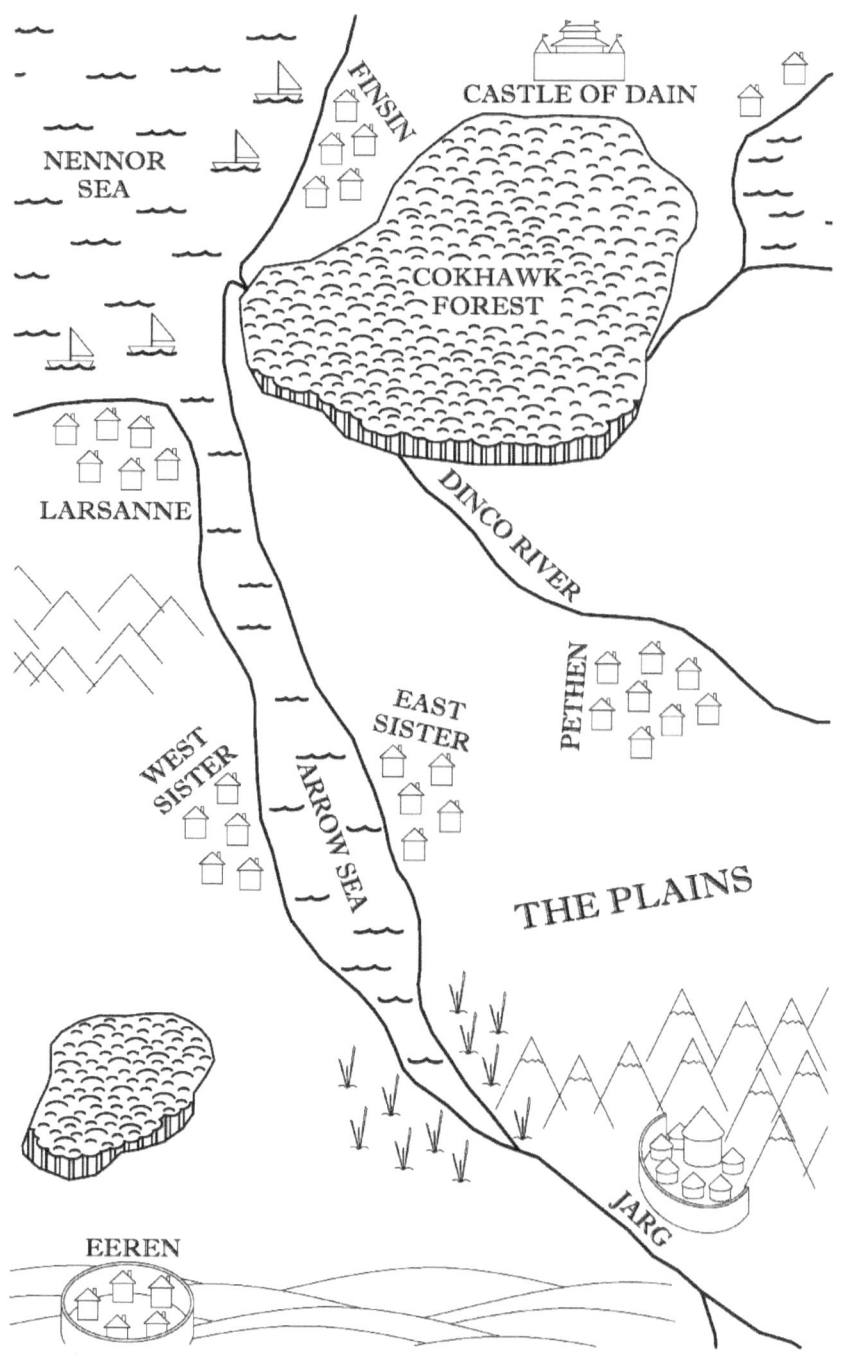

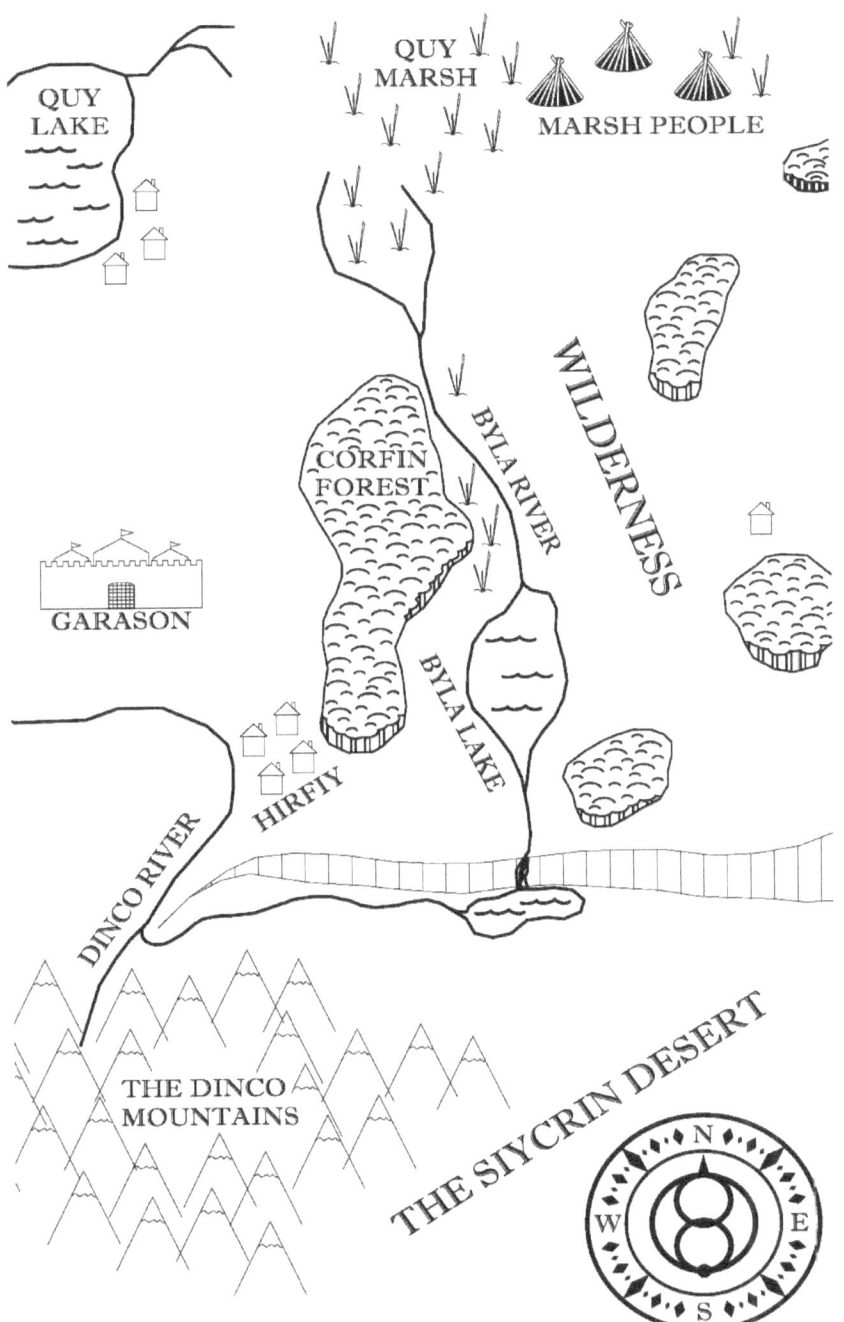

Chapter 1

Freedom

No one knows…no one need know.

No one will find out… No, this secret is safe. But if that were true, then why was Ree so nervous? She looked over her shoulder, but all was dark on the path behind her; nothing but the shadows - dark shadows that filled the spaces in between the tall pine trees and fern bushes. The cry of a Cokhawk split the night air. Ree jumped. Her heart beat like a drum, but she tried to calm herself. She looked ahead. Although she couldn't see it, she knew that the path would turn just ahead; and then it would just be a few more minutes and she would be home. The night would conceal what she had done, she thought to herself. The water from the stone well would wash away the evidence. The blood on her knife would not betray her. She turned the corner and there in the shadows she knew her cottage sat. She washed up as fast as she could, then she slipped into the cottage taking care not to wake her mother. She left the shadows of the Cokhawk Forest behind her, to sleep until morning light.

Freedom… at birth she was given the Namesake of Freedom, and Ree had always liked her Namesake. As a child she had decided that she would always be free. Free from what others thought she should be like. Free from what they thought she should do. Yes freedom would always be hers.

'FREEDOM!' she could still hear the way Gra had shrieked her Namesake the night before. But she would be free from his dying scream, just as she was finally free from him… Ree awoke the next morn surprisingly rested and calm. After dressing in a comfortable dress she made her way down the narrow, steep stairs from her attic room, smoothing down her short black hair as she went. Looking up she saw her mother was at the fire, stirring a pot of soup. Her Namesake was Difference. Feren was a tiny person, frail and delicate, she worked as a serf for a lord (as did most everyone in the Cokhawk.) But Feren had worked hard all her life and had literally bought her daughter's freedom several years ago.

Ree had always thought of her mother as a dear old soul, and thought with a smile that she would drop dead if she knew what had happened the night before! But she wouldn't find out.... No one would. Ree spent the rest of the day inside, doing odds and ends like a good forest maiden- it was safer that way. She slept well that night and arose early the following morn. She went into the kitchen alongside her mother to help prepare the morning meal.

Feren looked over at her and asked, "Did you hear about Gra?"

Careful... Ree told herself. Grace and she had been engaged to be married - but that had all ended – rather abruptly - months ago when Gra had shamed her by calling it all off. Her mother must know by now what had happened two nights ago. Careful....

"No..." she replied, munching on a carrot not looking at her.

"He's dead....the neighbors think he was murdered."

Ree did her best to look surprised, hoping it looked natural. Feren looked like she would say something more, but instead went back to kneading the bread. Ree breathed a silent sigh of relief.

The next day was the forest market day, when the forest people from all around would come to buy and sell. To Ree, who had gone alone that day, market day was exciting and busy. But, in all honesty, it was just a forest clearing where neighbors and relatives gathered to buy, sell and trade things that they grew in their own gardens and made in their own homes. They came every Tuesday and Thursday to gossip about what had happened the week before.

But all this slipped Ree's mind, for on this fine Tuesday something was different; there were Tarven soldiers in the market clearing. Although the Cokhawk was a large forest, it was not the whole world; the Cokhawk Forest was in the country of Garatin. Even if she was just a simple forest maiden, Ree knew of the proud Tarven King from over the sea. He had come over the sea with sword and flaming arrow, and a will to conquer the world. It had been some sixty years since Tarva had claimed Garatin for its own. Since then it had been an occupied country. Even still it was strange to see Tarven soldiers in such a remote place as the Cokhawk Forest. Ree felt her chest tighten. Did they know? Everyone knew of Gra's death by now - but did they know about her? She wanted to run! She had to get away! They knew.

'No stay calm', she told herself. They couldn't know…they didn't. She made herself pay attention to the stand in front of her. It had a display of woven towels, but all the same she felt sweat trickle down her spine. She couldn't help it, and she glanced up; two of the soldiers were talking to a man a couple stands away. Just then, the man shrugged and pointed right at her! She spun round, a wild look in her eye, only to come face to face with another soldier! She shoved past him and ran. Ree saw faces loom up in front of her, heard someone ordering her to stop. It all turned into a wild panic before her eyes. She knocked over tables and jumped around barrels. But before a chase had really begun she was safe away into the forest.

Ree didn't stop running for a good time, and when she did she had to stop and catch her breath. Then, she continued on to her cottage. The pine needles crunched under foot as she made her way on foot paths through the tall white pines until she stood but a few feet from the clearing where her cottage stood. She caught her breath in a gasp; they had found out where she lived. For there in front of the little thatched roofed and shuttered cottage stood a group of six soldiers and their mounts. Feren stood in the doorway talking to one of them. Ree inched closer but she couldn't hear what was being said. Her mother shook her head and the soldier said something. Her mother nodded and then returned inside closing the door behind her. But the soldiers didn't move. Ree took a short breath; she had to get inside - but how?

A few minutes later, the soldiers all looked up to see someone running through the forest towards them. It looked to be a boy of thirteen, with short black hair, and tunic and pants (typical clothes for a Cokhawken). The youth jumped over a clump of ferns then stopped short before coming out into the sunlight. He dropped down to his knees. Trying hard to catch his breath he managed to point behind him.

"I come from the cottage down the path - the woman you're

looking for - broke in - you must hurry to catch her!" the boy said between gasps of air.

The soldiers looked suspicious for a moment, and then four of them swung up onto their horses and rode away, leaving two soldiers behind. These two looked after them for a moment as they thundered down the path. Then they turned towards the boy with further questions on their lips... But he was gone!

Ree slipped around the back of the little cottage without a noise. For Ree it had been who had sent the soldiers on a wild goose chase; now it was possible to get inside. Having grown up in the forest she knew how to be silent in the underbrush. Once through the back door she went straight up to her attic room. She threw some extra clothes into a traveling bag (she had no saddle bags for she had no horse) and grabbed a hunting bow and some arrows, and her knife. She then went back down the creaky stairs to the pantry to pack previsions.

"Ree what are you doing?" Feren asked when she saw her daughter. But without waiting for an answer she went on to say, "There are soldiers out front looking for you. What am I to think? Why do they want you?" she demanded.

Ree looked up at her for a moment then went back to packing while saying, "I'm leaving, I can't stay here."

"Then it's true..." Feren whispered.

Ree sprang to her feet and shouted, "NO! I DIDN'T DO IT!" She calmed herself down with a deep breath; she then gathered her bags and said, "I'll return in a few months' time." She turned to go when Feren spoke with a broken sob.

"You needn't come back, Freedom."

Ree turned toward her mother and saw tears glisten in her eyes as she said, "Not until it's made right."

Ree could hardly believe her ears; made right? Did her mother expect her to go to prison!? It was in that moment when the very last part of Ree's heart died and turned to stone.

Her face hardened and her eyes went cold. "I won't come back!"

she shouted at Feren. She then spun on her heels and left. As she walked away from her cottage, Ree could hear her mother weeping and she hated her for it! She was so weak!

Just then Feren called out in a broken sob, "SOLDIERS!"

Ree spun round in dismay and surprise. Her mother was stronger than she had ever thought! She then broke into a run and disappeared into the forest, feeling hurt and betrayed.

Fornor was little more than a village without even a keep to protect it. But it was the biggest town that Ree had ever been to. It was a ramshackle collection of pine shacks and dirt streets on the edge of the forest. It would take her three days to get there, but not everything went as planned. On her second night on the run, Ree was sitting by a small fire on the side of the foot path she was on when something happened that would change her life forever.

She looked up as a twig snapped in the shadows - had the soldiers found her!? Much to her relief, a woman stepped out into the firelight. At first Ree thought she was rather old, but when she came closer Ree realized that she was quite young, or was she? It was hard to tell in this light. She was dressed much like Ree herself but with her long brown hair pulled up in a bun.

"May I join you?" the woman asked.

Ree looked around, certain that soldiers would jump out at any moment. But the shadows told nothing, so she nodded and carefully checked to make sure that the knife in her boot was ready. The woman sat down across from her and the flames danced between them. The silence stretched on broken only by the fire crackling. Ree could take it no more.

"What's your Namesake?" she asked.

The woman stared into the fire for a moment before saying,

"My name is An."

Ree looked at her a little confused, her name? But what was her Namesake? Oh well, perhaps this woman was not quite right in the head. "And mine is Ree" she decided to play along.

"No… you will not be free."

Ree looked up at her with a frown. What did this woman mean?! An got up and came around the fire to stand in front of Ree.

She took Ree's hand and said, "You will make a prison for yourself, with your own hands Freedom." She rubbed Rees palm, and then she turned and disappeared into the night. Ree looked after her, stricken. How did this woman know her Namesake? This, Ree did not know, but what she did know, was that An knew! She knew…

Sleep was elusive that night and Ree started out early the next morn. Thinking of the night before and the strange woman, she looked down at her hand. An's touch had sent shivers down Ree's spine. But as she looked at her hand now she got a chill. In the middle of her hand was a black mark - ebony black, darker then the blackest night. It looked like a hole into - nothing! It was a black mark that would not rub off, nor wash off - no matter how hard she tried! Her pace had been swift that day but it took till nightfall before she was looking on the town of Fornor from the forest edge. Dusk was fading and she looked down at her hand again only to find IT had grown…

She feared that it was poison and clenched her wrist in the hope of slowing its spread. As fate would have it an herb man resided there. Ree had heard of him, and went straight to his cottage. It was an old and broken down cottage (even more so than the others.) The only thing that made it different from the others was a sign hanging above the door. It swung on rusty hinges and read "Healer". Ree looked up and down the muddy street. It was only lit by one small lamp further down the street. She let go of her infected hand only long enough to knock on the door under the sign. It creaked open showing an old, weather worn gray face.

"I'm looking for the herb man who calls himself Healer."

"I am he, but please, call me Ler", he replied with a pleasant enough smile. Then he beckoned her inside and closed the door. There were no interior walls and it was small and dimly lit inside. In the far corner was a sunken bed with a window with closed shutters above it and there were book shelves with dusty old volumes. But what drew the eye was a table along the wall covered with candles, parchment, boxes, jars, and bottles.

The herb man was old (no one knew just how old.) He was short and shuffled more than walked. He had the vague look of someone who was not quite honest all the time. He sat down at the table and bid Ree to do the same. She reluctantly showed him her hand. Ler looked at it closely and he poked and pinched it. He then put some kind of oil on it from a blue bottle. Ree relaxed and leaned back in her chair. She closed her eyes. Everything would be all right and Ler would make it go away.

She was startled when Ler suddenly pushed back his chair, grabbed a stack of books from the table and without a word, shuffled across the room to a bookshelf.

"I'm sorry, I cannot help you," he mumbled.

Frowning, Ree got up and walked over to him. Grabbing his arm she turned him towards her. His stack of books fell with a thud.

"What do you mean?" she demanded.

He flinched at her touch. She was surprised at his reaction but looking down she understood. She had grabbed him with her infected hand. She let go uncertain; what was happening to her!?

"There is no cure for this," he mumbled again avoiding her intense gaze.

"Then…. You know what it is?"

"No I…." it was clear he was lying.

Ree narrowed her eyes and grabbed his arm with her other hand. This time, with a tighter grip, she could feel his thin arm beneath her grasp - he winced.

"It's a….. Heart stain!" he confessed, " a black magic of old that has been long forgotten… I once treated a man who suffered from it…. Long ago…"

Ree was starting to get scared. "What will it do?" she asked.

"Nothing… it will just spread." There was a silence as though Ler was uncertain if he should say this next part. But a hard glitter came into his eyes and he looked up into Ree's face as he said, "The man I treated… had murdered someone."

She fell back from him, terrified. 'No, this can't be!' she thought in desperation. He looked at her as if he KNEW! She then screamed at him, "I've murdered no one!!" She grabbed her bags and fled. She ran down the street in the dark. How many others knew of this - this heart stain? She glanced up at closed shutters with the glow of lights shining from behind them. They would know! They would find out! She made her way as fast as she could to the nearest inn. She looked down at it - it had grown and now was curling around to the back of her hand…

She was running, running away from the darkness; But she could not get away from it… there was a voice, it was Gra… 'You're not who I thought you were…' there was more to what he said, but she ran away from it. She didn't want to hear it again! The darkness was all around! She could not get away from it! They would know. They would all find out - but she would cover it up! Freedom would still be hers!

Ree awoke in a cold sweat and looked about the dark, unfamiliar room that she had rented only a few hours ago. "Just a dream" she breathed, just a dream… The stain had now covered her whole hand in a blackness that would never go away. Why was this happening to her!? A black magic of old- why her? She bit her lip as a fear took her, but it gave way to anger; this had all started with An! (What was her Namesake?) An had done something to her. What had she said? 'You will not be free… you will make a prison for yourself.' Yes this was all An's fault!

But it didn't matter! Ree would cover it; this dark stain would not betray her. The next morning she went to the market and bought some white silk. Concealed in her room at the inn she then put her seamstress skills to work and made for herself a cloak. The cloak covered her from head to toe, and along with it she made a pair of long white leather gloves. It was perfect; she thought as she slipped it over her head for the first time. No one would see the stain, no matter how much it grew. No one would know… she would have to leave Fornor she thought as she opened up the shutters and looked out of the window. The risk was too great to stay. She would go to the biggest city in the east. She would run, and unlike her dream;

she would get away from this darkness. She would lose herself and hide in the city of Garason.

Chapter 2

Wilderness

The wind ran across the fields, skipped down the rivers, danced in the grass and whispered among the scattered trees. Then finally, it gently blew on Wilder's face. 'This is home...' he thought to himself. He looked over the vast land called the Byla Wilderness, and knew in his heart that he would never leave this place... Things had changed indeed from the old days. Dark days they were, until he had met Eam... He smiled gently as he remembered her. It had been a hesitant love at first- but it turned into something sure and strong. He was from a rich family. So when he asked, Eam's family had given their permission for them to marry. They found love but little happiness. Although they lived as Tarvens they both had Garatin blood, and they found the life of a Tarven mundane and pointless.

They became curious and longed to know more about their Garatin ancestors. For as long as birds have made nests, the nation of Garatin had put all their pride, strength and confidence into one being: they had given him the name of Eloi. They believed him greater than any. He was from ancient times, even though some thought him a mere myth. Wilder and Eam were desperate, and so they embraced this legend of old and became believers in Eloi.

After they had dedicated themselves to Eloi nothing was the same again. They saw everything differently! They saw their family's differently, their culture, and their very lives. Their transformation was so complete that they decided to leave their home in the city of Garason. Everyone they knew was against it- but they could not be dissuaded. They disappeared from the west lands into the far east of the Byla Wilderness.

Yes, Wilderness and Dream had disappeared into the wilderness, for those were their Namesake's. It had not been easy to carve a living out of the rough land, but they had been determined that it would work and so it had! Theirs was a lovely home indeed. Then, they had had a daughter; and they gave her the Namesake of Destination.

Copper colored hair would float behind her as she carelessly ran through the tall grass of their home. They had never been happier! Desti was their pride and joy, even more so when they realized that Eam could not seem to have another child. If they had still lived in the west lands it would have been a disgrace not to have a son. But here in their domain, life was perfect. For seven years they lived as though in a dream, a dream in which life was fair and Eloi was kind to them. But all things must have an end…

When Desti was seven years old, she and her mother fell ill with a fever. Wilder had never felt so helpless before in his life! What could he do? He was no herb man! He had no understanding of medicine, or of illnesses, and there was no herb man in all of the Byla! Desti was worse than Eam, indeed she was burning up with a fever. What are a mother and father to do when faced with the death of their only child? There are no words for the pain they endured.

For many a night Wilder and Eam braced themselves for their last farewells to their daughter. It did not seem possible that they could lose their little girl. And indeed it was Eam who succumbed to the fever in the end. One dark night Wilder held his wife in his arms one last time. He promised her that Desti would get better and that he would make sure that she was always happy. Eam died soon thereafter, with his name on her lips.

As if the death of her mother had taken all hope with her, Desti grew worse in the following days. Wilder would have gladly died with his wife and daughter. But as though Eloi had changed his mind at the last minute, Desti recovered. But it was too late for Wilder, he had lost all interest in living- even if Desti lived how could he go on without his Eam? He blamed Eloi for what happened, and his bitterness was strong: wasn't Eloi supposed to take care of him and those he loved? But in the years that followed, as he watched Desti grow he felt a desire to live on, and slowly his bitterness turned to sorrow. Slowly he learned to trust Eloi again. Meanwhile, little Desti grew to be the spitting image of Eam. At eighteen she was a beautiful young maiden, full of blissful happiness.

All these things faded from Wilder's mind, for he had caught sight of someone as he looked over the land that had been his home for over eighteen years. He watched as a horse and rider approached over the gentle hills. He watched for a half hour as the man rode slowly towards him. 'Who was this man?' he wondered; it was not often one got visitors out here!

Wilder had no fear of this stranger. He had his weapons with him and Desti was safe back at the main cottage. But when the rider came up over a little hill, it turned out to be the last person Wilder ever thought to see again; it was Courage. It was as though the man came riding up out of the past. Memories stirred in Wilder's mind, things that he thought he had forgotten long ago, perhaps things best left forgotten. What was Courage doing here!?

Rage came up in front of him and nodded. "Wilder," he said in a low voice and then he dismounted his black stallion.

"Rage..." Wilder returned the greeting as he looked the other man in the eye; he was having a hard time believing it really was Rage.

They looked at each other with stern faces... then both broke into smiles and embraced. "It's been a long time, Wilder!"

"Yes, indeed it has," Wilder said looking at his old friend; it had been twenty years at least! Yet time had not done much to Rage, other than a bit of gray in his otherwise short black hair and beard. Rage had hardly changed and his dark skin looked healthier than ever. They began to walk together towards the main thatched roofed cottage (it was built of logs-which was impressive in itself since there were not many trees about!) Courage's horse followed along behind them with his reins trailing along in the packed dirt.

"So this is where you've been hiding all these years!" Rage said with a laugh as he looked about at the different out buildings. Then he added more seriously, "How is your wife?"

Wilder stopped in his tracks and looked at his friend.

"She died," he paused, "eleven years ago."

"I'm sorry..." Rage managed, he then looked away feeling quite shocked at this news.

Just than Desti came out from the front door of the cottage, Wilder pulled himself together with a deep breath.

"Rage this is my daughter, Destination. Desti this is Courage, an old friend," he said waving a hand towards Desti; she looked at Rage with open curiosity.

"You're the spitting image of your mother," Rage said with a smile.

"Thank you," Desti breathed in surprise as the two men passed by her; she then followed them inside. She quietly arranged some fresh pastries on a platter for her father and his visitor.

"Tell me," Wilder began as the two of them sat at a scarred table, "what news from the west?" He could tell that his old friend found the simple surroundings uncomfortable.

"Oh, you know, that fool Dain still rules in the north," Rage said taking his eyes from the room they sat in that (to him) looked more like a servant's room.

"Dain? Who is he?" Wilder asked.

"Oh you remember him; the so called King Ordained, whose father was practically banished to rule in the north many years ago," Wilder nodded as he remembered.

"The fool has declared himself a full blooded Garatin!" Rage said with a snort.

"You can't be serious Rage! He comes from the Vinan Mountains, does he not? He married into the Garatin crown."

"Yes that's right, but he's king and he'll do as he likes. You know some are saying that he's gone mad."

"I could have told you that even before we left Garason!" Wilder said with a chuckle.

"Indeed, the only way he's tolerated is because he'll do anything to please the Tarven government! Although we Tarvens could use a bit more of that now a days," he looked at his friend hard.

Wilder sighed, "Must we always be arguing about that?"

"Only because you disagree with me." There was a moment of strained silence as they looked at each other, then they both broke out laughing. "But really Wilder-," Rage said catching his breath- "have you changed your political thinking at all?" he asked with a hopeful air.

"You know where I stand, Rage," Wilder said with reluctance. "My father was a Tarven and my mother was a Garatin..."

Rage cut in sharply, "Yes I know, you don't stand! You sit quite comfortably on the fence; you are neither for nor against Tarven occupation. After you married Eam you (how do you say?) gave over to this Garatin myth, a complete and total waste if you ask me, but that's just it isn't it? You didn't ask me!" He had to stop so as to catch his breath.

Wilder spoke with a calm and collected air, "What can I say old friend? I've changed." There was a silence as Wilder waited for Rage to calm down, then he spoke again, "But you didn't come all this way just to argue with me. Why have you come?"

"Well I..." Rage stopped and looked over at Desti who had been making herself busy with the fire.

Wilder spoke to his daughter, "Desti, would you go and see to Rage's horse? Thank you dear."

Desti went to the door and looked back with curiosity then left.

"So... she doesn't know?" Rage asked in a low voice.

"There's no need for her to know, that's all behind me now."

Rage toke a deep breath, "That's why I've come, Wilder."

Wilder looked at him with a wary eye.

"There is a man, I think his Namesake is Deliverance, he's a Garatin and like you, he's given over to Eloi. He's stirring up trouble with the people, raising that old belief that a man will rise up and drive the Tarvens out of the east completely. A typical rebel of the worst kind, he believes that Eloi will become mortal and set Garatin free."

Wilder looked at him with renewed interest, "That is a man to reckon with!"

"That's what the Tarven General thinks. He has asked me to... take care of him. And you're the only man that I know I can trust to do that job."

Wilder stood to his feet abruptly, going to the fire he leaned against the mantel. "I left that line of work nineteen years ago, Rage," he whispered fiercely then turned about to face him. "You can't ask me to go back!"

"But I have to Wilder!" Rage said to match his friend's voice.

"Recently I have lost two of the best men I had! You're the only man I know who can do this!"

"I can't! No man can claim to be given over to Eloi, and then kill someone!"

Rage took a settling breath, "Listen, Wilder," he said with passion in a low voice. "This must be done! If this man isn't stopped, then we believe a revolution will break out! Thousands of innocent people will die! Wilder, I know what you think, but Tarva has kept peace in Garatin for over sixty years, that peace is at risk! You! You can save it! I know that you love your country Wilder, but no amount of love will be able to save it."

There was silence for a long time.

Rage stood up and said, "Some assassinations are necessary. I must return to Garason. If you have not come by the new moon, I will look for someone else to do the job," he ended softly looking at his friend.

Desti was just finishing up with the visitor's horse; she looked at the cottage, the shutters were all half closed and she could not see inside. Who was this man? And what were they talking about that her father didn't want her to hear? 'Oh well,' she thought, he would tell her about it all later; there were no secrets between her and her father.

Just then Rage came outside and walked up to his horse, "Thank you for the trouble, but I must be leaving now," he said heavily.

She nodded and gave him the reins, then went to stand by her father who had stepped outside. He put his arm around her shoulders. Rage saddled and mounted up, and then turned to face them.

"Should I look for you in Garason?" he asked.

"Perhaps…" Wilder replied thoughtfully.

Rage looked at him and smiled, despite all their differences they were still friends. "Farewell then, Wilderness," he said softly.

"Farewell Courage."

Then Desti and her father watched as Rage rode away towards the west lands. Desti looked up at her father and was surprised to see that he almost looked sad.

"Who is he, father?" she asked.

"An old friend," he said without taking his eyes from Courage.

"A Tarven?" she pressed for more.

"Yes…" he answered elusively then turned and went back inside. Desti looked on at this 'old friend' of her fathers. What had he meant by his parting words? 'Should I look for you in Garason?' Her father had never in all her life gone west of the Byla River, why would he do so now? At first she had thought that her father would tell her about this stranger, but now it did not look like he would! She returned inside.

Over the next two weeks, Desti came no closer to finding out about her father's 'old friend.' But it was as if her horizons had been widened just by watching Rage ride into the west. She wanted to know of the lands beyond the Byla River. How big was the city of Garason, how many people lived there, how far away was it? But what she wanted to know most of all was would her father go to Garason? Desti sat in the high grass looking at the sky and pondered these things. The wind blew in her waist length copper colored hair and bent the grass around her.

"Destination?" she heard her father call. She smirked at the irony of her own Namesake, as if she was going anywhere in her life! She wasn't bitter about it, after all she could not have asked for a better life! She loved this place with its fields and rivers…but all the same she could not help but wonder when her life would begin. She just longed for something more. With a soft sigh she got up and went to her father.

Later that night they sat across from each other for dinner at their rough little table. Little did Desti know that things were about to change forever.

"Desti…"Wilder began suddenly, "you'll be nineteen in five months."

Desti looked at him and waited for more. "Yes?" she prodded after a moment.

Wilder looked up at her. "I think," he paused again before continuing, "I think that you're old enough to take care of this place on your own."

Desti was confused, what was he talking about?

"What I mean is, just for a few weeks," he clarified.

Desti narrowed her eyes, "You're going away father?" she stated more then asked. He nodded. 'That's it?' she thought in annoyance. "Where? Why!?" she asked in a rush.

"I'm going to be doing something for a friend."

"Courage?" she knew the answer before she asked. "You're going to Garason... aren't you?"

Wilder sighed and nodded, "Yes, I am."

"What are you going to be doing there?"

"That is something you don't need to know," he said sternly.

Desti knew he wouldn't talk about it anymore, so there was no point in asking further.

"When will you leave?" she asked, poking at her food.

"I'll have to leave soon, to get there for the new moon."

It would take two weeks hard travel to get out of the Byla, and four more days to Garason from there, but Desti didn't know any of this. All she knew was that Garason was far, far from home; away to the west somewhere.

"The cold room is full, so you should be fine; even if you do run out you're good with the bow. Taking care of the animals is about all you need to do. I'll be back in one and a half months."

They finished their dinner in silence. This was all new to Desti, her father had never kept secrets from her before. Or had he? She could not sleep that night; she just lay there thinking about it all. With her father leaving in the morning, she should be excited! All on her own for a whole month! But she wasn't excited. What did it all mean? The next morning Desti watched as her father rode away into the west; she hugged herself as if trying to hold on to the warmth of his last embrace. It was early morning but she could tell that it would be overcast that day.

"What are you hiding from me, father?" she whispered into the wind.

24

Chapter 3

Destination

"I'm not going," Desti firmly said to her horse Willow, "I can't go Will!" her voice turned to a pleading tone. Will blinked, with seemingly no interest. Desti marched over to the cold room with a determined step, to empty the saddle bag she had recently filled. A few minutes later she returned to stand in front of Will (the bag was still full). "Well... he didn't forbid me to go, right?" she asked uncertainly, Will blinked again. "You're right, Willow! I'll never get another chance!" she said as if just realizing it, she then tied down her bag to the saddle. But her sudden burst of inspiration died quickly, for after getting that done she promptly stooped down and undid his girth strap. "I should stay here and... and enjoy myself!" she told Willow, as if he were arguing with her.

A look of stubbornness came back to her face and without a second thought she swung up onto Willow. At least she tried, but the girth strap was still undone, so the saddle slipped off and landed in her lap as she hit the ground. Will side-stepped away from her. Desti sighed as she stood up and secured the saddle back onto Willow's back. Then she turned on her heels and marched over to the main cottage, muttering something about "I'm going inside and I'm not coming back out again!" But Will only snorted at her declaration.

It was only a few minutes later when she returned with another bag in her hand. She fastened it onto the saddle and then mounted up. But no sooner was she in the saddle then she glanced back over her shoulder, "It's not too late to turn back," she told herself, "not yet..." The wind picked up and whipped her hair around; it was blowing into the west as though pushing her onwards.

Desti turned her face from her home and looked towards the west. She would come within a few miles of their only neighbors so she would leave a note in a sack on a tree asking them to care for the animals; hopefully they would pass by that way soon. She would then follow her father closely, only making herself known to him after they crossed over the Byla River. By then they would be too far for him to turn her back; he would have to take her with him to Garason! Will snorted again; his mistress was acting a little strange this morning.

*   *   *

Ree pulled off her white leather glove finger by finger. The light was shining off of her white silk cloak making it shimmer. But she did not notice; she was looking intently at IT. She pushed her sleeve up; the stain now went up past her elbow, and was beginning to infect her right hand as well. There seemed to be no stopping its spread. Stone faced she moved to put her glove back on, when the light on her sleeve caught her eye. But-no, this couldn't be! But it was. Her white silk cloak shimmered black… No, no! She wanted to scream! She was seeing things, and that was all. She put her glove back on. No one knows… she reminded herself.

But it was a lie and she knew it! How many people knew, she wondered. "There is my mother-I mean Feren," Ree went over all the people who knew, "The Tarven soldiers, just about everyone in the forest by now, Ler and whoever else that he has told, and then there's An." An was the one who had made the stain start; it was her fault.

She looked out of her window at the narrow street below; upon arriving in the city of Garason she had found a landlord who had an empty room at his inn- it was a crumby old place with holes in the thatched roof and rats in the cellar. But, it was all she could afford. At first she had felt small and alone in this big city, but now she felt quite at home here! She was even finding odd jobs to do here and there as a seamstress to pay for the rent. But as comfortable as she might be, she could not help but feel anxious and look over her shoulder every so often; had that man recognized her? Was that soldier following her? Did that woman know about her? There was no escape… not from her fear. She took a deep breath.

*   *   *

For the first nine days that Desti traveled, she was able to see the smoke from her father's nightly fire. But she had been too scared that he would see the smoke from her own fire so she went without (which gets quite tiresome and cold after nine days). But on the tenth morning she over slept, and as a result could not see the smoke from her father's fire that night. It took her five more days to come in view of the Byla River.

Tired and worn out she was hoping against hope that she would be able to see her father on the further shore. But when Willow crested the top of a little rise overlooking the river an entire world opened up before her-one that she had never known even existed. It took her breath away as she sat there. The river stretched out both north and south until it disappeared into a haze, and beyond the river was the Corfin Forest dark and entangled. Beyond that? Desti had not a clue. But to her disappointment; her father was nowhere in sight...

"I'm lost..." the words were out of her mouth before she knew it. Will snorted (not for the last time) as if to say 'What else is new?' Desti took a deep breath, and then nudged Will down the hill towards the river.

The crossing of which, was truly a disastrous affair; both Desti and Will got terribly wet on the way over. By ill luck or perhaps unfair fate, the further shore was more or less a swamp. Desti discovered this when she tried to climb up onto the bank. She was almost knee deep in mud before she knew it! But there was nothing for it, so she pulled at Willow's reins and stretched her neck trying to see over the bulrushes. Her dress became dreadfully dirty, and Will was making it quite clear that he was not enjoying himself.

Looking down to where she was about to step Desti jumped backwards and screamed at what she saw; there was an Idrcoon at her feet. Idrcoons are strange creatures to be sure; they live in the Quy Marsh and surrounding area. They resemble raccoons, but instead have webbed toes, and both their floppy ears are covered with long greasy hair, which catches flies and various bugs in much the same way a spider web does. Desti had had these creatures described to her before by her father but she had never seen one before, and they are not incredibly nice to look at. So who can blame her for screaming? And it was hardly Willow's fault that he was spooked by her scream and made a run for it, yanking the reins from Desti's hand and causing her to fall face down into the mud. Needless to say, when they finally got to dry ground again they were wet, cold and grumpy, understandably so. As if to make it more miserable, the sun was setting. Grumpy hardly describes how Desti was feeling that night, but to her credit she did do her best to wash off Will.

After eating a meal of rabbit stew, and finding out that even if she could catch rabbits- her stews were no good, she lay down beside her small fire and wondered if there were any more Idrcoons around. Her dress and cloak were stiff with mud but her eyes were heavy and she fell asleep soon thereafter on the cold hard ground. It took her all the next morning to wash up in the River, but at last she was back in the saddle, and a new problem presented itself; where was she to go from here?

The Corfin Forest loomed up in front her like a monster waiting for dinner... what way had her father gone? She did not know of the lands that lay south of where she was, but she did know that to the north was the Quy Marsh. Just thinking of running into another Idrcoon made her shudder! And there was no way she would go into that dark forest! Her reasoning may have been foolish but she went south and followed the River until noon. It was then that she came upon a lake; she decided that it must be Byla Lake.

She sat there looking at the forest, thinking about how tiresome this whole thing was becoming when she spoke, "Will, would you say that that Forest has thinned out?" Will stomped his hoof in reply. The forest had in fact thinned out and when they got closer to it they found a foot trail. Desti was feeling quite brave, (or impatient as the case may be.) she decided to go through the forest, seeing as how there seemed to be no end to the forest to the north.

She really had no idea just how lucky she was that she made it through to the other side; for that stretch of the Corfin Forest was notorious for slave traders and highway men. But she did make it through without incident; it took four hours before she found herself on the west side of the Corfin. From where she sat on top of a little rise, she could see a town in the distance. She sighed in relief, "Look, Will; It's Garason!" In two more awfully long hours she reached it.

The town had no walls or keep, it began with farms on the outskirts and then turned into crooked cobbled streets sided by little cottages with shuttered windows and sunken roofs; to Desti's eyes it was huge! But, it was not Garason; it was the town of Hirfly. She was told so by a group of merchants in the town square. They would be traveling to Garason on the morrow, and they agreed to allow her to come along. It would take two more days to reach the city, but she comforted herself in thinking, 'I'll be able to find father once we get there, Garason can't be that big!'

The night that Desti spent on the road to the city was the night after the new moon, and the night that Wilder arrived in Garason. He was stopped at the gates by a Tarven soldier for breaking curfew, but luckily Wilder had brought with him his old Tarven credentials. The soldier looked embarrassed and quickly wished him on his way. The darkness shadowed the great city of old and hid him as he quietly rode through the still streets. He felt like he was a phantom from the past, one who had no right to visit again. Faces and voices came up and rode beside him, then they would vanish into the night; memories of the past that seemed as foreign to him as he was to this city. 'What am I doing here?' he wondered to himself. The manor of Courage was just as Wilder remembered; tall stone ramparts surrounding a courtyard, complete with a stable, a private black smith, an armory and many out buildings. The manor itself was huge! But nothing more than any other Tarven lived in. Grand stone walls and marble pillars, thick window panes with swirls of color, double oak doorways with brass hinges led to many a chamber, with more than one secret passageway hidden in that labyrinth. Of this, Wilder had no doubt!

With his horse being taken care of by a stable boy, Wilder entered the grand manor and was led by a servant to the library. The doors opened and a large fire lit room opened up. Every wall was covered with bookshelves, and behind a huge desk sat Rage.

"Wilder!" he said standing in surprise. A smile spread across his face when he said, "I did not think you'd come.

"His Namesake is Deliverance," Rage wasted no time in filling Wilder in on his assignment, "He is known as Liveran. He is a street teacher by profession and a busybody by habit. He started teaching in the Quy Lake region, where he lives, about five months ago, but right now he is in the city."

"What does he teach?" Wilder asked.

"That Eloi will come and live among man."

"Why do the Tarven officials care about that? They have no interest in Eloi."

"No we don't," Rage stated flatly, "In fact, we couldn't care less what personal beliefs the people have. But it has gone too far! The people are beginning to believe that this Eloi-man will liberate the whole country from Tarven rule!"

"A war…" Wilder said softly.

"Yes, exactly, and worse yet, there are rumors that the people believe Liveran is this man!"

"I see," Wilder spoke thoughtfully, "And Tarva can't touch him because he has become too popular with the people. But why have the Garatin leaders let him be? We have strict laws about those sorts of things. Claiming to be Eloi is no laughing matter!"

"That's the problem, no one can touch him! The entire city is head-over-heels for him; if we tried to arrest him we would have a full-fledged rebellion on our hands! And on top of all this, he isn't always within our reach!" Rage was losing his temper.

Wilder spoke, calm as ever, "Well, that makes him either very smart or a mad man."

Rage had always found it amusing that Wilder could always be so calm, 'that's what makes him a good assassin', he thought with a smile. "Precisely, but back to your question; he himself has not claimed to be Eloi. However, about one, no two months ago, right after I left to find you, Liveran was teaching in some tiny little village not far from here. He was saying much the same stuff - that Eloi would come; and my spies tell me that at that moment, Liveran pointed to a man in the crowd and declared it to be him!"

Wilder raised his eyebrows. "And what did this man do?" he asked.

"He went up to Liveran, said something to him. Confounded spies! What use are they if they can't tell me exactly what happened? Then Liveran resumed teaching again."

"Who was this alleged Eloi-man? A known rebel no doubt?"

"That's the strange thing about it, his Namesake is Eternity, he's known as Nity, and he comes from the Quy Lake region; that's about all there IS to know about him. He's a no-one from nowhere!"

"And where is this man now?"

"Back where he lives as far as I know, he disappeared after the incident, ran in fear of his life is my guess. I'm told that he's become a street teacher too, but he's a small fish in this sea. We must keep our attention on Deliverance. He has said some upsetting things lately. He is a reckless and impulsive man; and therefore, dangerous."

A long silence followed.

"So you need him taken care of," Wilder said.

"Yes," Rage replied.

Wilder stood to leave, "I haven't said that I'll take the job," he warned, "but I will look into it."

"That's all I'm asking, Wilderness." Rage stood and then walked Wilder out into the hallway.

"DADDY!" A young voice called out. A girl came running into Rage's arms.

"Mise!" Rage cried as he lifted the girl up. "Why aren't you asleep?" The girl only giggled, her governess stood in the shadows going very red in the face.

"Wilder, this is my daughter Promise." Rage said as he put Mise back on the carpeted floor. Mise was a sweet little girl of eleven, she had black curly, wavy hair and her big cinnamon brown eyes peeked at him from around Rage.

"Good evening, Promise", Wilder said gravely.

"Courage, introduce me to your friend", a woman said as she approached them.

"That's not necessary Loyal, surely you remember Wilderness?"

"And so I do", she said with a smile as she came up to stand by her husband.

Wilder remembered her as well. Loy was a case of classic Tarven beauty; her tanned skin complemented her long wavy black\brown hair and her cinnamon eyes glowed in a long face.

"My lady, it is a pleasure to meet you again", luckily Wilder remembered proper protocol and bowed over her outstretched hand.

"And I you sir; it has been a long time."

Obviously Rage had told his wife about Eam's death, otherwise she would have asked about her, the two of them had been friends. A few minutes later and Wilder was crossing the court yard towards the stables. Oddly enough he was not thinking about Liveran; instead he was thinking about Rage and his happy family. Loy and Rage had been wed the summer before Wilder and his beloved Eam had. But poor Rage and Loy could not have any children, or so it had seemed then. They must have had little Promise some ten years after Wilder had left the west lands. Mise was their only child and that they loved her dearly was quite obvious to Wilder, even if she was only a girl, almost as much as he loved Desti. He shook himself out of his thoughts as he neared the stables. He had to find a place to stay for the night and then in the morning he would find out all he could about Liveran.

*   *   *

The darkness was all around- but Ree did not fear it anymore. It was just so much easier to embrace the darkness than to run from it. The darkness was comforting and securing, as Ree walked down the path that Gra had asked to meet her on, on that terrible night…

"But why?" she had pleaded him.

"Because Ree, you're not who I thought you were."

Ree had stepped back from him, a hurt look on her face. "And what's so different now, from when you loved me?" She would never forget the look on his face as he replied.

"You've turned cold Ree; I don't think you're capable of love anymore."

He had cut her deep, so deep… but not as deep as she would cut him- Ree awoke with a start even before the thought had finished, she took a few breaths to steady herself, "Just another dream", she assured herself; but in truth- the nightmare had just begun. She looked down and was sure that the early morning twilight was playing tricks on her eyes, for it looked as if her cloak had turned black! For a moment she did not believe it, it could not be true!

But as sure as the dawn she realized that it was true; both her ivory cloak and gloves had turned black. More of the dark magic at work. All she wanted was to get out! In a moment of frenzy she tore at the neckline- desperate to get away from it. But it would not tear. Her nails bent over backwards as she tried, but the pain made her stop, she was terrified! Again she clawed at it, 'I must get out!' her mind screamed. The darkness was closing in; she wanted to run! At last in frustration she ripped a glove from her hand- but stopped short when she saw IT. She knelt there in her bed, panting, holding up her stained hand.

No… this cloak was better than the stain that lay beneath. A sob escaped her as she gave up trying to escape and instead covered her face with her stained hands and wept bitter tears.

Later that day Ree came across a man who was teaching in the streets. Many said that he was mad, and Ree was inclined to agree with them. But… there was something about him, something few could describe, he held Ree captive by his words and passion. She could not help but wonder. His namesake was Deliverance…

Wilder stood in a dark corner of the square. Leaning up against a wall, he was an imposing figure to be sure! He wore knee-high boots with baggy pants that he tucked into them and a gray tunic with a long brown vest falling to his knees. It was hard to say if his hair was blond or brown. Inherited from his Garatin mother, wispy and perpetually straight, it fell just above his broad shoulders; he had a long chin and a firm mouth and heavy eyebrows over gray eyes that could be described as sad. His face was finished off with a straight nose. He had left his short sword behind and replaced it with the old weapons of an assassin provided by Rage; there was a brace of throwing knifes strapped to his back and a double bladed knife hidden in his boot. He could feel the knives pressing into his back as he leaned against the wall. All morning he had been struggling with the feelings that came with the weapons that he wore. He felt unstoppable, and dark- and oh so dangerous. He almost wished that he could put the weapons to good use- he wanted to use the power at his fingertips; and that scared him.

He crossed his arms over his chest and put one boot in front of the other. He pushed the thoughts from his mind and looked around the square that Liveran was teaching in. It was filled to overflowing, most of whom were Garatins. Women leaned out of windows and men stood in the doorways of ale houses; some stood on the outskirts, while others sat around Liveran himself, who sat on a barrel.

As Wilder swept the square with his eyes, he made eye contact with a figure all in black, deep in the shadows… a dangerous sort to be sure, Liveran attracted all kinds.

Wilder now saw why the Tarvens were concerned about this man; everyone in the square listened as though in a trance! He spoke with a fire in his words; no one could doubt that he believed what he said. Even the few children standing about paid attention to him. This man was a born leader! People were drawn to him, like flies to an Idrcoon!

And the things he said! Things like: 'Eloi is near to us. Get ready for him, for the true King of Garason will come soon! And he will change everything!' Garatins are touchy about anything to do with Eloi: all it would take was for Liveran to say one thing that the people did not think right and proper about Eloi- and his crowed of admirers would quickly turn into a bloodthirsty mob, anxious to avenge Eloi's good name. Yes, Liveran walked a thin line, but he fervently believed all he said and that's what drew people to him. Yes, Wilder now saw why this man was a threat to the Tarven government in Garason. But, was he a threat to Wilder? Ah, the old conflict within Wilder's heart.

34

As a Garatin given over to Eloi he should rejoice! For the things Liveran said were at the heart of every Garatin; Wilder should in fact join this man! After all they believed the same thing. But as a Tarven, who served his country, he was against Liveran, and it was his duty to do all in his power to stop this mad man! With a Tarven father and a Garatin mother, where did Wilder's loyalty lie? This had been the reason he and Eam had left twenty years ago. There was no simple answer to this. But he must decide now: was Liveran truly given over to Eloi and simply a wishful thinker? Or was he a rebel impostor set on bringing about unnecessary war? Could Wilder really prevent thousands from dying, as Rage said? Could Wilder do this one last job of old and pick up the tools of an assassin one last time?

Chapter 4
Treasure

A few short streets away from the square with the "mad man" teaching in it, was the market square bursting with life on that sunny day, a fine picture of life in the city. There was a Garatin butcher who determined his prices depending on who was buying. There was a blind old woman selling homemade blankets, most made it a sport to see how many items they could steal from her. There were several violinists who competed with one another all day long and a dozen or so boys who made a living off of pick-pocketing. All this and many more things were watched from above on a roof top with bored indifference. The watcher was a young man of perhaps twenty, he himself did not know for sure, for he had never known a father or mother - indeed the streets of Garason had raised him and taught him all he knew. He was a Garatin and his Namesake was Treasure, that's about all he knew about himself. He was a simple street urchin, not unlike many in the market below.

Many people in the city knew Treas, he would do all kinds of work in exchange for food or a place to sleep; there were many people all over the city who owed him some favor or other. But so often, like now, he did not have one coin in his pocket. But then no one could steal from him. And not two sticks to make a fire with. He had always lived this way, it did not bother him. For the past twenty minutes he had been watching a young maiden wander the market below. She had copper colored hair that was wild about her as she looked around at everything with wide eyed wonder; she obviously was lost.

He watched with little interest as she left the market and entered an alley, but he tensed at what he saw. There were two rough looking men in the alley ahead of her; he knew what would happen before it even did happen! One of the men grabbed her and stopped her scream, while the other grabbed her bag and went through it. Treas watched it all in horror. Worst of all, he was the only one who saw it! He jumped to his feet, no longer thinking like himself. He had to do something!

Desti had gone to the market first thing to make some purchases. But the size of the place and all the people disoriented her, and she clean forgot the way she had come. She had been afraid that she wouldn't be able to find her way back to her inn, and now she urgently tried to find the alley she had come in by. But instead of her inn, she found just plain trouble. The two men came at her just too fast and her scream too late. One of the thugs held her from behind and put a big smelly hand over both her mouth and nose- she couldn't breathe! Her mind began to go blank and her vision went blurry.

"Oh Eloi… send help…" she silently pleaded. But despair quickly filled her mind. "No help will come…" but she did not have time to finish the thought for just then something fell and landed on the brute that stood in front of her. The hand over her mouth shifted and she gulped in air. As a result her vision cleared a little and she could see that there was a struggle going on at her feet. Two men rolled about on the cobble stones. The man holding her said an oath under his breath and shifted as if wishing he could join in; Desti could only watch helplessly. The attacker, she noticed, was a much smaller man but seemed to be keeping his own. Then she saw a bright flash; the other man had pulled out a knife! Her rescuer was quick though, and he kicked it from the hand of the other, and then finished him off with a great blow. Next, he then spun round to take on the one who held her, but there was no need for he was more of a coward then the other. He flung Desti at her rescuer and made a run for it. Desti didn't even have time to catch her breath before the other brute (who had been momentarily stunned) was coming to his feet and was madder than a hornet!

Her rescuer stooped to scoop up her bag than grabbed her arm and said, "Come on!" He led her at top speed back out into the busy market, and he did not stop until they were in the middle of the crowd. He then turned to look back. Desti did the same but all she could see was the crowd closing about them.

"Are you all right?" he asked out of breath.

It was the first time that she got a good look at him, and was surprised to see that he was not much older than her. He was a half foot taller than her, had a square jawbone, wonderfully blue eyes and brown hair much like her fathers. He wore simple and worn clothes that were too small for him; he carried no sword, cloak or bag.

"Yes, thank you," she replied breathlessly.

"You're not hurt?" he made sure.

"No - but are you!? I saw a knife!"

"Ah, never touched me," he assured her, and handed back her bag.

She took it as though coming out of a trance, at last she said all at once, "Thank you, so much! You- you could have been hurt and I …" she looked at him in amazement, "I don't even know your Namesake…" If Desti hadn't been so shaken she would have realized how scattered she was and would have seen just how awkward he was feeling.

"Treasure, most call me Treas," he said.

"And I'm Destination, and I truly do owe you something!" she insisted.

"Don't think any more of it, how about I take you to wherever you were going?" he said, glad to change the subject.

"Well I …" Desti said a little confused. "I came to get a few things but I forgot the way back to my inn…" her voice trailed off. She looked around as if the inn would jump out at her.

"I see," Treas said in a way that suggested he didn't. Never the less for the next little while he followed her around as she went to the different stands and shops getting the things she had come for. To help her calm down he began asking her simple questions. "So, do you live in Garason?"

"Oh, no! I live over there," she said absently, pointing eastward.

Treas thought she meant Hirfly.

"And what about you, Where do you live?" she asked, getting her whit's about her again.

"Oh I live here," he answered vaguely.

"I think that's all I need," Desti said a little later, after she had bought a few things. She was still not quite herself.

Treas nodded and said, "The nearest inn is over this way." He pointed to a street.

Desti was more than happy to let Treas lead the way after the morning she just had. She had only arrived late last night and had been blown away by the mere size of the city!

It was foolish on Desti's part to trust a stranger and this time her foolishness caught up with her. Even if Treas had her best interest at heart, he could not stop what happened next. They had not even left the market when a man pointed at Treas and shouted, "Hey! That's the boy what run off with a loaf from my bakery, not two hours ago!" Treas looked at him like a fox caught in the hen house! The man continued to yell; getting the attention of two Tarven soldiers who came on the run! Treas grabbed Desti by the arm and made a dash down a side street. To Desti it all happened too fast! She hardly knew what was happening. Trying to stop and tell Treas that this was none of her business simply wasn't an option! She was too busy running.

"Stupid, stupid, STUPID!" Treas told himself as he ran down another alley, pulling Desti behind him by the hand. But, he could not think about that now. At the end of this alley they would turn right, and because it was still morning, or was it? There would be a ladder up against a wall and they would go along the rooftops for a bit. But wait - there would be women up there doing their wash, so… they would just have to go left up ahead, and risk the open street? No, they would go up on the rooftops. He glanced over his shoulder; Desti was wide eyed but was keeping up.

"Quick! Up the ladder!" he said as they reached it. He looked back down the alley; he could hear the sounds of pursuit. He hurried up after Desti. Both of them ran past washing women and jumped over their baskets. At one point Treas got a face full of blanket and was very nearly clothes lined! How long did it go on for?! Treas had lost track, he was too busy thinking where they would go next, but soon, he stopped thinking about even that! He had known that it was only a matter of time before the soldiers had had enough of him- and now he was paying the price. They were running across another rooftop with the soldiers following below when suddenly he realized; that if they did not get to the other ladder in time; they would be trapped!

Reaching the ladder he skidded to a stop, and slid down, at the bottom he ducked into a nearby door that stood open. Desti came down after him (going painfully slow), but she had not seen where he had gone - she was standing out in the middle of the side street! His heart pounded in his ears; the soldiers would round the corner any moment! He reached out and pulled her in, just as the soldiers came into view! They pressed themselves against the dark wall as the soldiers ran past; safe, at last!

Treas relaxed and noticed that he was holding his hand firmly over Desti's mouth. He removed his hand. He then looked around at their newly found hiding place. It was pitch black, but as his eyes adjusted he could see that they were standing at the top of three steps that lead down to a sunken room. He realized then that it was an abandoned wine cellar. In case the soldiers returned, he and Desti went all the way down into it and there they sat down on the last step breathing hard wishing that their hearts would slow down. The next thing they wished for was a drink of water.

Treas broke the silence by asking, "You all right?" He was still out of breath, and so apparently was she, for she only nodded.

It was some time later when she asked in a whisper, "What time is it?"

Treas ventured up the steps and glanced out the door. All he could see was the wall of the building across from them, it was in shadow. He was hungry, but that did not mean that it was any particular time of day- he was always hungry. He shook his head and went back down the steps.

"Oh!" Desti made a small sound. Treas looked at her, she held up her bag. "I forgot I was still carrying this! Here-" she offered him a hunk of bread.

Treas shook his head. "No, I-" but Desti interrupted, "I insist, you must be as hungry as I am."

Well, he could not argue with that, so he took the bread and thought back to that morning. This was how it all started, just a bit of bread! He had been hungry, he reasoned with himself. What choice had he had? It was either steal or starve! It happened every day in this city- but what a mess he had made this time! He looked over at Desti; she was absently nibbling at her bread. He had never wanted to involve her into all this. Yes, quite stupid! He had stolen some bread that morning and then sat on a roof top to eat it. He had been feeling guilty, and that's why he had jumped to Desti's rescue. Now, she thought of him as a hero; some hero he made! After saving her he had dragged her into this big mess!

And yet… she shared her bread with him; now he felt even worse! All he wanted to do was part from her company as soon as he could get her back to her inn. A half hour later Treas poked his head out of the narrow side street; where were they!? He wondered in confusion as he didn't recognize anything!

The street was quiet and peaceful, there was a man sweeping in his pottery shop, a woman collecting her wash from a roof top, and a man driving a horse and cart down the street. And not a Tarven in sight! Both he and Desti stepped out onto the street.

"Where are we?" Desti asked.

"Ahh…well…" he was a little embarrassed that he didn't know where they were. Without answering they walked up the street a little. At last he saw something familiar, now he knew where they were! But, "Oh no," he said under his breath. They were on the other end of the city from where they started! It would take… two hours to walk back the way they had come! He looked up at the sun; it was three hours past noon. He glanced at Desti, she was exhausted! And besides that it wasn't safe for him to be out and about just yet.

"So, where are we?" Desti asked again.

"A long way from your inn," he replied.

"Oh," she sounded quite dismayed.

Treas thought for a moment, "I know a place where we can rest though, this way."

A few streets over and Treas found what he was looking for; a stable. He had been in there before and knew that there was a hay loft. The only problem was that the only doorway was right beside the front door of the cottage. So they would have to go in through the window of the loft. There was a ladder nearby, Treas pulled it over beneath the window.

"Do you live here?" Desti asked without any note of accusation.

It made Treas stop dead in his tracks, had she not guessed? Didn't she know yet who and what he was?

"Ah, yeah, something like that," he added under his breath as he climbed up the ladder. He was pleased to find that the shutters opened easily. Looking inside he saw that no one was there. "Come on up," he called softly.

A few minutes later and they were both comfortably sitting in the hay. Desti was looking around with a bit of a puzzled expression.

'Oh no!' thought Treas, 'she's going to start asking questions soon!'

"So!" Treas said just as she was opening her mouth, "Where did you say you lived?"

"Oh, I told you, east of here," She replied, completely forgetting her own question.

"You mean Hirfly?"

"Oh no! I live much further east then that! I live beyond the Byla River."

Treasure's eyes nearly popped out of his head! "Oh... that far east," was all he could manage. Desti smiled.

"So why are you here in Garason?" Treas asked.

"Oh, it-it's a long story," she said, looking a little embarrassed.

Treas believed it. He had never met anyone who lived that Far East before! He had never given the Byla Wilderness much thought before, so much so that he did not know what to say! There was silence for a moment. Treas noticed that Desti looked worried about something.

"Say, don't worry about finding your inn again, I can show you the way back on the morrow," he offered.

"Oh thank you, but that's not what I'm worried about."

"What then?" he asked.

She bit her lip, "I-I need to find someone," she admitted.

"Who?" he asked.

"My father," she replied. She then went on to explain about the last two weeks. When she was done Treas nodded as if to say 'you got problems!' Desti must not have noticed for she looked at him in a curious way and asked, "Could you help me find my father?"

Treas almost laughed in her face! It would be like looking for a needle in a haystack. There was a simple answer; No and no! He wasn't about to waste his time looking for someone who may or may not even be in Garason! He just about told Desti all that too, but… she was looking at him with such hopefulness!

"I could try." He regretted it as soon as it came out of his mouth! But there was no turning back now. "Do you know where he was going?" Treas asked with an effort.

"Um…here?" Desti offered.

Yes, Treas regretted this. "But where in Garason?" he tried making himself clearer.

"I …don't know," she said in a little voice.

Treas took a deep breath, "Do you know why he came here?"

"Oh, yes I know that! He came to see a Tarven friend by the Namesake of Courage. Do you know him?" she asked hopefully.

"Well you saw how big the city is!" he almost laughed.

She nodded, suddenly looking weary.

"But don't worry about that now. You look tired, get some sleep."

With sleeping out of doors for two weeks and not nearly enough sleep the night before, Desti was asleep in the hay in less than two minutes. The last thing Treas remembered thinking before falling asleep himself was 'How on earth will I find her father? Some hero I am!'

Chapter 5

Dark and Light

'Where am I? Ahh yes, in the darkness. Deep in the darkness, deep in the black silk, Safe- but not free. No never free again...' She looked up, what was that? Oh yes, the light. Yes she remembered now, the light had been there for some time now. But it stayed away from her, as if waiting for her to go to it. Could she go to it? She wanted too. She wanted to discover what this light was- but... she daren't try! In the light everyone would see, everyone would know. 'I must stay here, safe. I will be safe in the darkness'; in this dark prison she would be safe. No one would find out...

Ree opened her eyes; the dream was familiar to her, the darkness was her constant companion. Freedom, her persistent wish; fear of them finding out, her everlasting plague. What dream? That was her life! The one thing that did not fit was the strange light, where had it come from? What did it all mean? Or did it mean anything? Ree sat up and looked around the dingy room she rented. How long had she been here? A month? Too long, she hated this place! This was all An's fault! That witch had done this to her! What was her Namesake? Oh well, Namesakes did not mean much to Ree anymore. Her Namesake, 'Freedom', no longer held the meaning it once had had for her. Freedom had been taken from her! It was all An's fault. It was Feren's fault. It was Gra's and Ler's fault! They had done this to her!

Later that day Ree found herself in a Garatin ale house listening to the mad man teacher, along with many others. The door and the shutters were wide open and the room was packed. The ale house keeper did not mind that his establishment had been taken over by a street teacher- he was just glad for all the customers and he rushed about the room taking care of orders. Some sat and talked in low tones paying no heed to Liveran; but most listened carefully. Why? Ree wondered as she looked around, but she wasn't sure. Why did people come to him? Perhaps it was because he talked about freedom from the Tarvens, or maybe freedom of a different sort... Ree was not sure. Ree had heard of the incident that happened three months ago, who had not heard? It had been the talk of the city! Liveran had

44

declared that Eloi had come! But the man he had declared to be him had left town, disappeared, and gone back to where ever it was that he lived. Everyone who had seen this man had all agreed that he was no rebel. How could that simple man lead a rebellion and drive out the Tarvens?

The rumors said that the man's Namesake was Eternity, and that he, like Liveran, had become a street teacher. But as far as Ree could tell the rumors said nothing about a rebellion. As far as Ree was concerned Liveran had finally cracked! But she was here! Once again listening to him, she could not stay away! She could sense that Liveran had something that she herself had lost... could she get it back? Was Liveran the light she had dreamed of? If he was, then she should stay away from him! But she couldn't... She felt like a moth, drawn to a flame, which would kill her. Even so she could not make herself stay away. Yes, it was true. The flame that burned in Liveran's eyes would draw her to her death.

Wilder was there also that day, sitting in a far corner eating a meal and looking for the world like a vagabond in dirty clothes and an over grown beard. A disguise he was quite good at. All the while keeping up his act he listened closely to Liveran. But unlike Ree, he had sensed something else in the air; a tension. Liveran was the kind of man who was not afraid of speaking out about what others pretended not to see. And that was dangerous. He spoke out about the corruption in both the Tarven and Garatin governments, corruption that had been ignored for years. Storm clouds were forming on the horizon; Liveran would not stop for anything! Wilder had been in the city for three days now, and Rage wanted an answer as to whether he would take the job. Wilder had decided; he would do the job. Liveran had to be silenced, Wilder reasoned, otherwise the storm of war would come. It was a matter of sacrificing the one to save the many.

Wilder did not like it, but there was no other way about it. He himself did not have anything against Liveran; in fact he agreed with much of what he said about Eloi and the corruption in Garatin. But, Liveran also spoke of rebellion. Wilder truly wished he was not involved, he wished that he could just go home to Desti. It would be so much easier if he had not promised his wife, Eam, that he would do no more assassinations. But he felt he had to do this job, regardless of the promise. He would let Rage know of his decision on the morrow.

It was almost high noon and Garason was in full swing. Shops were open, tradesmen from faraway places were in the market, Tarven soldiers were on patrol, and women were doing their wash on the roof tops. No one paid any attention to the young man and maiden walking down the street together.

'Which is quite all right!' thought Treas to himself. He and Desti had almost reached Desti's inn, where she would pay the landlord and collect Willow. 'I wish finding her father were as easy as finding her horse!' Treas thought. Again he went over all he knew about her father. 'His Namesake is Wilderness, he's Garatin, he arrived a few days ago and he's visiting a Tarven friend by the Namesake of Courage.' Treas sighed; this would be no piece of cake! Upon arriving at her inn, Desti paid the rather grumpy landlord; they then went to the stable.

"Willow, this is Treasure," Desti said after she had taken care of Will's food.

Willow, who had not been fed for the past day, wasn't in a very good mood and his only greeting was an ill-tempered snort as he munched on oats. "So, what's next?" Desti asked brightly.

"Well..." Treas felt tired already, how was he going to keep his word? He leaned up against the stall wall. "We can start by asking a few people I know who might know who your father's friend is."

And so they saddled up Will and started out. But success did not come on the first try or on the second try... indeed it went on all day. However it did not seem to bother Desti, she began to ask questions as they rode along the streets on Will.

"So, why are there Tarvens in Garatin?" she asked simply.

Treas who had been enjoying riding a horse turned in the saddle and looked at her like she had grown a second nose! But when he saw that she was serious he tried to explain, but he felt idiotic about it. "Well..." he did not know what to say!

"Where are they from?" Desti asked.

"They're from Tarva!" Treas said, thinking about how ridiculous this was.

"Where is Tarva?"

"It's over there," he said waving his arm in no general direction," Don't you know?!"

"No," Desti said truthfully.

"Oh," Treas said a little surprised. He then did his best to explain how Garatin was an occupied country and had been for sixty years. But there had never really been a war, the Garatin king at that time had surrendered before a challenge had even been sent. "Tarva has kept the peace with an iron fist," Treas said darkly.

Desti had vaguely known all this before, but that was the extent of her western knowledge. "Is there still a king of Garatin?" she asked.

"Yeah, but he doesn't rule in Garason."

"But it's the capital isn't it?"

Treas nodded, "When Tarva came the royal line was relieved of their duties and given the Quy Lake region to rule."

"And who is the king?" Desti asked.

"His Majesty Ordained," Treas replied with mock pomp.

"Oh my! That is quite the Namesake!" Desti said with a laugh.

"I guess that's what happens when you are born a prince," he said dryly.

"You don't like him?" Desti said, leaning over to see his face.

"Let's just say that not very many adore him," he said with heavy sarcasm. "He'll act shocked and dismayed when a crime is done, but in all truth he was probably the mastermind behind the crime. He's just sorry it was found out and stopped and then he has the gall to say that he's devotedly given over to Eloi!"

"Is everyone given over to Eloi?" Desti asked quietly.

"Every Garatin is, or says that he is."

"Are you?"

It made Treas pause, was he given over to Eloi? He did not like to ask himself those kinds of questions. "All good Garatins are," he replied.

There was silence for a bit, until Desti asked. "Is there a Tarven king in Garason?"

Treas was glad for the subject change, "Not a king, an ambassador, Sinister is his Namesake."

"Oh, you people in the west sure do know how to pick Namesakes!" Desti laughed.

"The rumor is that he was given it after his first battle. Ister sure isn't the type one invites to a banquet! Let's just say that his Namesake suit's him. His way to deal with anyone who does not see things his way is to execute them on the spot! He is supposed to be the peace keeper but most know him as a war general."

"I see... as you said, peace-keepers with an iron fist," Desti said in dreary voice. In an attempt to change the subject to something not quite so dreary she said, "What's this?"

They were crossing a main street, but along the center of it all the cobble stones looked as if something big and heavy was frequently dragged along them. Treas winced, it wasn't pleasant. "It's the path way of the stone," he said quietly. "It's where the public executions take place."

Desti looked at the street in confusion, "What do you mean?"

Treas sighed, "It's the execution for murderers and other big trouble makers; first the prisoner is whipped with poison coated whips that will slowly kill them. After the flogging they are made to drag a large stone through the city and out into the hills of Dumah. If they are still alive, they then lay on the stone until death. They are then flung into a pit and the blood stained stone is pushed over them, a last mockery that they should drag their own tomb stone through the streets before they die."

Desti looked back at the street, 'how horrid!' was her thought.

"The Tarvens invented it," Treas finished. They did not talk again for some time after that.

They continued the search for Desti's father all day long.

"I assume that the reason you've come here is to tell me that you'll do the job."

"Indeed I will," Wilder answered. He was once again in Rage's library.

"If you were any other of my men, I would ask 'when, where and how', but you're not. I know that you will get the job done," Rage said with confidence.

"I promised Desti that I would return soon."

Rage knew what he meant; it would be done by the end of the week, the problem taken care of, the entire city would be in an uproar and a man would be dead.

"Just a warning, Liveran has many who, if given the chance, would die or kill for him. When it's done I suggest you leave as soon as possible," Rage said with a hint of concern for his friend.

"When it's done?" Wilder asked showing how uncertain he was about it all.

"Yes, when it's done," Rage reassured in a deep voice. "I have no doubt that you can do it, old friend."

Wilder nodded, as he looked at Rage.

"Here, this is for you." Rage said coming to his feet and crossing the room with a mahogany wooden box he had taken from the mantelpiece; he handed it to Wilder.

Wilder frowned in confusion as he took it, it was a shallow, long and narrow box. He opened it with reluctance, somehow he knew what it was; inside was a familiar thing indeed. It was a long knife that in the old days he use to carry with him everywhere. But he had left it behind with Rage when he and Eam had left- so long ago. Wilder had never expected to see it again; he had never wanted to, so many lives had he taken with that knife. It was part of the life he had forsaken. He couldn't even bring himself to touch it. The room seemed to close around him in a trap.

"Father!" Mise squealed as she slowly entered the room. She was being very careful because she was holding a small flower pot. "Look, father.

Look!" She held it up for Rage to see.

"Yes Promise, I see," Rage said with a smile.

Wilder shook himself and closed the box with a click. Swallowing hard he then looked over to what little Mise held up. What he saw was a tiny yellow-green shoot, not more than an inch high. But Wilder knew what it was; the Cres`aren, the Garatin national flower! Some might think it strange that a Tarven would allow his daughter to even have that flower, a symbol of ancient Garatin. But Rage had grown up here, indeed Garason was his home as much as any Garatin.

"Father when will it bloom?" Mise asked with a tiny frown.

"Not for a long time yet, Mise," Rage told his daughter, it would be a very long time indeed! It takes three years for the Cres`aren to bloom.

"Now it's late, off to bed with you!" Rage softly scolded her.

"Yes father," Mise said as she left the room.

"I'm afraid that we spoil her terribly," Rage said when she was out of sight.

Wilder didn't respond. He was still thinking of the box he held in his hands; it felt heavy. All he wanted to do was put it down somewhere-where he didn't have to touch it. He turned to leave.

"Wilder?" Rage spoke up, "Why don't you sleep here for the night? I don't think that there's any real risk in it." He could tell that Wilder was troubled.

Wilder nodded his agreement, and he was led up to his chambers by a servant. The chamber was the size of his entire cottage back in the Byla! There was a huge bed with a silk canopy, an oak dresser, a wood and silver trunk, and behind a changing screen a big brass tub. Wilder thought it all too much as he walked across the room to the trunk. Slowly, one by one he removed his many weapons and laid them on the trunk along with the wooden box and its contents- but he still felt just as heavy. He then went to stand by the window, the thick glass made everything beyond look twisted and disjointed. He released the brass latch and the heavy window pane swung open; the sun was just setting and its red light shone over the city. His heart ached. Oh! How he wished he was home! Soon he could return, soon he would see his dear sweet Desti, and then he would never leave again: just this one last job to do, and then never again. He wondered to himself, not for the first time, if he could really do it one last time; his skill was still as sharp as ever but- he was a different man, wasn't he? Yes, he was, he had changed. He had given himself over to Eloi and in so doing had given up the life of an assassin. He had even promised Eam that he would never do it again. So why did he feel driven to do it again? He had escaped from that dark life once; it was a dangerous game to go back into; what if the darkness and death did not release him this time? What if he couldn't walk away a second time? He closed his eyes, oh how he wished he knew what to do!

Only a few short streets away Treas and Desti also watched the sun sink below the horizon. It had been a long day for them! They had searched and searched in vain. Finally they decided to give up till the morrow. Treas had found another inn for Desti to stay at; they now sat on the inn's roof top enjoying the view of roof tops and the hills beyond. Willow was snug in the stable below, and Desti was pleased with her room as well. Treas was surprised that Desti had not guessed what he was, what would she do when she found out? Or worse, what would her father do? Surely her father would not approve of him, a street urchin and a thief. He looked over at Desti, the pink light of the setting sun lit up her face, and she looked so innocent. 'I wish this would never end,' Treas sighed silently. But it would end, just as soon as they found her father, and then he would never see her again. Treas knew a lot people, but never had he meet anyone like Desti. Never had he opened up to anyone like he had to her. Why? Because Desti could not hurt him, there wasn't a cruel bone in her body! He could trust her like no one else. It was not fair that it had to end so soon! But did it have to end? What if they didn't find her father for another couple days? What would be the harm in that? He didn't have to say farewell- not yet!

Desti sighed then said, "Well, I'd better turn in. Where did you say you were going to stay for the night?"

"Yeah, you look tired," he said skirting the subject. "I'll be here in the morning to continue our search," Treas said as he stood up.

"But where are you staying?" Desti repeated as she too came to her feet.

"I know someone who lives near here." It was true he did know someone nearby. But, what he didn't say was that he wasn't staying there for the night, instead he would sleep on the roof of the inn: Desti didn't have to know that though.

Wilder's business mind took over as he concealed his old assassins knife in a hidden pocket of his pants, the sun was yet to rise when he set out through a back doorway and slipped out into the street, his disguise in place and his mind set. He hoped to find out how many loyal men Liveran had at his side at all times. This meant not letting Liveran out of his sight for a single moment all day long. Wilder must get this job done soon; he felt he would go mad otherwise! This was his fourth day here- and already he felt he had been there too long. Wilder's mind had not rested all night long, Rage had told him to not worry about this man called Eternity, and to keep his mind on the job at hand.

It was all very strange to Wilder; he had decided that Liveran was what he said he was, and that everything would come to pass just as he said- including what he said about Nity leading a rebellion. But if Liveran had been wrong about Nity, then Liveran must be mad, like everyone said.

Chapter 6

The Truth

That very same morning a tense little drama was taking place but a few short streets away. As was his habit, Treas had awoken early that morn and had gone for a walk. He was just on his way back to the inn so he and Desti could begin the search again when he overheard two Tarven women talking. All he heard was one word, but that was all it took! 'Courage' said one of the two women. Treas stopped so fast that if someone had been walking behind him, they would have run right in to him! The next moment he was leaning up against a wall and looking for the entire world as if he had been there all morning long, with his eyes looking off into the distance and his ears tuned to the two women.

One of the women was in the doorway of a bakery shop and the other was facing her. She wore an apron and had a basket hanging off of one arm.

"Yes, Courage is my master." The woman with the basket said to the other.

"And he's a knight, isn't he?" said the other.

"How should I know? All I know is that I've just about had it!"

"What's happened now?" the woman asked.

"Late last night I was told that the master had a visitor, so I had better have breakfast for him."

"And?" The woman said, turning to knead a lump of bread dough on the counter.

"Well of course I had it ready this morning, but no sooner is it on the table than I'm told that the visitor has gone! And he won't return till late tonight. Now, how can I run a house-?"

Treas wasn't listening anymore; his mind was reeling at this news. What had Desti said when he had asked why her father had come? 'He came to see a Tarven friend by the Namesake of Courage'. How many could there be in Garason with the Namesake of Courage? Treas did not know, but it was worth a try.

He followed the woman with the basket at a safe distance, out of the market area and into the Tarven district. He was surprised to find that it was not far to her master's house. He peeked around a corner and watched as she disappeared through a side gate of a tall wall. He could see the manor (or castle) that lay beyond and high up at the tips of the towers banners and a Tarven flag snapped in the wind. He knew at once that only a very rich Tarven indeed would live in that kind of place. Beyond all shadow of a doubt this was where Courage the Tarven lived, and that his visitor must be Wilderness; Desti's father. But Treas did not feel relief about finding the needle in the hay stack; instead he felt a sense of loss… He would never see Desti again! He started on his way back to the inn feeling like he had been kicked in the stomach, when a sudden thought hit him; the woman said that the visitor would not return till very late… So, he did not have to tell Desti till that night! She would not be able to see him till the morrow anyway, so what was the harm? He would tell Desti later that night and pretend that he had just found it out. It was prefect! He and Desti could have fun all day long!

∗   ∗   ∗

"Where are we going?" Desti asked for the third time.

"You'll see," Treas replied from the front of Willow.

"Not with my eyes closed!" Desti laughed.

"Be patient! And no peeking!" he told her in mock sternness. They had been riding through the city for almost two hours when Treas had told Desti to close her eyes. But now they had arrived. "All right, open," he said bringing Willow to a stop.

She did and what she saw made her gasp in delight! "Oh! What is this place?" she breathed.

Treas smiled, pleased that she liked it. "It's the gardens of Jes`reel," he told her.

What Desti saw was something that she had never before imagined! The gardens of Jes`reel was an ancient place indeed, it was said that the first seeds had been planted when Garason was still only a manor and village! The garden lay beyond the city ramparts on the south east side. It took up an entire rolling hill and faced the city as if showing off its bright colors and intricate pathways. Desti and Treas jumped from Willow's back and left Will to graze on the lush grass. The two of them entered under an arch covered with ivy. Treas slowly led the way along the older parts of the garden, along stone path ways lined with bushes that passed under arches over grown with rose vines that had huge luscious blooms, and past old gnarled trees that somehow bloomed every spring. The paths wound this way and that, circling flower beds like a maze. Desti couldn't withhold her excitement, with every twist and turn the path made she felt as though she was discovering something new and wild. Her pace quickened and soon Treas was all but running to keep up with her! She guessed their way with hardly enough time to take everything in. Soon the older parts of the garden gave way to the new, with bushes cut into the shapes of ships, dragons and Cokhawks, and trees twisted and tangled together creating a leafy canopy overhead. The Cres'aren grew everywhere thick in the flower beds and trailing along the arches even stretching across the path at times. But the newest of all these and the most spectacular, was a Tarven invention; great big fountains, flowing out into a dozen little rivers that watered the whole garden! It was said the city of Tarva was full of such fountains.

Treas told Desti that there once had been an underground river that had run from the Quy Marsh to join the Dinco River west, and it now it bubbled up into the fountains. Desti's eyes nearly popped right out of her head when they breathlessly rounded a corner and beheld the fountains. Some of them spilled out and pooled onto big smooth stone slabs before running out into the gardens and on hot summer days children would play under the fountains on the stone slabs. On that day there was a little Garatin boy and his sister who were playing there. Desti watched with wide eyes as the two children splashed in the water.

"Jealous?" Treas asked with a laugh.

Just then the little girl called out to them. "Do you want to play with us?"

Desti didn't even hesitate. Treas laughed as she ran to join the children, but no sooner had she reached them she turned about and beckoned him to come. He hesitated only long enough to make sure that no one else was about. Satisfied that no one would see him he quickly joined them. He and Desti made quick friends with the two children and for hours they played with them splashing about in the water like children themselves! However after a time of splashing about in the cold water, Desti's dress was drenched and she and the little girl stood to the side to watch- but Treas would have none of it and soon he and the little boy were chasing the two of them through the gardens. Being the fastest Treas caught them often, and dragged whomever he caught back to the fountains. With much laughter and squeals by the girls Treas and the boy would splash them mercilessly; they played as if they had not a care in the world!

It was the best day of Desti's life, and Treas could not remember if he had ever been happier. Every so often Will would look up from munching on the grass and would sigh when he saw his mistress running about like a fool. A few hours later the mother of the two children came for them and Treas and Desti reluctantly wished them farewell. As they were heading back to Willow, Desti looked behind her at Treas; he had a mischievous look in his eye, with a squeal Desti ran away just in time. Treas chased her all the way out of the gardens. The chase ended in an exhausted giggling heap on the grass; at last Treas picked himself up and pulled Desti to her feet as well. Then they turned to Willow, but he had apparently developed a sense of humor. For at the very sight of two dripping wet humans approaching him with the intentions of mounting, he promptly ran away. With much laughter the two of them chased and caught him again, then mounted up. It was then that Treas realized just how much he enjoyed making Desti laugh, he didn't want this to ever end.

"Thank you, Treas. I really enjoyed today," Desti said when she had caught her breath.

"You're welcome," he replied looking up at her in the saddle. "Maybe tomorrow I can show you the coliseum," he said as he climbed up in front of her.

"What's that?" Desti asked.

"It's a big old coliseum used for horse racing, tournaments and other such things; it's on the other side of Garason from here," he explained as they rode into the city. The two of them talked and laughed lightly until they were almost back to Desti's inn, the sun was well on its way to setting when Treas suddenly remembered that he had to pretend to find Desti's father; he bit his lip as he thought about how he would do it. He pulled Will off to the side of the street.

"Stay here a minute," he said slipping off of Will. "I just thought of someone who lives near here who might know your father's friend," he said vaguely and then turned to go when Desti spoke.

"Treas?" he looked back up at her. "I want to thank you, for doing all this for me. I know it isn't the easiest thing, looking for my father I mean, but you're trying, so thank you."

Treas felt his conscience prick him, it felt more like a punch though, how could he mislead her like this!? She trusted him so much... What would she do if she knew the truth?

"I know where your father is!" Treas said the words before he could stop himself, there was no going back now! Either Desti would forgive him or she would treat him the way he deserved.

A small frown appeared on her face. "You...? What do you mean?" she asked at last.

"I know where he is, I found out this morning." Here it comes, he thought as he watched her reaction.

"Why didn't you tell me?" she asked simply in a calm voice.

Treas had been expecting anger and accusations, as it was he was little surprised. "I-I..." he stuttered, "I didn't want to say farewell just yet... I'm sorry."

For a moment she only looked down at him, as if searching for something. Finally after what seemed a life time she bent over and grabbed his hand and said, "I understand, thank you for telling me the truth."

"You're not mad?" he asked hopefully.

"No," she broke into a smile and sat back up. "I still need you to show me the coliseum," she said ruefully.

Treas smiled too. She forgave him, and everything would be all right now! "You got it!" he said as he climbed back up onto Will, who had begun to accept all this weirdness as normal city behavior. Will only sighed when Treas nudged him on again.

"So are you taking me to see him now?" Desti asked, leaning around to see Treasure's face.

"Well that's just it! I can't!" he hurriedly explained what he had overheard that morning and Desti agreed that it would be awkward at best to show up uninvited at a Tarven's door and ask to wait till her father arrived; they agreed it was best to wait till the morrow.

"Desti, I am really sorry about not telling you," Treas said anxiously.

"You're forgiven, just promise me no more secrets!" she laughed.

Treas tried to laugh too- but his conscience would not leave him alone. No more secrets? It seemed to say, what about the one about you being a thief? But that was different; he argued with himself, she would not understand that! Would she? The sun had almost set when they arrived back at Desti's inn; the two of them unsaddled Willow and gave him a rub down before Treas wished Desti a goodnight.

"I'll come to get you in the morning," he told her as he left, and without her knowledge went to the roof to sleep. Below, Desti smiled to herself as she went up a narrow set of stairs to her room. Despite Treasure's unpleasant confession, she still counted it as one of the best days of her life.

If only the same could be said for Wilder. Early that day Wilder walked down the slanted streets in the gray light of morning. He knew where he was going because Liveran had said the day before where he would be the next day; it was necessary that he find out how many body guards Liveran had at all times. He turned the corner and looked into the square where Liveran said he would be... It was empty. Wilder waited, and waited. The sun was high in the sky when Wilder finally found out where Liveran was, by that time the crowds were thick and there was not a chance of finding out what he needed to know.

He had had more luck when darkness came that night; Wilder had been able to follow Liveran and a group of men, eight strong, back to where they were staying; a small inn. Wilder sized up each man as he entered in through the back door, from this he decided the owner of the inn must support Liveran. He then memorized where the inn was and made note of how many exits there were and then left. It was late indeed when he returned to Rage's manor, no one was there to greet him, and he went straight to his chamber with a deep frown upon his face. He washed off the dirt and grime that he had rubbed on his face that morning for his disguise. He then removed his weapons one by one with a heavy heart. The silk canopy and brass tubs were of little comfort to him. Even the silvery moonlight shining through the thick glass and billowing drapes could not penetrate his thoughts, dark thoughts they were.

Liveran had said dangerous words that day, even treasonous words… Words that had made many of his admirers very angry, and made others shout for joy. Some might have thought it a rebellious mob, rather than a crowd listening to a teacher. Liveran had spoken out against the Tarven government; he had said things about King Ordained, none of which were pleasant. The tension around this fiery eyed man was so thick it could be cut with a knife… Wilder had decided that he would do the job the day after tomorrow. He would make certain tomorrow of where Liveran would be staying, and then much before dawn the next day he would go to the inn where Liveran was staying and he would slip inside in the dark of the night… he would leave as soon as it was finished. This would quiet the cry for rebellion; thousands would be spared; only one would die.

This was right, he told himself. It needed to be done. At last Wilder closed his eyes as he lay down, blocking out Garason, Liveran, rebellions and the tools known only to an assassin. Instead he focused on far off places and long lost days; of sun shine and laughter, and of the wind blowing over fields. The harsh life of the present faded and gave way to happier days of long ago. It had been eleven years since he had seen his wife's face, but it came clear and vivid to his mind. Just as it had since the night she died; he dreamed of Eam that night.

*   *   *

It hurts… it hurts me! Please, STOP. 'You're not who I thought you were.' No! Stop, please! I don't want to hear this again…not again. 'You've turned cold, Ree. I don't think you're capable of love anymore.' No! Gra you're hurting me! You cut me so deep, so deep. She remembered how she had nursed her wounded heart until love turned to hate, she would cut him deeper still- No! I don't want to remember! She burrowed deeper into the darkness, a sudden thought occurred to her; would it suffice her? "I don't care!" she whispered, fiercely. "It's better than the light!" she turned to look at it, as deep as she was the light was still there, shining bright, threatening to reveal what she had done. "I must go deeper still!"

Ree awoke gasping for air! She sat there in her bed, with the dark silk all around her, her lungs burned. A shaft of light sprung on her, she screamed and threw up her arms to protect herself! Then she relaxed, this was not the light that hunted her in sleep, but instead just the light of morning that had escaped through the curtains. She sighed in relief, and then got up. "I can't stay here all day," she said under her breath. After securing a belt about her hips she left and closed her room door behind her. She had no key but she did not have anything worth stealing. Then she turned and went down the narrow, dingy stairwell until she reached the room below; it was full of tables and benches and chars, but it was still too early for anyone to be about and she made her way through the empty room to the open door.

"Hey! Reed!" a voice called.

Ree clenched her teeth, how annoying she thought. "It's Ree," she said with open irritation to her landlord, who had waddled over from behind the counter. He wore a dirty apron and his grimy face didn't look like it had been washed in an age.

"That's none of my business! But what is my business is your rent! It's due tomorrow," he said in a thick voice.

"Then you'll get it tomorrow," she said over her shoulder as she went through the door and out into the street, barely holding her temper in check. She did not know it but what Gra once said was true; she was cold. Wandering through the streets she had not meant to run into Liveran and his crowd of eager listeners, in fact she had meant to stay away from him, and from the hunting light in his eyes. But here she was once again, the moth transfixed by the beautiful, yet deadly flame… He spoke of freedom, oh how she longed to be free! But she could not forget what freedom would cost her.

Chapter 7

Flight and Arrest

"The Garatin visitor? No, he left early this morn. Don't know when he'll be returning, sorry."

Desti blinked, she couldn't believe her ears! She stared at the stable boy in disbelieve.

"Oh…" Treas said at last. "Thanks anyways," he said turning away from the courtyard and back into the street, Desti followed holding on to Willows reins. They walked down the street, neither one said a word. Treas felt like an idiot, after lying to Desti, reasoning that she would be able to see her father today; her father had left early. The stable boy's words played again in Desti's ears; she wondered vaguely what her father was doing so early in the morning. But oh! How guilty she felt! Everything seemed to be going wrong, how would she explain it all to him? If she found him before he left. It was a nasty thought! But oh, so true. What if he did leave before she found him? He would be so worried when he got home only to find her missing. Oh she would have to make the long journey home all by herself! It made her shudder just to think of it all, the Corfin Forest, the Byla River, and Idercoons! –

"Desti?" Treas interrupted her thoughts.

"Oh, yes? I didn't hear you," she said trying hard to pay attention.

Treas gave her a concerned look. "I said not to worry about your father, after we've eaten we can go back and ask to see your father's friend and ask him where your father went." Treas did not much like the idea himself, but it was the least he could do.

Desti smiled, even if he had not been truthful yesterday, he was trying now. He did have a point; she herself did not want to wish him a farewell so soon.

"What's that!?" Desti asked; they had made their way to the market square, and Desti was looking at a crowd all in one corner. They appeared to be listening to someone, but Desti could not see who it was.

"Oh, just some street teacher who thinks he knows something the rest of us don't," Treas said with little interest. "I think it's the rebel Liveran."

"A rebel!?" Desti asked, curious.

"Well, that's what some hope he is," he said ruefully.

"And what do you think?"

"He's not a rebel, just a charlatan," he said darkly. Treas had little to no respect for street teachers.

Desti was just about to ask why he did not like Liveran, when she heard a familiar voice.

"Destination!?" her Namesake being called in this unfamiliar place made her spin round to see to whom the voice belonged.

Treas watched as Desti's face lit up like the sky on a starry night, dropping Wills reins she then broke into a run towards a Garatin man Treas had never seen before. The man was average height with broad shoulders. He was dressed similar to Treas himself in old looking clothes, and he had a bit of a straggly beard. Treas guessed him to be middle aged, but still a formidable enemy; the thought came so sudden Treas did not know what to do with it! There was no doubt, the evidence was there; the high cheek bones and diamond shaped jaw bone. This was Desti's father.

Wilder had arisen even earlier that morning with a sense of foreboding. He had followed Liveran from where he had stayed the night before to where he was now; in a market square. Indeed, Wilder had been his shadow all morning. Liveran had been directly accusing King Dain all that morning. All of what Liveran said was true; for in truth, King Dain was one of the biggest criminals in all the country. Liveran was the only one brave enough to say it in public though, and the people rallied to him; a restless people, looking for a leader. Yes, Liveran needed to be stopped, and he would be, that night.

Wilder looked around at the crowd, he knew he had been here too long when the faces were all becoming familiar to him: there was a group of young men who were loud and always looked restless, there was the old man at the back of the crowd, who was always grumbling about something or other, and always in a dark corner was a figure all in black. Future rebels one and all, Wilder thought bleakly. He himself looked like a very poor man indeed, he was wearing simple rags- but each one of his weapons was carefully concealed. He still felt uncomfortable with so many weapons- but he was getting used to it and that scared him. He turned away from watching Liveran and before his eyes was a vision of loveliness… a maiden with copper colored hair, and gray-green eyes, there was an innocent and graceful air about her- it was his beloved Eam! But not as he had last seen her cold and pale in her grave, nor even tired and drawn as she had been on her death bed, but young, and very much alive! She walked among the living in the streets of Garason, just as she had when they had first met, time went back and he could hear her soft voice. But 'NO!' Dream was eleven years dead, he reminded himself; this must be instead the precious gift she left behind.

"Destination!?" he called out, hardly daring to believe it to be true, but as if to prove him wrong the bright eyed vision turned at his call and ran through the crowd to his embrace. A flood of emotion over took him, at first it was joy at the sight of his daughter, then it was fear, she might have been hurt! Then a over whelming sense of pride, his daughter had made it all the way from the Byla to Garason all on her own!

He held her tightly in his arms, than he noticed a young man standing a few feet away, holding on to Desti's horse's reins. He was looking down in an awkward way. Wilder knew without being told that this man was accompanying his daughter. He was Garatin, and he had a square jaw and a firm mouth, neither slender nor built and his clothes were falling apart at the seams. He had the look of someone who did not take life seriously. The young man looked up and locked onto Wilder's eyes.

"Daddy!" Desti whispered. "Father this is Treasure," she said, clear that she thought highly of him. Wilder only glanced at Treas, then dismissed him from his mind.

"Desti what are you doing here!?" he asked looking steadily into her eyes.

She swallowed as if bracing herself. "Ah, well…I-I it's a long story," she said at last.

"Never mind then, we'll talk of it later, I'm just glad that you're not hurt." Wilder said.

"It's to Treas that I owe my safety!" she beamed, turning to him. Wilder turned to him as well, and looked Treas up and down, sensing Treasure's uneasiness.

"Thank you for looking after my daughter, young man," he said shaking his hand. "A deed for which I could never repay you, but none the less, accept this." He handed him a small sack of coins and at the same time he grabbed Will's halter. Treas held on to Will's reins a moment longer then he should have had. There followed a moment of awkward silence. Wilder thought quickly as to what he was to do. He was loathe to leave Liveran but he would not feel at ease until Desti was safe inside Courage's manor, and there was his disguise; what was Desti thinking? "If our paths ever cross again do not hesitate to ask any favor," Wilder said, breaking the silence

Desti looked confused for a moment then said, "Ah, goodbye Treas. Thank you." She ended with a smile.

Treas glanced at Wilder then said to Desti, "I'll see you on the morrow."

Wilder then led his daughter away.

Desti walked across the thick carpet and sighed as she leaned up against her west facing window. She had opened the double window panes wide, and she now beheld the sight below; three stories up and Desti could see everything from the rich Tarven castles to the thatched roofed Garatin slums, out to the city walls and the green rolling hills beyond. She could even see what must be the great coliseum! Desti had managed to explain everything to her father. At first she had been afraid that he would not understand, but in the end all was forgiven: even if trust would have to be built up between them again. She frowned, why had her father not liked Treas? He had not said it, but she was not blind. There had been a tension between them, even if they had both been civil, why couldn't the two most important men in her life get along?

After bringing her to Courage's manor and hearing her story, her father had left saying he would return soon. But that had been five hours ago! Desti would have gone out and found Treas, excepted she did not want to rock the boat where her father was concerned. Just what was her father up to? Why had he come to Garason? And why in the name of all that is good did he look like a vagabond!? She would ask Treas what he thought when she saw him tomorrow.

Wilder lay awake in his bed late that night, how long he had been like that he did not know. In a few hours he would rise and get ready for the long dark walk to where Liveran was staying, he would have to be careful not to be seen by the curfew guard; he could not let anyone see him this night. They would have to leave the city as soon as the assassination was done. What would he tell Desti? He had intentionally stayed out later then he had to so that Desti would be fast asleep when returned. A knock at his door interrupted his thoughts. Who would be knocking at his door at this hour!? He opened the door to find a manservant there.

"My master asked that you come," he said quietly.

Wilder got dressed quickly and then was led down to the library; the manservant left and took the candle he held with him. Wilder waited till he was out of sight then looked to the closed library doors; he could see fire light coming from underneath it. He entered, Rage stood in front of the lit fireplace; it was the only light in the room, not even a candle was lit.

"Ah, Wilder," he said as Wilder approached. "I apologize for the late hour, but something has happened."

Wilder narrowed his eyes.

Rage held his hands behind his back and spoke in a matter-of-fact way. "It seems that Dain took offense at what Liveran has been saying about him. Liveran has been arrested by Dain's soldiers, this very hour, and no doubt is being taken to Dain in the north as we speak."

Wilder felt relief wash over him, Liveran arrested- and by Dain, no one that far north would care about what happens to Liveran! No assassination was needed! But then… why this mysterious meeting? "So why wake me at this hour? What's gone wrong?" he asked steadily.

"It's leaked," Rage stated. "Word got out that an assassination was planned. I don't know what will happen come morning, but you and your daughter had best get out while you still can."

The fire crackled and its light flickered on Wilder's face. He knew what Rage meant; this news would not go over well with the public. Wilder and Desti had to leave, and leave now! Even if Desti did not understand, she did not need to know what would have happened that night! They had to leave.

*   *   *

Treas jumped out of the way as a group of Garatin men recklessly ran past shouting, "Down with Tarva!" Treas frowned, what were they so uptight about? He made his way to the rampart that surrounded Courage's manor; he knocked on what he knew to be the cook's door, the back of the manor made up part of the wall that circled the front half. The door opened slowly and a cook's maid looked out, she looked surprised to see him, almost frightened.

"Please! I'm looking for the Garatin maiden who came here yesterday," he said before she could close the door.

She shook her head and said, "She's gone."

"Gone! What do you mean gone!? " Treas asked in bewilderment.

"I don't know!" the poor girl said as if to say how should I know? "All I know is that the Garatin man and his daughter left late last night and they won't be returning."

Treas could not believe his ears. Gone! She was gone, without even saying farewell.

"A good idea if you ask me," the girl said.

"What do mean?" he asked, confused.

"Leaving the city! Escape the riots while you still can."

Dazed he asked, "What riots!?"

"Don't you know!?" she asked as if everyone knew. "Do you think that everyone is just shouting in the streets for fun? The riots over Liveran's arrest and how someone planned to assassinate him! About time he got what was coming to him if you ask me, but most of you Garatins don't think that way. It's going to get violent in this city before long, now you had best leave before the cook sees you!"

Treas wandered away back into the street, he felt completely stunned. Gone! She was gone without so much as a wave farewell! Was it possible that they had just gone to an inn? No, why would they have left at such an hour? More than this he knew it in his heart, Desti was lost to him. Her father had taken her back to the Byla Wilderness; it might as well be the other side of the world! He was out on the main street now and people were jostling him as they rushed by in their rioting. He was oblivious to it all; Desti the only person he had ever trusted, the only person he had ever cared about, was forever gone! He felt numb inside, how could she?

Chapter 8

Home

The wind blew over gentle grassy hills and tugged at the stunted trees, moving the gray clouds across the sky at a quick pace. A four horned deer lifted his head and sniffed the wind, there were two horses and their riders coming towards him, the deer stood still for a moment then bounded off.

Destination and her father had been traveling for three days now; they had crossed the Byla River at noon and were now several miles east of it. Desti marveled at how easy the trek had been up to this point, compared to when she had undertaken it alone. Wilder had taken them through the Corfin Forest and across the Byla River without incident (or Idrcoons). She looked over at her father; the closest friend she had ever known and yet he was still a stranger.

"What were you doing in Garason, father?" she asked, breaking the silence. Not much had been said since they left three days ago.

Wilder sighed, "There are some things in my past that are best left just there; in the past." He looked over at her, "You don't need to know about them, Desti."

It was clear from the way he said it that that was the end of the conversation. Desti could have argued that he had been to Garason! The things of the past were no longer left behind!

But she had too much respect for him to argue, instead she asked, "But why did we have to leave like that!? Leaving in the middle of the night like we were fugitives!" It was all so strange to her, none of it made any sense!

"I had been planning to depart soon anyhow and then I learned that there would be riots in the city come morning, I thought it best we leave as soon as possible."

Desti interrupted him, "RIOTS! About what!?" she asked.

"An important man had been arrested that night," he answered vaguely.

"Who?" she asked, curiously.

"A Garatin man; Deliverance," he said, hoping that that would be the end of her questions.

"Liveran! The street teacher?" she said in surprise.

Wilder looked at her, he was surprised that she had learned so much in so little time. "Yes," he replied.

Desti thought of that for a moment, but it was not long before she exclaimed, "But leaving in the middle of the night like that! I can't imagine what Treas must think!" she said more to herself than to her father, poor Treas.

"Does it matter so much to you what he thinks?" Wilder gave his daughter a sharp look.

She looked away, did it matter? What was Treas to her anyway? Just a friend! She answered herself with irritation, a friend she would have liked to say farewell to.

"Will you ever return to Garason?" Desti changed the subject.

Wilder looked at her as if guessing her motive. "I promise if I do, I'll take you with me."

Desti seemed pleased with this and smiled.

'Better with me than by herself,' Wilder thought. The thought that she could have been hurt broke his heart and at the same time made him seethe with anger that she had even done such a thing- but he was never one to let his emotions get away with him. The trip passed quickly with no more said about their late night departure. Instead, Desti told of her many adventures: like the disastrous crossing of the Byla River, which Wilder had a hearty laugh over and for a moment the tension eased. But things were still not quite right between them; Desti could not get the thought out of her head that her father was hiding something dreadful from her. But if it was so dreadful, did she really want to know what it was?

Two weeks after leaving Garason Desti was finally looking upon a familiar site; Home. And with it came a mix of emotions for her. On the one hand she missed Treas and the excitement that she had known while in Garason. She could believe that she did really have a destination when she was with him; on the other hand it was good to be home, and to know that there would be no unpleasant surprises here. It really was not so bad to step out of one life style and into another, to go back to the way life use to be, when it was simple and when her father had no secrets. But she would miss Treasure; perhaps she would see him again. Willow snorted as if he could read her thoughts on the matter; then he trotted on ahead to the cottage. He at least was completely content to be back at home, even if his mistress wasn't.

Wilder sighed, home; the place he had vowed never to leave, indeed he was happy to stay here until death, but he saw now that Desti wasn't. Watching her ride on ahead, he was reminded that she was no longer a child. Yes, perhaps there would be more trips to Garason and other places in the future, for Desti's sake.

*   *   *

Treasure hunkered down into his cloak against the wind; he was cold and wet. He thought moodily that the weather matched his life quite effectively; dark and raining. He had tried to sneak into a stable for the afternoon but had been caught. Now he had to settle for a narrow alley; that the wind seemed to be fond of blowing down. Well, home sweet home,' he muttered under his breath, feeling cynical. Since Desti had disappeared two weeks ago, he had wandered all over the city like a snail that had lost its shell, half the time feeling sorry for himself and wishing that he could see Desti again; and the other half scolding himself for caring so much for her! If he had only guarded his heart against her, this would not be so hard! But he had cared and she had packed up in the middle of the night and left! Just like that. Well, that's what he got for opening up his heart to someone.

But it had been her father who had made her leave like that! Hadn't it? She would not do that to him on purpose, or would she? He had to get his mind off of all this! After all, there were no answers. He pushed off the wall and walked out onto the street and into the wind. There was a tavern near, the owner of which was a friend of his (friend in the loosest sort of terms) and would sometimes give Treas a free meal if he offered his service's for a few hours.

Two hours later and Treas was sitting down to a warm meal, the first he had had in quite some time. While he was wolfing down his food, a group of Tarven soldiers came in and sat down at a table. They ordered their food and since it was a Tarven establishment, went on talking rather loudly. Treas paid them no heed, that is, until they said, "Courage..." Treasure's head snapped round! He looked away quickly before they noticed him, and listened carefully.

"I heard that he had something to do with the arrest," said one of the soldiers.

"No, don't believe a word of it," said another.

"Nothing doing!" a third said loudly, "I know the rumors are true, I used to serve under him before I was transferred!"

The others all quieted down as this man got their attention.

"Aye, we know that Courage was a war general years ago, he fought in the Five Island Uprising when he was young, but he is also the leader of Tarva's most deadly assassins!"

Treasure's skin crawled.

"No! I tell you it's true!" the speaker said when the others laughed. "I was once asked to train to become one!"

The others all laughed again, but Treas could not shrug it off so easily. He finished his meal quickly; he had to get out of here! Standing up and nodding to the tavern keeper, he walked quickly past the table of soldiers. Once out into the street he turned into the wind and a shiver went up his spine but it was not from the rain. Treas believed the rumors about an assassination being planned for Liveran, and if Courage was indeed the leader of assassins, then it would have been one of his men who would have done it. A horrid thought grew in his mind; what if Desti's father had been the assassin? He had just shown up and then disappeared again when Liveran was arrested. What was it Desti said about her father being in Garason? 'To see a Tarven friend by the Namesake of Courage', those had been her very words. Treas had thought it strange that a man, who had not left his home for eighteen years, had traveled all the way from the Byla Wilderness just to see a friend. Was it not more likely that he had come to do something, perhaps of a sinister nature? It had been painfully obvious that Desti herself had not known the true reason why her father had come. Was Desti's father, Wilder, an assassin? Did Desti know about her own father? Should she not be told!? Treas had a wild impulse to tell her! Just then he slipped into an ally escaping the cold wind, yes this was Home.

Chapter 9

As Time Goes By

'Oh! That hurt! I can't see…it's too dark, I can't see! It's too close, the darkness it's too close. I can't breathe! I'll suffocate! Why can't I see? Where is it? What's missing!?' Ree woke with her arms out in front of her, as if searching for something among the twisted blankets and black silk, but for what? The dream was just like the others, the feeling of suffocation, the pain, the darkness; wait, the Darkness? But where was the light!? The realization came to her in a rush; the light was gone just like the street teacher. The flame was extinguished; the threat was subdued; the light was faded; the hope was gone.

'Why would I think that?' she asked herself. But the answer was more than she was prepared to face, it came unbidden; she had gotten used to that unhealthy relationship between the moth and the flame. The answer came as a shock to her; the light had threatened to expose the past and what happened, why should she mourn its disappearance? Well, at least she had not been stumbling about in darkness, she reasoned with bitterness. But now, it was gone and she was left alone in the silky blackness. Alone with Gra, no one else had heard his last shriek of terror, 'No! I will not think of this!' She squeezed her eyes shut but it still came, vivid and clear! 'FREEDOM' she brought her knife down, to silence him once and for all. To cut him as deep as he had cut her.

*   *   *

'It's a ridiculous idea!' Treas said to himself, almost hysterical. 'Someone should talk me out of it; I should talk myself out of it!' He looked down at his small collection of belongings; a worn out cloak, an old knife, a small leather bag with two copper coins that he had found as a boy, a piece of flint, and a dented tin cup along with a bit of food wrapped in some cloth. 'What have I got to pack?' he said out loud, then laughed at himself, what indeed! 'Don't want to forget anything!' he was feeling light hearted, even care free!

He had finally decided that he was miserable, and that he would not let one hurt destroy him, yes he would love and he would care; he would find Desti! Everything of what he had learned in life told him to forget her! And to never trust nor care for anyone ever again, then no one could hurt him again. But he could not forget. What would he say to Desti? That is if he could find her! And what would he say to her father!? He did not know, and he did not care! What he did know, was that he had to see her again! He wanted to know what it was like to care about someone other than himself; it was a whole new world to him!

He was tired of living alone, and there was only one way to find out what this new world was like; he must go and find Desti. He swung the cloak over one shoulder, and shoved the knife into one boot and the cup into his only pocket that didn't have any holes; the bag went onto his belt along with his food. He took a deep breath. Then he left the aLey and stepped out onto the street. He would go first to Hirfly, and then turn east towards the Corfin Forest, the Byla River and Desti; how hard could it be? Sure it would take longer on foot, but Desti was not going anywhere! Was she?

Half way down the street he stopped, Desti was the only person he wanted to explore this new world with, but did she see it the same way? What if she did not feel the same as he? Even worse, what if she had already forgotten him!? But even that fear could not hold him back! He set his face and started down the street again, he must find out for sure. He looked up and made eye contact with a woman coming towards him, she wore all black. He looked into her eyes, and what he saw made his skin crawl, the brown eyes did not have the warmth that they should have had, instead they were uncommonly cold and lifeless. The moment passed, she looked away and he shook his unease off.

It seemed as if dusk came early that night and found him only a few miles south of the city gates. But Treas made the best of it that he could, and since there was not much in the way of fuel he went without a fire and slept on the ground. Lying on the cold hard ground would be enough to dampen anyone's spirits, especially with the promise of dew in the morning. But somehow looking up at the night full of stars, he felt invigorated as if he could take on the world and anything it had to throw at him. The only question was; was he prepared to take on anything that Eloi had to throw at him? Still nothing could deter him, how could he have known that his life was about to change forever?

Four long days later, Treas reached the town without walls; Hirfly. He had run out of his meager food supply the day before, so the first order of business was to find some food. Normally in a strange place he would just steal; after all, how else was he supposes to survive? But on this quest for a new life he wanted to do things right, and as it was, there was a man in town by the Namesake of Challenge. He was a blacksmith but was unable to do his work because he had recently injured his arm. He was willing to give Treas food as payment to do some work; some dried meat and the like. Treas could not have been happier; this was almost an honest living! It made him believe that this new world was not so far out of reach.

He worked for Chall for four days, all the while Chall asked him many questions about himself. Treas would have done better if he had stuck to his policy of 'don't trust anyone'. Perhaps it was his new mind frame; if he was a good person then everyone else would be too. Chall learned that Treas was homeless, had no family, and was traveling into the Byla, at which point Chall told him that the best way to get there was through the Corfin Forest, he even told him which path to use!

"What's this?" Treas asked as he brought something over to the anvil.

"It's a brand," answered Chall, from across the forge.

"For cattle?" Treas asked, showing just how naive he was.

Chall laughed then said, "No, for slaves!" Treas looked up at him startled, and then back at the brand in his hand, there was the letters D and V on it, nothing else. It made him shiver; slaves. Chall told him to make a duplicate of the brand, Treas did it as fast as he could. After four days of work Chall's arm was better, and Treas decided that he had enough food provisions to get him to where ever it was that Desti lived. So he started out again, it was midafternoon when Treas entered the Corfin Forest on the path that Chall had recommended. The path was easy to follow and a pleasant stroll at that, he had been walking along for an hour when he came to a fork in the meandering path that led off to the south. Beside this path there was a rather large man leaning up against a tree. Treas pretended to take no notice of him and began to walk by when the man spoke.

"Are you Treasure?" he said in a startling deep voice.

Treas stopped, how did this man know who he was?! "I might be, and then again I might not," he said cautiously.

"I'm looking for the boy who worked for Challenge the blacksmith in Hirfly," the man said, straightening up as he pushed off of the tree.

Treas looked him up and down; he was neither Garatin nor Tarven that was plain, even in the poor lighting of the forest. Treas noted again how tall and big this stranger was. The man took a step towards him. Treas heard a warning go off in his head; the same as when he was about to be mugged. The hair on his neck stood on end; he knew that he would be hard pressed to win any fight with this man, and he would never get far running!

"Look boy, this doesn't have to be done the hard way."

Treas jumped at him while the man's guard was down, his knife was out in a moment and for a few minutes he had the upper hand, but it did not last. Despite his brave effort, the man's brute strength and mere size outdid Treas in a matter of minutes. Treas was clubbed over the back of his head, a sharp pain went down his spine, and his eyes flashed open before his world went dark.

Treas awoke to a burning sensation but he could not tell from where it came. His head throbbed as he looked around from where he lay on the ground; it was dark but there were no stars, still in the forest then. There was a fire a few meters away with a group of men around it. One of them was the man who had attacked him. In his confusion they all looked bigger than life, or were they? He looked away, he had to run! Now was his chance! He sprang up to make a break! But something caught his foot and he was thrown to the ground. The men all laughed at him as he lay sprawled out. In his daze he looked at his foot, what had tripped him? There was a chain around his foot and the other end was held by one of the men by the fire.

"You're not going anywhere!" he said.

Another man added with a laugh, "Except to the Dinco silver mines!" They all laughed again.

The burning, it was coming from his right shoulder! He looked at it; his sleeve was torn away to reveal a red welt; in the middle was the letters D V. He had been branded as a slave! Chall had betrayed him! Sold him to slave traders! The smell of burnt flesh made him feel sick, the pain was too much, his head spun, a black mist came over his eyes and again the blackness took him.

Over grass and stone, through water and sand, cross hill and field, by ruin and village, the long hours of the days merged into one and the nights slipped through the grasp of tired fingers. His boots wore thin and his skin was burnt by the sun, weak with hunger by day and chilled by the wind at night, on he trudged. At one point Treasure glanced over his shoulder and was surprised to see ten or twelve more just like him. He had the vague idea that they had joined his company when crossing the Dinco River West, but he did not know for sure. For westward it was that they traveled, or it was when Treas had lost track.

The faces of the other slaves faded and the jingle of their chains was lost on him, they were just poor unfortunate souls like him. All he saw was the same red, blistering brand that he had, on every shoulder. Treasure knew it to be true that sticks and stones break bones, but the name of 'slave' worked its way far deeper than any brand could ever go, down to his very soul, until it became his identity. Until it became impossible to not be true; he was a slave. West and south they traveled across the Plains where it seemed as though you could see on forever. The grass grew too fast for any path to be worn here and it grew almost up past Treasure's shoulders at times and he tripped often. Three weeks of misery and they came to the ruins of the old keep of Pat`ion, old watch towers and crumbling walls were all there was to see. Only then did Treas realize just how far south they had come. They rested there for the night under the crumbling walls and among giant blocks of stone. Treas couldn't help but think of it as a grave yard.

In another nine days they came to the eastern Sister town, on the shore of the Arrow Sea. He and the rest of the slaves were given their first real meal that they had had in three weeks; up to this point it had just been scraps of bread. It was just watery soup, but to Treas it was like a feast. Treas felt like he had just come out of a trance and he really took in his surroundings for the first time, like he had just woken up from a nightmare only to find out that it was real after all. The town had no walls and it all sloped down to the lake. By the water's edge was a watch tower with a beacon on top, and every time a ship left its harbor for western Sister town on the other side they would light the beacon as a sign that it was a friendly ship.

He and the other slaves slept outside that night on the outskirts of town. Their chains were linked onto poles driven into the ground and they were watched all night long by more big men. Treas lay there shivering in the dark. The slaves were not given a fire to sleep by and Treasure's cloak had been taken from him that first night along with all his other belongings. So he shivered and wondered what would become of him? He would soon find out.

The next day the slaves were led through the town down to the water. Treas noted the different nationalities in this strange town that he had only heard of before; there were pale tall men like his slavers, there were Tarvens and also people with darker skin from the forest of Niben. But none of the town's people seemed to care about the line of slaves going past them, and they didn't even pause what they were doing. At the waterfront Treas and about fifteen other slaves were loaded onto a flat bottom raft, and then chained to rings in the raft. He wondered what would happen if the raft sunk.

For two days they floated south-east, for Treas it was the most terrifying thing yet. Never had he seen such a large expanse of water before let alone been out in the middle of it. What if a storm came!? But the water remained calm and only a few waves splashed over the rim of the raft. It was out in the middle of this sea that he got his first glimpse of the mountains, and every day they grew closer.

After two days the sea narrowed into a river and a marsh. The big slavers, again he noted how big they were, got out poles and began to push the raft along through the mud and bulrushes; they seemed to know this waterway quite well. It took four days for them to emerge from the Arrow marshes into a swift moving river. One morning Treas awoke in shadow, he looked up and saw the mountains looming over them like a warrior over the dead body of his enemy; the Dinco Mountains.

In two days the river made a bend to the right, and as they rounded the corner a great castle hewn from the mountain side was revealed, larger than seemed possible! In twenty minutes they had come alongside huge docks. They were loaded off onto them, and then made to march towards the board walks that lined the ramparts that protected the stone town beyond. It was there, under the shadow of the ramparts, that Treas got his first glimpse of the inhabitants; a huge nine foot man walked by, tall and stocky, his hands Treas felt sure could engulf his own head! Treas remembered the stories of the far south; Jarg was a great castle and its village nestled between the Dincos and the Arrow River. The people who lived there were Giants! It all made sense now! The slavers and the one with whom he fought with, must be half giant, that's why the castle looked so big! Treas swallowed hard, he also remembered that the castle of Jarg was known for its silver mines.

*   *   *

The rumors had spread through the city like wild fire; everyone in the city had heard them it seemed, including Ree. It seemed as though Eternity had stepped into the public eye, yes the man whom Liveran had declared to be the 'Eloi-man' come to liberate Garatin, had finally done something that matched up to the expectations. He had become a street teacher, and there was more.

He was going about the Quy Lake region where he lived, and was doing the impossible; there was a small fishing village on the north side of the lake, reports had said that there had been an outbreak of the black plague there. No one went near there and no one came from there, it was well understood that everyone living there would die in a matter of months;

a black death. But Nity had stunned everyone when he had disappeared into this town. No one had any hope that he would come out again. Everyone had had such high hopes for him, but apparently Liveran had been wrong about him; this man was a fool.

But two days later, Nity had come out again, along with a large number of villagers from the infected village; all signs of the black plague had vanished! Not one had died. Could the rumors be true? Had Liveran been right? Was Nity the man that Eloi promised? The villagers of Quy Lake thought so. Ree was not so sure, all she knew was that on the day she had heard the rumors, that same night she had had a dream. In the dream she had been stumbling about same as before, suffocating in the silk, when far away a light had dawned; far, far away. When she woke, Ree could only describe it as hope.

*   *   *

Time must go on and it stops for no one, it has no regrets, it gives nothing back. As time goes by it pulls us along with it, leaving no one behind no matter how much they might plead. Or so it seemed to Desti. But life is different, although anyone can have it; it can be cut short. Life has many regrets even if it can give anything. Life passes many by, for not all who breathe, live. For Desti it seemed as though time slipped through her fingers and life was beyond her grasp. Her Namesake became a mockery instead of the legacy it should have been. Destination, as if she had one, out here in the wilderness.

Her nineteenth birthday had come and gone, it had been on the tip of her tongue to ask of her father for the one thing that she wanted; to return to Garason. But Garason was so far away, so far from her life now. What happened there was so distant; she did not belong there anymore, and the further they stayed away from Garason the safer they would be. Her father was hiding something, something dreadful! A dark secret about the past, she did not want to know what it was! They were happy here, life was just fine how it was; why should it change? This dark secret would indeed change everything! Nothing would ever be the same again if she was to learn what this secret was. It was like a curtain that was between her and her father;

81

the curtain must remain intact, the closer they got to Garason the more risk there was of this curtain being torn away, even if she tried to hold it in place. As much as she wanted something more in life, it was safer to stay here. As time goes by, it changes many things.

*   *   *

Ree had heard of an archery tournament that was being held in the city. She was short on money and there was a prize for the winner of the tournament. She decided that she didn't have anything to lose by going. The courtyard where it was being held was small and not many came to compete. Ree did not have much difficulty winning; she had always been good with a bow. When she was awarded the prize all the other archers had glared at her as she had stolen it. But one man had come up to her with a smile.

"You're very good with the bow," he said smiling. "You are a Cokhawk forest maiden aren't you?" Ree looked at him suspiciously then answered.

"Yes," she didn't offer anything else.

"My Namesake is Devotion." He paused but she only looked at him coldly.

"I think I can trust you," he said bluntly. "I and some friends of mine have need of someone with your skills." Ree narrowed her eyes.

"If you're interested, come to the Whistle Valley Ale House at dusk tonight." He then nodded his head and walked away.

Her curiosity got the better of her that night and she made her way to the place Devo had told her about. The ale house was dark except for one or two lanterns. It was silent as she knocked on the closed door, which was soon opened by a stern faced man.

"We're closed!" he said bluntly.

But a voice called out from inside, "It's all right, I invited her here." The speaker was of course Devo. He led her past empty tables and chairs into a back room. "I'm glad you decided to come," he said as he opened up a door; the room on the other side was full of Garatin's, men and women alike, it was then that Ree fully understood what this was; secret rebel meeting! At first she had felt out of place with these fiery-eyed rebels, but their passion had made her skin tingle and her soul burn. She was angry at the world, angry that freedom had been taken from her! Anger was her way of trying to forget the truth, anything to forget that she was really angry, at herself! She had killed freedom the day she had done the same to Gra! She would do anything to forget that! She had to direct her anger at someone, and the rebels were angry too. So she would join them in their struggle, after all, they were searching for freedom too. Later that night after she had sneaked through the streets to avoid the curfew guard, she slipped into her inn by the back door. She now stood by her window looking out at the dark city, a figure etched in stone; she said aloud, "As time goes by, we'll search together for freedom."

*   *   *

Days had lost their meaning to Treas; one more day only meant a lifetime of misery. It only meant more whip lashes on the back. It meant waking up to the nightmare one more time. There was not a slave among them who did not at some point or other prefer death to one more day in the mines.

Upon arriving, the slaves were marched through the gigantic town, and up into the hills under the shadow of the mountain. After they arrived at the mines, they were counted, then they entered the dark hole. If Treas had known it, he would have savored his last breath of fresh air a little longer, for by design slaves did not come back out again. The new slaves were taken straight to their sleeping quarters; it was a low wooden door leading into the cave behind. It was known as 'the den'. It was here that their chains were broken off, none to gently. Inside the den there were thin coarse blankets scattered about the rough floor, there was a torch on the other side of the wooden wall but other than that it was dark.

No one slept much that night, if it was night, so terrified were they of what would happen next. When the guards came to get them again they were brought out into the mine, counted up then led to where they were to work: so began the nightmare. As far as Treas could tell shifts were six hours long; a horn would be blown and the slaves of that group would then leave their pickaxes in a barrel, be counted up then marched back to their 'den', to rest for another six hours and then begin all over again.

Treas woke up to the sound of the guards talking quietly outside the den. He looked at his right shoulder; he was somewhat surprised to see that his brand looked like an old scar! How long had he been here? Was it not only a few weeks ago that he had set out to find Desti? But then, had he not also been here forever? Had he not been mining silver forever and yet never seen a single coin, silver or otherwise? A horrid thought came to him, what if he woke up and could not remember anything!? He was a slave, yes, but there was escape in sleep. Yes, to sleep and dream of the past and of Desti, but what if it came to a point where he could no longer remember the past?

Chapter 10
Escape

Up came the pickaxe, and back down, bit by bit breaking down the stone and digging out the silver. Up; how long had he been here? Down; too long. Up, down. A chunk of stone broke off and went flying past his head, he didn't even flinch; yes, he had been here too long. A horn was blown, it was the end of his shift, Treas joined the line after dropping his axe in the barrel, and they began to march, in and out of the torch light often time in total darkness. There was no fear of hitting the roof of the caves, for all tunnels and mining caverns were made so the nine foot giants could walk about without stooping; indeed it was strange to have all that dark space above you, with who knows what living up there.

Treas had learned something interesting that day; all of the slaves slept inside the mines, except for a group of thirty-eight who slept outside in a wooden structure. When the mines first began that was the slave sleeping quarters, and in the many years since, they had just never changed it. Every slave wanted to be among the group who slept outside; the chance of sun shine and wind on your face and fresh air in your lungs but most of all, that much closer to escaping!

Treas arrived at the den and the slaves were counted up by a slaver, then one by one they all stooped into the den. The roof of the cave was much lower in the den, getting lower and lower the further back you went; at the furthest end it was hardly more than a crevice. Old worn out blankets were strewn about the uneven floor along with whatever belongings the slaves had. Treas and the others would lay there in the dark and talk quietly; Treas listened as a few of the others spoke in hushed tones.

"My Namesake?" said an older Garatin man when someone asked him. "It was King," he said proudly.

The others all laughed at him, as much as they could without disturbing the guards.

"No, it was!" the man insisted, "My parents had high hopes for me!"

Again they all laughed, Treas failed to see the humor in it all.

"I ran away from home when I was fifteen, then I was taken as a slave, that was nigh on forty years ago."

"How have you survived!?" asked a wide eyed seventeen year old.

"Most don't survive their first five years, but I have survived with a scrape here and a scratch there, and a little bit of 'know how' you learn how to work the system."

"What about you?" someone asked of an even older man.

"I was sold to repay a debt when I was very young," he answered quietly.

"No, what's your Namesake?" they clarified.

There was a silence and all eyes turned to the old man; he frowned. "I-I don't remember…"

No one laughed this time. Six hours later and Treas was back in the mines. Up, down; he had to get out of here! Just thinking of what that man had said- he had to get out. No, it was not just some foolish man being forgetful, he spoke first hand of the fear that every slave held in common. Just then Treas noticed that the slave beside him; the wide eyed seventeen year old, had bent over and picked up something. A bright flash of liquid fire caught Treasures eye; it was a ruby! Suddenly the words of the other man came to mind, the one who said his Namesake was King, in regards to surviving. 'You learn how to work the system.' The words echoed in his mind. When slaves found extra things like gems, they were rewarded by the slavers with special treatment. The boy put the gem in his pocket and went back to work no doubt intending to finish up for the day before handing over the gem.

Treas thought for a moment then turned away and walked towards the slaver who was keeping watch over the mining cavern; he looked Treas up and down and gripped his whip. Treas nodded towards the boy and said in a low voice, "He's hiding a ruby." The guard looked up at the boy and narrowed his eyes, than he stomped over to him. Treas turned away to work in a different part, an unpleasant smile was on his face and he turned a deaf ear to the boys cries. He knew that the guard would be giving him better treatment from now on, but he could not say the same for the seventeen year old.

Treas decided that he would 'work the system' to stay alive, no matter the cost. That night he was woken up by another whispered conversation in the den, he listened in.

"-and he just looked into the well and said 'this water will no longer poison anyone', and after that day it was just as Nity said!" the speaker was a new slave.

"Who's that?" Treas asked.

"The street teacher known as Eternity," the speaker answered.

"Who?" asked someone else.

"Nity! Don't you know?"

"Never heard of him."

"Never heard of Eternity!?" the slave said raising his voice.

"You forget I'm not a Garatin like you; I'm from the hill lands. And it's not like we hear very much here!"

Some laughed at his joke, Treas did not.

"Nity's a street teacher, he is, and a good one!" continued the new slave. "But that's not all he is, he also does the impossible! He walked right into a village crawling with the Black Death, and came out again!"

There was silence for a moment. "A wielder of black magic and sorcery!" someone muttered darkly.

"Aye! That's what I say! That one has made a deal with the very grave itself!" someone agreed with him, just then the slavers called out and ordered silence in the den; everyone obeyed.

Treas was about to roll over when he caught sight of the seventeen year old; a shaft of torch light from the front of the cave shone on his face, it was cut and bruised, his eyes were almost swollen shut, Treas felt a sense of power overwhelm him. Even as a slave he had found power. He had done this. He rolled over feeling pleased.

Up, down. Up, down. I must get out, I must escape! And this is my chance! A slave who slept in the outside quarters had died, and if Treas did it right, he would be able to slip into the column of slaves who were marched outside and when they were counted up and there was the same number of slaves as there was when they came into the mines - the slavers just might forget that one had died, just maybe escape was possible! It was not much of a plan, but who can say what a slave will do when escape is in his grasp?

The horn was sounded, Treas took a deep breath; it was now or never! The column of slaves started to form, the sound of their pickaxes being dropped into the barrel seemed to echo in his ears as Treas did the same with his pickaxe. He then took up position in the column. The other slaves took no notice of him, it had been a long day for them, they had worked for six hours-Treas on the other hand had just started an hour ago. No one would miss him until his column was counted up in five more hours! It was perfect! His heart pounded hard in his chest. 'Calm down!' he told himself, the last thing he needed was someone to take notice of him. They began to march in the darkness, on and on they went; it felt like forever! How long will it take to get out!?

He looked up, and over the heads of the slaves, he could see a light: and it wasn't the next lantern! It was a cold, silvery light; it was the moon! In a few moments they passed out of the wooden gate and he found himself blinking in the moon light and for the first time in, Treas did not know how long, he was outside!

A light breeze blew along the mountain and lightly ruffled his hair; he breathed in deep the fresh air. He looked down and noticed that there was dirt under his feet! He dug his toes into the cool dirt and almost smiled. What luck! Not only had he gotten this far, but it was night as well! But freedom was not his yet! A slaver was working his way down the line counting.

"Twenty eight, twenty nine, thirty, thirty one, thirty two-" he passed by, but Treas did not even dare to breathe a sigh of relief, indeed he did not breath at all!

"Thirty three, thirty four, thirty five, thirty six, thirty seven, thirty eight! Move out then!" They started walking again, the path winded down the mountain and in between big boulders; it would be easy to slip away among them, no, be patient. He looked wearily at an escort slaver walking along beside the column, a whip held tightly in his big hand.

They rounded a corner then stopped; the head of the column had come to the sleeping quarters. They were to be counted again.

"Thirty eight, same as this morning." The deep voice of the head guard could be heard talking to the guard in charge of the sleeping quarters.

"Thirty eight! Don't be more of a fool than you can help! A slave died today, there should only be thirty seven!" the other guard said. Treas tensed; was he about to be found out? He looked up; a cloud was moving over the moon.

"No t-that can't be…I-I counted thirty eight, I know I did!" the other slaver snorted in disgust then took charge. "You there! Count them up!" He shouted to an escort slaver. There was a tense moment as they were counted up in a hurry.

"Thirty seven!" the slaver called out; there was silence as all the guards looked at one another…

"You! Halt! I said halt!" a voice shouted out from further back in the line.

Treas ran as hard as he could! I must get away! I must escape! He heard shouts behind him, his blood pounded in his ears, the hair on the back of his neck stood on end, his legs felt weak; this was the first time he had run in who knew how long! He scrambled along over rock and stone, his hands, bare feet and knees began to bleed. The fresh air that had seemed so wondrous before now stabbed at his lungs!

'ESCAPE! ESCAPE! ESCAPE!' his mind screamed! One of the slavers was close at his heels! No! Freedom was almost his! The life he had once known was just out of reach! Things flashed in his memory, things almost forgotten; the streets of Garason, independence, and-and something else- what was it? A figure, faded and elusive in the corners of his mind - sweet laughter, gray-green eyes, and copper hair, she had renewed his interest in life, it was Des-

Just than he was grabbed from behind by his ankle, he fell to the ground but he had no time to recover. He and the slaver rolled about on the sharp stones, locked in a death grip. No! I will not be taken back! I'll fight to the death… The silent vow he carved into his very soul! But death is not ours to command; it serves a greater master and will choose its own victims. A searing pain went down his back, and Treas could not see the moon anymore. 'Death, death, find me now.'

The strong breeze rippled down the Arrow River and onto the proud giant castle of Jarg. The fur trees on the mountain slopes bent and waved; and high on the ramparts and towers banners and flags were sent fluttering in the wind.

Yet another group of thirty some slaves were making their way from the docks and boardwalks into the town and then up to some mine or other, wide eyed and terrified, their shoulders still red from their new brands, were met with a gruesome sight. Just inside the gates was the town square in the middle of which was a stake, bound to it was a young man; he had been flogged. He hung limp and motionless, many believed him to be dead, but alive he still was- in a manner of speaking. For although life had betrayed him, death would not claim him. There for anyone to see, as plain as the brand on his skin; he had been punished, and likewise would anyone else found trying to escape. The slaves marched on.

It was late morning and the square was, for the most part, empty, except for a Five Isles merchant and his two customers. They were men from the north and after watching the column of slaves march through, one asked, "What's this lad done?" he nodding towards the middle of the square.

The merchant grunted, he had been witness to the flogging that morning, he wished that he hadn't; it had not been pretty. "Ah, he was caught trying to escape, I think." He for one was not used to such things. The two Garatin man looked at him.

"What will happen to him?" the younger of the two asked.

"Die," the merchant said bluntly. "If he isn't dead already," he added, aware of how cold it sounded.

This took the younger man by surprise. "Just for trying to escape!?" he asked in unbelief.

"He's an example, much the same as the last one and no different than the next one." The merchant explained sounding as if he wished it was not so.

The poor young man didn't know what to say, and was glad to change the subject and talk instead of the price of fruit from the Five Islands. But the older of the two, who was his brother, crossed the square and looked at the slave. He bent down to peer into his battered face, and was overcome with pity and something he knew to be compassion.

"Hey, you! Leave him be!" a voice boomed as a guard came to his feet and strode across the square.

Normally a nine foot giant invokes; obedience. But this man, who's Namesake was Quest, was known for his passion, high ideals and often times hasty actions, which were not always well thought out. But many times, like now, he was calm and cool and he was not about to back down to anyone; not even an angry nine foot giant.

"Will this lad stay here until he dies?" Est asked as soon as the giant was close enough to hear.

"If he's not dead already. Now I said-" Est cut him off with a calm voice, as if reassuring him.

"Oh, he's alive. How much does his master want for him?"

That took the guard by surprise, who would want to buy a half dead slave? But he was a shrewd man and he knew when a few coins might pass his way.

"How much are you willing to pay for him?" he said, looking down at Est much the same way a cat would a mouse before eating him. But Est refused to squirm; he felt his brother and the merchant watching.

"As I recall-" Est began as if just entering a game. "-the going price for a slave is fifty silver coins."

A greedy look came into the guards eyes.

"But since this lad is in, shall I say, less than good shape, I'll only pay a quarter that."

"Ah-" said the guard like he was giving away a good deal. "-but he's a young slave; he'll be as good as new in a few days! Half price," he stated in a flat voice that said 'that's the end of it.'

But Est was not intimidated, and he knew it to be a lie, this lad might not live through the night. "Look here, you can wait until he dies, then take care of the mess, or you can walk away now with twenty coins in your pocket."

There was a silence as the guard sized Est up; he obviously decided that Est was no fool.

"Done!" he said at last.

Est handed over the money, and as the guard walked away grinning Est went back to his brother.

"Fin, we're taking that slave with us, we'll have to be careful when carrying him; he's in bad shape." He half turned away when the merchant spoke up.

"Wait! I have a litter that you can carry him on." He then disappeared for a moment behind his stand, he then brought back the litter; a bit of leather stretched over two poles. "Free of charge," the merchant said as he gave it to Est.

Est paused, and then nodded; not everyone had a heart of stone. Quest and his brother then cut the slave loose from the stake and then carried him, face down, to their camp, located just outside of the town ramparts.

Chapter 11

Go Back

Treas opened his eyes. Why had death not claimed him yet? Why was he lying face down? Was he outside? Yes, he was; he could see the red light of the setting sun, how long had it been since he had seen it? And the light of a fire flickered on his face, his body felt like dead weight.

"He's waking up," a kind voice said from somewhere.

Treas tried to move, but the dead weight turned into white pain, the most he could do was a weak groan. A bit of damp cloth was pressed to his dry, cracked lips.

"Now we'll see if he lives the night," the voice said.

His eyes closed and the darkness took him again. How long he spent there he did not know. It felt like forever, blundering about in the hazy darkness, trying hard to remember something. But what that was he did not know. It was always just out of reach, and the darkness would not release him! It would not let him go and yet it would not destroy him. After what seemed a lifetime, the darkness lost its hold on him, and his eyes opened; he moaned softly.

"So lad, you're going to live after all!" the voice said.

Treas looked up as best he could; it was morning and outlined by the almost too bright sun light was a man, he was a Garatin!

"Here, I have a bit of broth for you." The man began to spoon feed Treas the best food that he had had in a long time, after living with hunger for so long it almost did not feel good to be full. When he had eaten as much as he could, Treas sighed. But even that caused too much pain; he didn't want to know what his back must look like.

"Very good, lad, now, my Namesake is Quest, and this is my brother, Finished," the man said, and then waited for Treas to say who he was.

Treas frowned, as he thought for a moment; what was his Namesake!? His panic must have shown on his face for all though they tried to hide it, both Quest and Fin had a look of horror as they realized that he did not remember! Treas squeezed his eyes shut, he must remember! He must.

"Treas-ure!" he said at last with effort, he breathed deeply even though it hurt; he had a Namesake, he was not just a slave among thousands!

Est smoothed the horror out from his face and smiled at Treas, in some small way he understood. Treas did not know it but he had spent two days in that darkness, in that time it had been uncertain if he would live. Over the next two weeks he drifted in and out of consciousness. Est and Fin did all that they could to nurse Treas back to health, indeed it might be said that they took him from the very clutches of death. When Treas was finally released from the darkness once and for all, he still could not move, and he hardly knew where he was, so there was not much discussion between him and his new masters.

Three weeks from the terrible flogging and Treas moaned as he sat up for the first time, his muscles were weak and he felt light headed, but he was determined to sit up. He did not like being dependent on anyone, he looked around and realized that their camp was outside of the town and between the tree line and the river. The mountains lay behind them and the river moved slowly as it wound past the castle walls. Treas could see the docks and boardwalks further down the shore.

"Go easy on yourself lad!" Est said as Treas fought against the pain.

To get his mind off the pain Treas spoke, "So, you two are Garatins?"

"Yes, we're from Quy Lake in fact," answered Fin.

Treas looked at them both from across their cold fire. "Why did you come here?! That is no small journey, even on horseback!" He could see that there were no horses in their camp.

"Which leads to the question as to how you got here, but as for us- it's a bit of a long story," Est began with a laugh. He went on to explain that they were sent by their leader.

Treas looked confused then asked, "Are you two knights?"

Fin laughed, "No! We're just farmers."

"But you have a leader?" Treas asked envisioning an old farmer holding carrots in one hand and group of farmers behind him vowing their allegiance.

"You see," Fin explained, "He's a street teacher-" Est who had grown quiet, interrupted his brother.

"Fin, you and I both know that he's more than that," he said quietly. Then to Treas he said, "His Namesake is Eternity and he has asked us to join him in his fight to set Garatin free."

"So you're rebels," Treas said flatly, he did not mean it as an insult; he was just merely trying to understand.

Fin smiled as if it was a joke.

"Call us what you will," Est said, "But Nity does no violence-" they went on to tell Treas about the town with the black plague, the poisoned well and many other such- unbelievable things. Treas thought Est and Fin foolish to believe such things. "But we were there," Est said when he saw the cynical look in Treasures eyes. "We saw these things with our own eyes, we can't not believe!"

Treas was still skeptical, could anyone do such things? To him they made good stories, but they were impossible, they could not have really happened. But that would mean that Est and Fin were liars. That night Treas awoke from a deep sleep, looking up at the stars he remembered the dream that he had had; in the dream Est had taken him back to Garatin and put him to work in a mine. The dream made no sense; there were no mines in Garatin, but the reality hit him in the face. He was still a slave; he just had a new master.

Treas spent another week flat on his front hardly daring to move his back. Four weeks out of the mines and Treas finally got around to shaving off his overgrown, straggly beard, after doing so he looked into a cup of water and was shocked at what he saw. He recognized his own face of course, but it was so much older than what he remembered! But what scared him were his eyes, so cold and lifeless... he had seen eyes like this before, in a face of stone belonging to a woman dressed in black, he had seen her the day he had left Garason however long ago that was! How he remembered it when so many other things had been forgotten, he did not know; all he knew was that he did not like that look in his own eyes. So hard and callous, was it too late to change? A few days ago he had worked it out with Fin; Treas had been in the mines for two years, was it too late to change?

"So Treas…" Est said, calling him back to the present, "It would appear that life is not done with you yet, what will you do now?"

For Treas it had been easy to forget, after all Est and Fin treated him just like any other man. But he must face the truth of it; he was still a slave.

"I am your slave now," he said looking down at his reflection in the cup of water. "I must do as you say." He finished, and he remembered the dream that he had had; he emptied the cup into the grass.

There as a moment of silence.

"Nonsense!-" Est broke it, "I will have no slave! You, Treasure, are free to do as you wish," he said it with a half-smile.

Treas looked up at him, being careful not to move his back. He wondered if he could have heard wrong, he looked past Est at the smiling face of Fin, than back at Est. "But-but I have no means to repay this debt…" he said, all confused, he did not have anything to buy his freedom with!

"No, you don't," Est agreed with him gravely.

Treas waited for Est to say that he had to work for him for the next five years. "Your freedom is a gift, Treas," Quest said simply.

"Why?" Treas asked bewildered, why would anyone do such a thing?

"Because the teachings of Nity say that you are a man; like any other. He sent us out to do as he does; he said that we would find someone in need of freedom. Naturally we thought of freedom in a different sort of way. I can see now that we were wrong; as always."

It was far beyond Treas's understanding as to why men would do such things for poor wretches like him; there was no profit in it. Who was this strange man, Nity, who believed that slaves were men and that freedom, was for everyone?

The next day Est went into Jarg and came back with things for Treas; new clothes, a cloak, and a bag full of traveling supplies. He walked into their camp and put the things down in front of Treas.

"I assume that you will be leaving Jarg at some point, and I do not want to hear about needing to repay me for these," Est said when Treas tried to protest. Treas closed his mouth and slowly went through the things feeling grateful and stunned all at once. Est sat down close by and said. "And now that we're down to it, Fin and I must leave and return to Garatin. We wish you the best and that your future will be better than your past: may Eloi guide you in it."

Treas was startled by the name of Eloi, why would Eloi take interest in him? But he spoke before anything else could be said, "Quest, Fin I-I... I owe you both not only my freedom but my life, and I will find a way to repay that debt, some day."

Est had been surprised when Treas had spoken up, but now he pressed his lips together and said, "Now, we all know that it was Nity who sent us-" Treas interrupted him.

"This is why I must see him."

Est and Fin both paused.

"I'm asking you to take me with you, please."

Est frowned and asked, "Are you sure Treas?"

"Yes, I am." And so it was that Treas began a new life, little did he know where it would take him. Treas, the slave, would have thought nothing of taking advantage of Est and Fin, but perhaps it was such intense kindness that gave him the desire to meet their inspiration, or perhaps he felt an obligation to thank this strange man known as Nity. Or maybe he just wanted to stay close to Est and Fin, and find out where they had gotten the happiness that they so clearly had. Treas himself did not know which one it was that drove him to go with Est and Fin; he just knew that he had to.

Two days later all three of them packed up and took a raft up the Arrow River. They stayed at the eastern Sister town, and instead of crossing the plains they decided to go by the coastal road; along the Nennor Sea. Treas felt as though a new chapter were being opened in his life, as if anything were within reach: what lay in store for him in this new life? Would he ever remember what his old life had been like? Would he ever find what it was that he had been searching for in the darkness?

Far from the dust and poverty of the streets in Garason, high in a room of silk and velvet, in an unmistakable Tarven environment, Loy sat quietly and listened as her husband Courage explained the latest orders from the Ambassador Ister. Loy nodded, she had not asked why Rage had to leave, indeed she never asked questions when it had something to do with his work, but this time he had volunteered the information; he was going into the Byla once more in the hopes that Wilder would return with him. If he did so then the unrest in the country would settle. That was all she needed to know and indeed it was more than she wanted to know.

"And you believe he will return with you" she asked carefully.

Rage was silent for a moment. "I think he will…" he said at last. "He did the last time."

Loy nodded, "When shall I look for your return?"

"A little over a month perhaps," he answered.

Loy smiled ruefully as she skillfully changed the subject, "Mise will be fit to be tied if her flower blooms while you are away."

Rage laughed, Mise had become quite excited the past few months; her flower, the Cres`aren, had grown and would bloom in the next few months.

There was a moment of silence, and then Loy said, "Well… I shall await your home coming eagerly in the knowledge that you will bring back hope for this sad country."

"Yes…" Rage agreed softly, "Wilder is our only hope."

*   *   *

The wind played in her copper hair as Desti watched the horizon. A horse and rider were approaching the little cottage, and Desti watched in amazement as she realized who it was; it was Courage. What was he doing here!? It had been two and a half years since Desti and her father had returned from Garason, but there was no mistaking him. This was indeed her father's old friend; back from the past, once again. He rode up and came through their little gate, he then dismounted before her.

"Good morrow, Destination," Rage said after looking at her for a moment.

"Good morrow, sir." she answered in bewilderment. "M-May I take your horse?" she then asked, if there was one thing she knew in all of this; it was that Rage had not come all this way to wish a good morrow to her!

Rage nodded and handed her the reins to his stallion then went on to the main cottage. There was a time when Desti would have rushed the grooming of Courage's horse so as to go into the cottage in the hopes of hearing what was being said. But if there was one thing that she had learned it was this; her father's past held a dark secret, and he had worked hard to pull a curtain in between her and this dark past. Why should she pull that curtain aside? They were happy now! Yes, life was mundane, but also stable, predictable and safe. All that would change if this curtain was torn away-Rage was part of the secret and it seemed as though his very presence brought a stiff breeze that made the curtain ripple: Desti felt as though she was holding the curtain in place, she didn't want to know what lay behind it!

"She looks even more like Dream than when last I saw her," Rage told Wilder after their greetings.

"Yes... she does," Wilder said looking out through the half open shutters at his daughter. He shook himself and turned to his friend. "I must say that I'm surprised to see you Rage."

"I wish I could say that I just came to see an old friend, but that's not entirely true..." Rage began, he sat down at the rough table and Wilder joined him. "I'll get right to the point, Wilder. You remember Nity?"

Wilder thought for a moment then nodded, "What's become of Liveran? Did Dain release him?"

"No, he had him executed a little over a year ago, I don't know the details," Rage answered.

Wilder nodded, "What has Nity got to do with all this then, I thought you were assured that he was no threat."

Wilder was being kind and Rage knew it. It had been Rage who had assured Wilder that Nity was no threat and Wilder was the one who had doubted, now it appeared that those doubts had some merit to them.

"Well, he has become a bit of a problem…" Rage said delicately, he hated to admit that he was wrong.

"In what way?"

"You might recall that he too became a street teacher, but he-he… he does the impossible!" Rage told him about the many stories of Nity's activities.

"And whose robe has he treaded upon?" Wilder knew that Nity had to have upset someone important; otherwise Rage would not be here.

"The Garatin leaders seem to have a problem with him," Rage said it in a way that suggested that the Garatin leaders had problems with lots of people. "And they cried on Ister's shoulder and he in turn came to me, and I have come… to you," he finished looking into Wilder's gray eyes.

"And what has he done that they have a problem with him?"

"That's what makes this so difficult; the man is above reproach in everything! No one can find any true dirt on him other than that he was born out of wedlock. He defies old standing Garatin traditions, and outright denounces Garatin laws! And when accused of this he has some older law to back him up, he seems to thrive on loop holes!"

"Why have the Garatin leaders come to you? Isn't that their problem?"

"Well, yes it is, and when I said that they came to Ister. Well what I meant is that Ister went to them and told them that they had better take care of him before he causes trouble, but the only solution is to silence him, and as you know the Garatins have no authority to do executions. And they want something not quite so public-"

"So Ister came to you," Wilder finished for him.

"Yes, the long and short of it is that he is a cock who has crowed too loudly," Rage said his voice full of meaning; he was a little out of breath.

"Is Tarva in the habit of silencing every out of tune rooster?" Wilder asked calmly.

"No-" Rage answered, aware of his friend's views of these things, "-just the ones who have a hen house to cheer them on."

"What do you mean?"

"Currently there are three major rebel groups in the area who have sworn allegiance to Nity should he need them, along with the oath that they will drive the Tarvens from Garatin forever or die trying. Nity has not made a move to revolution – yet. But if he does, the entire country will answer his call! We can't let that happen!" Rage finished with passion.

There followed a moment of silence, Wilder was gazing out the window; his face giving away nothing of the intense debate within his soul.

"I will think on this Rage," he said at last. "When do you plan to return?" he asked.

"When you come with me," Rage answered with a straight face.

Wilder paused and looked at him, then they both smiled. Wilder looked back out the window, what would Desti think of all this?

Wilder could not sleep that night and he found himself outside instead. The long grass brushed his legs and the stars shone in the sky like rain drops on a rose petal, each one seemed to be earnestly trying to tell Wilder something, only lacking the voice to say it. Surprisingly enough his thoughts were not on the problem that Rage had presented. No, Wilder had already made up his mind on that matter. Rage had come with dark news; the storm had not passed away. Instead the wind brought whispers of rebellion and unrest. Could Wilder passively stand by? Nity must be stopped!

Yes, Wilder's mind was made up. His thoughts were instead on Desti; he still could not find it in him to tell her about himself. He would rather her stay here; uninvolved. But then there was his promise, that he would take her with him if he ever returned to Garason. He had not forgotten it even if they had not spoken of it in a year and he was sure that she had not forgotten it either, he could not go back on his word! If there was one thing that he treasured it was his daughter's respect for him With a sigh he returned inside, passing her room he noticed that there was a light coming from underneath Desti's door. He knocked softly on her door then cracked it open. She was sitting on the floor leaning against her bed; a candle, sitting on its brass plate flickered beside her, casting a warm light upon her. She looked up and smiled at him as he eased himself down beside her.

"My thoughts will not rest tonight," she explained softly.

He nodded, "I think I know why." He gave her a knowing look; he then leaned his head back and looked up at the thatched roof. He wasn't sure but he thought he could see stars twinkling through. He wondered vaguely if the rain also leaked into her room. "You might as well know that Rage has asked me to return to Garason with him," he said softly.

"Why?" she asked with a frown.

He heaved a deep sigh and turned his eyes once again upon her, and then asked, "Desti, do you trust me?"

The sad look that Desti found in his eyes broke her heart! "Of course I do." How could she answer any differently? Already she regretted even asking him why; she did not want to know!

"Then trust me when I say, you don't need to know, Desti," he spoke in earnest, looking into her eyes.

Relieved, she rested her head on his shoulder.

"And will you do as he asked?" she asked after a moment.

"Yes, we will leave on the morrow- or the next day."

Desti did not say anything.

"I once promised you that I would take you with me if I ever went back," he said and waited for her response; he was not disappointed. She looked up at him in surprise he looked back at her gravely, as if to prove that he was serious.

"Thank you, Daddy," she whispered as she rested her head back on his shoulder.

The next morning the three of them made their plans; Rage was not really surprised at the news that Wilder's daughter would be accompanying them, he knew how distraught his friend had been two years ago when he had found that his daughter had wandered about Garason by herself for a week; it had terrified Wilder. They would leave at first light the next day.

Desti had not been this excited for years, two and a half to be exact. To go back to Garason! But would it be like last time? What if she could not find Treas? Or worse, what if he did not remember her? No, Desti was not without doubts. But the most important question to her was; could she hold the curtain in place while in Garason?

The next day they started out across the plains, she could tell that Rage and her father wanted to discuss something important, but not with her there! That was fine with her; she did not want to know. Instead Rage told them that a week after they arrived in Garason he and his wife were going up to the Quy Lake region, to where they had just bought a summer manor. They would be staying there for some time, Desti and her father would of course accompany them. That's when Desti gave up all hope of running into Treas; since he did not live in Quy, well… maybe not all hope.

*   *   *

Thunder crackled and the sky was rent in two, for a brief moment the darkness was lit up in an eerie light, then it ebbed away into darkness. A creature of the darkness reemerged and ran on, frenetically searching for a better hiding place to wait out the storm before the next strike of lightning. The storm raged on and rain fell in torrents, deranging the miserable creature, threatening to lay bare all the evils it had done. The creature stumbled over something, lighting flashed again and it was lit up. It was Gra's dead body… The creature shrieked and ran on blindly, but there was no hope; this storm would go on for all of eternity.

Wait! That was it, this storm was Nity! The creature of darkness also had a Namesake, but it no longer had meaning in her life.

Ree was jolted awake by the answering clap of thunder; she calmed down when she realized that it was just a horse and cart going down the street. For almost three years now, dreams had tortured her by night, they refused to do what she had succeeded in doing; forgetting. No, Nity would not forget what had happened, she did not know how, but he knew! She breathed deeply; this storm would destroy her.

Chapter 12

Copper

The sun beat down on the busy market square full of Garatins and Tarvens alike, flies were brushed away from goods for sale, women swished colorful fans, children darted amongst the crowd and many voices blended together in a loud but pleasant way; it was a typical market for Garason. Treasure watched it like he was a stranger to it all. Although having arrived in Garason a week ago with Est and Fin, Treas felt like an unwanted guest in his own home. It was as though Garason had forgotten him and over the last two and a half years had gotten on quite well without him.

At first, it had felt like he had finally come home, and he had promptly gone out for a walk, thinking to reacquaint himself with all the old streets that he had grown up on. But to his surprise and lasting dismay he did not remember the old streets and passage ways and he had gotten lost; it took him hours to find his way back to the inn that he was staying at with Est and his brother. Yes, Garason had forgotten him, and likewise he had forgotten Garason.

Treas hated being so dependent on Est and Fin, but if it had not been for them, Treas would never have made it this far. Again and again the brothers proved that their kindness was unconditional, they held nothing back. Many times over Treas had wondered how they could open up like that. How they could make themselves so vulnerable? Didn't they ever get hurt? They must! And yet it did not stop them.

Traveling north along the shore of Nennor, they passed through many fishing villages and towns. Never once did Est and Fin pass up the chance of helping someone, whether it was helping to build a new cottage or to bring in a large load of fish. They never hesitated to pitch-in and help. Once they even stayed in one town for a week to care for an old woman who had fallen ill. But as long as he lived Treas would never forget what happened when they were going through the town of Finsin.

They were on the outskirts when they came across a man who was flogging his slave. Upon seeing it Treasure's chest had tightened and his breath would not come. The scars of hardly healed wounds on his own back had burned with remembrance and the day he should have died came back with shocking clarity. He looked away, his emotion choking him. Est had approached the man and asked him why he was punishing his slave. The man said that he had a field of wheat that needed to be harvested but the slave had not been doing it fast enough. Fin had without hesitation volunteered to do the slave's work for that day. The master of the slave was quite bewildered but after a few moments of stunned silence, he let Fin do the slaves work and allowed Est care for the slave as he disappeared on his own business.

Treas had not wanted ever to do any work for anyone again, but that was the first day that he did 'slave' work after the mines. He could not stay with Est and help care for the slave, it was too much for him. Instead, he went along with Fin into the field. At the end of the day Treas and Fin returned where they had left Est at the man's cottage. Even though the slave's wounds were not nearly as bad as Treasures had been, Treas expected the slave to be flat on his stomach wincing with pain as Est brushed away flies. But instead when the two of them stepped through the door of the little shack where the slave slept- the slave was sitting up! And his wounds looked like old scars! No sooner had they stepped into the room than they were followed by the slave's master, and again the poor man was stunned into silence at the sight he beheld.

The man vowed from that day on never again to flog his slave. Treas was astonished, so much so that he could not speak! Not much was said that night as the three of them sat around a fire in their camp. Est did not speak at all that night or the next morning ether! It almost was like he was just as astonished as everyone else, Treas remembered looking at him from across the fire that night and thinking that Nity must be able to do the impossible; because he had seen Est do the same.

None the less, nothing could have prepared him for meeting Nity himself. Somehow Treasure had envisioned a man with gray hair, wise eyes and a stern voice and never without a book of the old Garatin laws in his hands; but nothing could be further from the truth! Nity was a man no more than thirty, a Garatin through and through and as such had blond-brown hair, which was cut much the same as Treasures and of average height and build.

Two things caught his attention right away; the first was a raw energy within Nity, as though he was just waiting to do something big and important. The other thing, were his eyes, they seemed like they were pools of wisdom and when Nity looked at him, Treas felt transparent - as though Nity knew everything about him! "As if he knows that I'm a man without honor... but that would be impossible!" Treas had thought at the time. But then didn't Nity do the impossible?

Treas had decided then and there that he must stay away from Nity; it was too dangerous to be with him, what if Nity called him out on all his lies? As grateful as Treas was to Nity for his freedom, he must stay away from him! Nity demanded too much of people, you just couldn't hang about him; you were either for him or against him, there was no in between. Treas had vowed never to commit to anyone ever again, never trust anyone and he would be protected from all betrayal and pain. But that was not good enough for Nity, he did not tolerate fakers. How long would he put up with Treas sitting on the fence?

They had met up with Nity in a little town between the Cokhawk forest and the city of Garason and since then the group of them, about fifteen strong, had traveled together into Garason. But soon Nity would be returning to his home in the Quy Lake region, along with Est and the others. Nity had asked Treas to come along too. Treas had not yet told him that he would not be going with them, but he would, at some point. There was no way that he was going to go with Nity! Treas's thoughts were brought back to the busy market as his stomach made an unhappy sound. Normally he would eat with Est and Fin, but they were with Nity, and right now Treas would rather go hungry than be around Nity!

Up ahead of him there was a barrel of apples and the man selling them had just turned his back. Treas walked by the barrel without looking at it and no one saw him take a big red apple. He was about to take a big bite out of it when he felt a prick at his conscience. There was a time when he had wanted to leave this lifestyle behind him - what had changed? He ignored the uncomfortable thought and leaned against a sun baked wall as he ate the apple. A few moments later he threw away the core and watched the people rush by, he sighed; would he ever belong here again?

Pushing off the wall he turned to leave the market when a horse came trotting towards him. The crowd made way for the horse but pressed close again when the horse was past. There was no one on the horse and Treas was about to sidestep it, when the horse stretched out his neck and bit Treas on the shoulder! Treas grabbed his shoulder, he then gave the horse a look that said 'what was that for!?' The horse did not look one bit sorry for it ether! Treas forgot about his shoulder and grabbed the halter; this horse looked familiar somehow. Memories forgotten in the mines, slowly came back in clipped images; a day in the sun, cold water and chasing this horse with- someone, but who? Could it possibly be? The horse snorted. Just then he heard a voice coming from behind the horse.

"Oh, excuse me! I'm sorry." A young woman was making her way around the horse.

That voice! Could it possibly be!? Just then he caught sight of wild, copper hair.

"Treas!?" Desti felt sure that she was dreaming, any moment now she would wake up and smile at her own silliness, but she didn't wake.

"Destination?" he breathed in response. Yes! It was true!

"Oh!" she squealed in delight as she threw her arms around his neck. Treas stood still in shock with his arms hanging lose, Desti stepped back and looked at him, Treas put his hands on her shoulders and he looked at her as if she would disappear.

She laughed and said, "I can't believe it's you!"

At long last Treas smiled, "It is you".

"It's been so long, Treas! I… I," she did not know what to say, it had been so long - two and a half years! And time had indeed done its work on Treas. No more was he the streetwise lad who had never left Garason; he looked as strong as a dragon warrior! But it was his eyes that held her, blue as ever. And yet, something was wrong; he looked as though he had tasted the world and found it bitter. Desti pushed aside the thought, all that mattered now was that the impossible had happened!

Willow nuzzled his head in between Desti and Treas, breaking the magical world of which the two had found for just a few minutes. Desti suddenly became aware of the busy market around them.

"Walk with me?" Desti suggested more then asked, but Treas didn't protest. They began on their way out of the market square.

For a few moments Treas just stared at her, at a loss for words, then as if he suddenly remembered how to speak he said, "What are you doing back in Garason!?"

Desti bit the inside of her lip, what was she to say? In all truth she did not know why they were here, she fiddled with Willow's reins. 'Ah, well...' she had to say something! "My father came to visit his friend." It was true.

Treas waited a little before he asked, "The Tarven?"

"Yes," she said as if it did not matter, if she had been paying attention she would have seen Treas look down and frown as if he had remembered something- unpleasant.

"So, how long will you be staying here?" Treas asked, breaking the silence.

"Well, we arrived just a few days ago-"

Treas interrupted by asking, "Who's we?"

"Oh, my father and I and his friend Courage-" Again she did not notice it when Treasure frowned.

"But I'm afraid that we won't be staying long," she said with some distress. "We will be accompanying Rage to his summer manor soon."

"For how long? Will you be coming back to Garason?" Treas asked looking at her.

She shrugged her shoulders and said, "I don't know."

"Where is this manor?"

"Oh, um..." she thought for a moment, "In the Quy Lake region I think."

Treas snapped his head around to look at her!

"This is more than I've done in the past two and a half years!" Desti laughed, trying to put on a brave face in all this uncertainty. "What about you, what have you been up too?" she asked.

"Oh, you know…" Treas said looking away as if he was bored with this subject. "I've done a bit of traveling."

Desti raised her eyebrows, "Where have you gone?" she asked when he did not say anything more. There was silence for a moment as though Treas did not want to say.

"To the Dinco Mountains and the castle of Jarg," he finally admitted softly.

Desti did not say so but she had studied her father's maps, hungry to know more about the world around her. She knew where he was talking about. She thought it strange that Treas would go there. She waited for Treas to say more of his travels but he didn't. They walked on down the street with Will following them.

"It really is too bad that I have to leave so soon," Desti said.

"Well, I'll be here when you return."

Desti smiled, but both she and Treas knew that she might not return to Garason, they just did not want to talk about it.

"Just don't leave without saying farewell again," Treas said with a twinkle in his eye, but Desti did not see it and she turned to him in a rush.

"I am sorry about that Treas! I really did want to see you before we left, but I never got the chance because of the riots, father wanted to get away before they began. I truly hope that you can forgive me."

Treas looked at her and raised his eyebrows as if he was not sure if he would forgive her, but the terrified look in her eyes made him smile. "Desti!-" he said with a laugh. "I never could say no to you! How could I hold a grudge against you?!"

She laughed with relief, and without really knowing it, they had ended up in the shadow of Rage's manor. Just beyond where they stood was the double gate with iron enforcements and on its far side was the smaller postern; it stood open.

"Oh! Here we are," she said, surprised at how fast they had reached it.

"Oh yes, how could I forget this place?" Treas said looking over the wall at the great Tarven manor. Treas and Desti went on to talk about everything and nothing! Just the way two old friends can and it was noon when Desti finally made her way inside. Treas had promised to return the next day, although they had not discussed it, both of them knew why they had parted company so early in the day; they needed time to think, to work through this new change in their lives.

Walking down a carpeted hallway Desti noticed a flicker of light coming from the library, she knew that Rage would be away all that day so she peaked through the slightly open doors. Her suspicions were correct; her father was inside sitting in front of the fireplace. His arms were resting on his knees as he leaned toward the fire. The curtains were drawn casting the large room into shadow, and the fire that he was staring into was dying.

"Daddy?" she called softly, coming into the room.

He straightened and turned to her like he was awakening from a dream, yes, she thought, the dream from which he had never woke; Eam. She sat down beside him. He looked at her.

"What is it daughter? You look like you've just found a fairy!"

She bit her lip to try and hide the smile that came, it didn't work. "I think I have! Father, I-I found Treasure! We bumped into one another at the market!" She bit her lip again, what would he think? Why am I afraid? A little voice asked in her mind. "You remember him, don't you?" she asked when he didn't reply.

He looked at her long and hard than nodded. "I'm happy for you, it's not often one meets a friend on these streets," he said at last, and Desti decided that he was sincere, she smiled.

"But father-" she asked with concern, "We will be returning to Garason after we go to Quy- won't we?"

"I don't know Desti, perhaps."

She believed that he spoke the truth and that was enough for her. Up in her chamber she curled up on her cushioned stone window seat and swung open the brass framed windowpanes and watched the streets below,

110

a tender smile on her face. She felt in her heart that things had changed, perhaps her life did have a destination after all. She giggled to herself; she did feel like she had found a fairy.

Treas made his way up the back stairs of an inn; the owner was good friends with Nity and was allowing him and his company to stay at half price. Treas shared a room with Est and Fin and two other men by the Namesakes of Obedience (Dien) and Appeared (Peare), they too were brothers, and had grown up with Est and Fin in Quy, but right now the room was empty. Treas sank down on to his lumpy cot. He heaved a heavy sigh as he tried to work out what had just happened; at first he had not really remembered her. The Namesake Destination had just sort of popped out. She looked familiar to him but only from his dreams, but she seemed to know him! Then bit by bit it had come back as she spoke, it had felt like falling off a horse. For a few moments it was just terrifying free fall where nothing made sense. Then, he hit the ground and the memories knocked the wind out of him. Even now he was not sure that he remembered it all. It was like he was rediscovering his past, something that he had been without for some time now. The darkness and years of slavery faded for a moment as the life he had once known became clearer. He squeezed his eyes shut, where had he first met her? In the market? No in an alley, she was being mugged and he had saved her. The wild flight that he had led her on came back in shadowy images, then there were other memories, happier ones.

Sunshine, laughter, cold water, being out of breath, was it all a dream? Or had it really happened? Treas opened his eyes, not all memories of this copper haired girl were pleasant; she had hurt him! Yes he remembered it now, how she had disappeared without a word of farewell. He had let himself care too much, and in doing so had made himself vulnerable, weak, and susceptible to heartache. Well, now he knew better. He stood up and started to pace the small room. If there was one thing the silver mines had taught him it was that you could not survive with a soft heart. True she may not have meant to hurt him, but if she could do it accidentally once what was stopping her from doing it again?

'No Treas,' he said to himself through clenched teeth. 'If you were smart, you would stay away from her!' Another memory was fighting for clarity in his mind - something about her father, a secret of some sort - what was it? He shook his head, it did not matter; Desti was no longer part of his life. He suddenly remembered that he had promised to see her tomorrow; he paused, could he leave it just like that? Move on as if nothing had happened? Yes! And he would! 'I will not get hurt again!' he gritted his teeth. She would be leaving soon for Quy Lake, and that would be the end of it! So too would Nity, Est and Fin, and that was just fine, this had all gone on for too long! Treas was too dependent on Est as it was, and the sooner he broke ties with him the better it would be! Treas would live a new life style, he would be strong and vulnerable to no one, he would trust no one and live alone, and-and… he would be safe. He took a deep breath to strengthen his resolve.

Chapter 13

Bareback

"It is our hopes that he won't expect it in his own hometown. But being a stranger you will be watched," Rage explained to Wilder late at night. They were in his, oh so familiar library standing before a wall where a map of northern Garatin was pinned up. "Ister has stressed that this is to be as non-public as possible, so our only hope is to get him on the road. But that is unlikely since he travels with body guards where ever he goes. And as if things were not complicated enough, Ister is now not so sure this assassination is necessary - which I disagree with, but I do not give the orders," Rage expressed his frustrations. "He says that Nity has not been doing any damage lately, but all the same we cannot let the man out of our sight. He is too much of a risk just to ignore him. Ister thinks that Nity will just go home and become a 'good little boy' again. I disagree with him, but his orders are clear, to observe only and send regular reports on Nity's activities," Rage finished.

"I understand," Wilder said.

"I'm glad one of us does," Rage said with a smirk.

*   *   *

Nity's home town was really just a fishing village on the north-west side of Quy Lake. There were many such towns all around the lake, most everyone knew each other and some of the smaller villages were made up entirely of one family! To the north of the Quy Lake region was the castle and keep of his Majesty Ordained. But it was the Duke Consider who governed the region. His manor had a view of the mouth of the Quy River, and he also had a smaller manor in a town close to where Nity grew up. This was where Rage was taking Wilder, Desti and his own wife and daughter. The women had been told that they were going to a manor that Rage had just acquired and that they all would be staying there for some time. However Rage knew that his wife suspected differently. Loy knew of his work, she also knew never to ask questions about it. They had agreed long ago that it was never to be discussed - so much so that Mise had no idea about her father's dark life.

Through spies, Rage had learned that Nity and his company were planning to leave in two days. They would be followed, at a discreet distance, by Rage and company. There would always be someone watching Nity whether it was soldiers hiding in the shadows or Wilder and Rage themselves. Wilder sighed; it would soon be over, he told himself.

*   *   *

The next day Desti leaned out of her window. A frown was on her face as she looked below, the afternoon sun glared in her face. Turning from the window she walked across her large room, too large in her opinion. Still frowning, she opened up the big oak door and made her way down the hallways of Courage's manor. She breathed a sigh of relief when she found her way down to ground level. 'It's too easy to get lost in here,' she said under her breath. She made her way to the nearest servant door and went out into the courtyard; she crossed it and poked her head out of a side gate. She looked both up and down the street but she did not find what it was she was looking for. Where was Treasure? Turning back into the courtyard she asked a passing stable boy if there had been anyone about that day.

"No, sorry miss. No one's been about," he said then went on his way.

Desti hugged herself as if she had gotten a chill in the heat of the day, then with one last reluctant look at the gate she returned inside. Would Treas have forgotten? Had something happened to him? Why had he not come!? She could have almost believed that she had only imagined finding her fairy the day before! Where was Treasure!?

"No, I'll carry my flower." Mise informed her maid. Promise was newly turned thirteen and already resembled her mother in every way, a long face, beautifully tanned skin, brown-black curls that cascaded down her back and her eyes were the color of cinnamon. Although beautiful and sweet tempered, she was spoiled. After all she was the only daughter of a rich Tarven. Mise had placed the Cres'aren flower that she had been growing for the past two and a half years into a tiny little chest to keep it safe; still, she did not trust it to anyone.

Mise looked around the courtyard as if she was the sole owner of it. There was a group of servants carrying a rolled up pavilion, and they were trying to get by her. She stood oblivious to it all, they did not dare to ask the master's daughter to move, and instead they awkwardly tried to get around her. Then she saw Desti and walked toward her, the servants looked at each other in frustration as she cut off their path once again.

"What's wrong Desti?" Mise asked as she reached her, "Are you still waiting for your friend?"

Desti nodded, she had been wandering about hoping that Treas would just pop out. "I thought he would have come by now, but..." her voice trailed off as she looked around. She had been feeling rather useless all that morning, since she was not allowed to pack her own things. Loy would not stand for it. It had been three days now since she had seen Treas.

"Well... you could leave a message for him with one of the servants who are staying behind," Mise offered eager to be of help.

That did not really help, Desti wanted to see Treas. "Yes, thank you Mise, I'll try that," she said to humor her, and wandered off.

Mise smiled, quite pleased with how useful she was. She looked back at the servants busy at work in the courtyard, loading wagons with trunks and rolled up pavilions. A group of servants had left the day before so as to ready the manor before the master arrived. Four wagons of supplies would accompany the travelers; they would be leaving within the hour. It was a two week journey through the grass lands to the Quy Lake region and the King of Tarva insisted that Tarvens should travel in style! They would have several large tents for the family and guests to use, as well as tents for the servants. They would travel with a cook and a kitchen wagon. Among the many servants coming, there would be groomsmen to care for the horses, and personal servants for each of the family members. For safety, they would be escorted by a company of soldiers.

It was all quite typical of a rich, traveling Tarven lord, anything less and then something would have been amiss. Loy and Mise had never known anything but luxury, and Rage, although a soldier and a rugged man did not mind being pampered. Wilder on the other hand found it all quite ridiculous, seeing as how he had traveled much further distances with only what he could carry on the back of his own horse! He would have felt much more at home on the cold hard ground than on a feather bed!

Poor Desti felt awkward in the lap of luxury, cramped in her large tent and uncomfortable under warm fleece blankets. It took her three days to convince Loy that she really did not need a lady in waiting to help her get out of bed in the morning! She felt like she was being smothered. Her only saving grace was bareback riding! She would wake early in the morning and take Will out for a short gallop of pure joy, it made Desti shudder to think of what Loy would do if she found out.

Early on the fifth morning of their journey Desti slipped out of her tent as quiet as could be, and crept along through the camp to where Will was tied up with the rest of the mounts. She then led him through the camp with her heart beating fast. It just would not do to be caught. Loy had standards that just had to be met; something about what ladies do and don't do.

"What are you doing?"

Desti nearly jumped out of her skin! She spun round to see Mise standing there in her night dress.

"I- ah…I-" she suddenly realized how ridiculous this was, she wasn't going to cower to a girl! "I'm going for a ride," she answered truthfully.

"Without a saddle?" through the morning twilight Desti could see the confusion on Promise's face.

Desti nodded, than hesitated before asking, "Haven't you ever been bareback riding before?"

"No!" Mise said, shaking her head as if the whole thing was unfathomable!

"Would… would you like too?" Desti asked.

Mise looked at her with shining eyes. "May I!?" she asked.

Desti smiled. Will neighed softly as Desti helped Mise onto his back. She then pulled herself up in front of her, her wide riding skirt flowed over each side of Will. "Now hold on to me as tight as you like," Desti whispered over her shoulder.

Mise wrapped her arms around Desti's waist, holding her tightly. Desti than kicked Willow's sides and in few moments they were flying over the fields. Will neighed for joy as Mise let out a laugh. Copper and black curls were wild behind them, and Desti raised her face to the wind and felt her soul take flight. The camp was far behind them when Will slowed down to a trot, Desti and Mise bounced on his back and soon the both of them were giggling like children! Their laughter died away as Willow slowed to a stop. The grass lands that they traveled over reminded Desti of the Byla Wilderness, except that there were no rivers. It was all gentle rolling fields with high grass dotted with the odd tree. Out on the horizon the haze of forests could be seen. The road that they followed was well used and led to the manor of Governor Consider, but after that the road was less used and the high grass would disappear giving way to shrubs and willow trees. Desti took a deep breath and tears sprung to her eyes, this reminded her too much of the day she had spent with Treas in the gardens of Jes'reel. Oh why had he not come!?

"Do you miss your friend?" Mise asked.

Desti was a little surprised at first, she then heaved a heavy sigh. 'He said that he would come…' she whispered to herself. "Yes Mise, I do miss him," she answered over her shoulder.

Mise frowned to herself. "I don't have many friends," she said quietly.

Desti looked over her shoulder at her, the girl looked so mournful. "I'll be your friend, if you like," she offered without hesitation.

Mise looked up in surprise. "Really?" she asked a little skeptical.

"Well of course, Mise!" Desti reassured her.

Mise smiled, "I'd like that."

Back at the camp the rising sun touched Wilder as he stepped out of his tent and let the door flap fall back into place. He took in a deep breath and surveyed the landscape; he was a little surprised to see a horse and rider out in the field, but he smiled ruefully when he realized that it was his daughter and Mise romping about. He then made his way to a fire pit and began to poke the still glowing coals with a stick; the servants who were beginning to wake paid him no heed. Ten minutes later Desti came from around a tent, a little breathless and flushed, she stopped when she saw him.

"Good morrow father! I just woke up, isn't it beautiful!?" she said passing by him.

"No telling what Loy will do when she finds out you took her daughter out bare back riding and in her night dress to boot," he said still looking at the fire.

It made Desti stop in her tracks and spin around to look at him in mute horror!

"Not very lady like, is it?" he added gravely looking up at her.

Desti rushed to his side and knelt before him. "Daddy! You- you won't tell, will you!?" she pleaded desperately.

He could not hold back a smile. "Not a word," he whispered; she smiled too.

*   *   *

It had been twelve days since they had left Garason when they came within sight of Quy Lake. Only one of the many villages around Quy Lake actually had a name, and that was the one that belonged to the manor of Consider; it was called Dahin. They would arrive at it that night. Although still a day's ride away from the manor, Loy had put on a rich dress of red silk. The sleeves floated behind her gracefully, her hair was gathered at the back of her neck in gold net, and she rode on a full-blooded, black mare. Mise was her mirror image in deep brown, on a bay mare. The two of them boasted of everything that was lovely and delicate in Tarva.

Rage on the other hand, rode a black stallion, his elaborate black and silver clothing only emphasized the long broad sword that he wore on his belt; he boasted of everything that was strong and proud in Tarva. In his presence it was impossible to forget who the conqueror was and who was the defeated. Wilder noted that as they rode through the small village, that even though they continued about their daily chores the fear in the Garatin peasants' eyes was evident. Wilder comforted himself with the knowledge that although a war hardened knight and a man of action, Rage believed in peace, didn't he? Wilder wondered if Rage knew of the effect that he had on the peasants.

That morning Desti had turned down Loy's offer of a fancier dress to wear, and now she felt out done by how dressed up Loy and Mise were, but she thought all the up-to-do was just plain silly! After all, the village that they were riding through was just a couple of cottages! Desti could not help but get the feeling that Rage and his family enjoyed exercising their superiority. Was it just a feeling? Up ahead she could see the manor of Consider with its high ramparts and lonely towers, it was resting on a hill overlooking the village. She frowned when Mise unexpectedly covered up her mouth when she had a sudden coughing fit.

Chapter 14

Scars

"I took the liberty of having this dress made for you, I hope you will like it," Loy said as she came into Desti's chamber where she and Mise were both sitting on a day bed.

Mise clapped her hands excitedly as Desti stood to her feet with her mouth open as a servant brought in a lovely dress of light pastel green embellished with the same shade of yellow. The waist dipped down in the front and the skirt flowed down to a short train in the back. The many layers in the wispy sleeves fell away at the shoulder. Desti had never seen such a dress before and couldn't possibly imagine wearing it herself! She was about to say so to Loy when she looked at her and saw that she had a tiny hopeful smile; she was trying so hard to make her feel at home!

"Thank you Loy, it-it's beautiful," she managed to say with a smile. Loy looked relieved and nodded with satisfaction. "Shall we do the final fittings?" she said happily.

They had arrived at the manor of Consider the night before, and the governor had planned a grand banquet that night, in their honor. Up to this point Desti had not intended on going but she saw now that that was not an option, and she resigned herself to her fate. Mise had been so excited all day that she could talk of nothing else! This was to be the first banquet that she was being allowed to stay for the dancing, even though there would be no one that she could dance with!

When the banquet finally began Desti entered the great hall on her father's arm and had he not held on tightly she would have fled right there and then! Great long tables were set up parallel to one another and the governor sat at the head table with his court surrounding him. One end of the hall had great arched windows with no glass panes in them and they let in the night breeze. The chandeliers above were alight and torches were everywhere. After being seated Desti was so terrified during the meal that she would break some eating edict and embarrass poor Loy forever that she could not remember what it was she had eaten. When the meal was over and the dancing finally began the best she could do was sit in a corner and try to breathe in her tight clothing. She was thankful that no one really knew her, and so no one asked her for a dance; especially as she did not know how to dance. Her head hurt; the maid-servant that Loy had sent to her before the festivities had arranged Desti's hair in a way that it had never been in before and hopefully, never would be again! She sat there and tried hard not to look too miserable. Across the hall Rage and Wilder stood side by side.

"Your daughter is one of the prettiest maidens here and yet she has not danced once!" Rage observed.

Wilder smiled, "She does not know how too," he said quietly. Men were not supposed to know of such things. Rage looked at him in surprise than back at the dancers.

"She should have consulted my wife; she would have been glad to teach her," he said.

Wilder's smile softened. "She does not care for such things," he said just as softly as he looked at her.

Rage frowned, "She should know the ways of the court. You need to arrange a marriage for her soon."

Wilder was silent, how could he part with Desti? How could he part with his living memory of Eam? He nodded, even though he did not agree with Rage. He then made his way around the hall to Desti's side.

Desti looked up at her father as he came to stand beside her. "I feel so awkward and out of place here," she spoke her mind at once. He laughed softly.

"I'm afraid neither of us belongs in this lifestyle!" he did feel ever so uncomfortable in the rich clothing he wore.

Desti frowned; it made her wonder where she did belong. She looked up just in time to see Mise across the hall quickly turn away to hide a sudden coughing fit, Desti's frown deepened. Much to her relief, the banquet was not everlasting. The next morn they departed and arrived in two days' time at Courage's manor. It was a small and for the most part, a friendly looking manor; it sat on a little hill and looked over a small village like a guardian. The village itself was on the north-west side of the lake and it sat right by the water. It consisted of a community oven where everyone sent their dough to be baked and a blacksmith who was a jack of all trades. There was no well and it was the duty of every young man or maiden to go down to the shore two or three times a day to fetch water. There was no real market day, for everyone grew their own food. The real farming went on in the lands in between Quy Lake and Corfin Forest. Those farms fed the city of Garason, and indeed the main work in this nameless town was fishing. The village had one cobbled street and two dirt ones that lead off of it; at the end of one of these was the manor.

Desti really had no quarrel with Rage, Loy or Mise. Indeed she was beginning to think of Mise as a little sister. Loy was so gracious that Desti could pretend, just for a moment, that she was her mother. Desti found it hard not to admire Rage, proud stubborn Tarven that he was. But just the same Desti had come to know more and more that what her father had said was true; she did not belong here. That was the reason that the day after their arrival she took Will from the stables for some exercise and started to walk him through the village. She soon saw that she would have to walk very slowly if she wanted the walk to take up any amount of time. It was then that she saw him, and truth be told, she was not really surprised to see him at all!

"Treas?" she said coming up behind him.

He turned to her at the sound of his name; he did not look surprised to see her either.

"What are you doing here?" she asked putting her hands on her hips with mock discipline.

"It's a bit of a long story," he said with a smile.

"My, but there are a lot of stories that you have yet to tell me!" she laughed.

"What do you mean?"

"Well-" she began as they began to walk along together. "- there is the one of what you have been doing for the past two and a half years, but right now I'd settle for why you're here," she said with a grin.

"Ah, well... a few friends of mine were returning home and were passing through this area and they asked me to come along." The answer seemed a bit vague to Desti, but she did not say so.

"And where are these friends now?" she asked instead.

"Oh, well, they're somewhere about looking for a place to stay for a bit- would you believe that the inn here only has two rooms?"

"You could stay with us! Well I mean at Courage's manor!" she offered excitedly.

Treas glanced at the manor with its sturdy ramparts and blowing flags; he shook his head and said ruefully, "I don't think that we'd be welcome." Desti realized what it was that he meant; what Tarven Lord would welcome Garatin peasants into his home? She wanted to tell him that he was wrong about this Tarven- but was he?

"Treasure?" a voice called. They both looked up to see a man coming towards them down the little crooked street; he stopped a little ways away.

"Is that one of your friends?" Desti asked.

"Yeah, it's Quest," he replied.

"We've found a place to stay," Est called out.

"I'll catch up," Treas told him, the man nodded then turned back the way he had come.

"When will I see you again?" Desti asked feeling a little desperate.

Treas thought for a moment before turning to her. "My friends will be having a banquet tonight, will you come?"

"I-ah…" she looked back at the manor, "where is it?"

"I don't know.. I'll come to the manor tonight and bring you there."

"All right," Desti agreed with a smile.

"Until tonight then."

With a nod Treas turned to go when Will reached out and bit his tunic, as if to say 'Aren't you going to wish me a good morrow?' Treas laughed as he pulled his tunic from Willows teeth and gave him a pat, but Desti was not laughing. She had seen something on Treasure's shoulder when Will had pulled at his tunic; a big ugly, scar… But not just any random scar, from what she could see of it, it was a perfect circle. The moment passed and she could hear Treasure laughing again, she forced a laugh of her own.

"Well, until tonight, Desti," he said as he turned away.

Desti tried to think; what was that!? What could cause such a scar!?

'I will not get hurt again!' Those had been his very words, and Treas had stayed true to them- for two days! And then he could stand it no longer and he had told Est last minute that he wished to accompany him and Nity to Quy. If he had known then just how big Quy Lake was, he would have seen how foolish it was to think that he would just bump into Desti there. But he had not thought of that, all he could think of was how much he wanted to see Desti again. Now, he saw how strange it was that Rage and Nity should come to the same place. He brushed the thought away. He could kick himself! He was just asking for more pain and heartache by following Desti!

For the entire two weeks it took to get to Quy, Treas had been trying hard to remember the past, there was something about Desti's father that made him nervous- something dark and sinister- but he could not remember what it was! It had something to do with his Tarven friend, Courage. Why was that Namesake so very familiar? Somehow he knew that Desti herself had no idea of this dark secret- whatever it was. Treas had half a mind not bring Desti to the banquet that night, and just disappear from her life once and for all! But he couldn't...

Destination frowned again when Mise coughed, after she had caught her breath she asked, "When will you return?"

"In a few hours," Desti replied.

"Are you sure your father won't mind it?" Mise asked, skeptical.

"Why would he mind?" Desti asked genuinely puzzled. "It's just a banquet, and besides he's not here to ask, I'm sure he won't mind."

Just than a maid servant came in. "Mistress? There is a young man at the cook's door asking to see you, shall I send him away?" she sounded a little too eager.

"No, that won't be necessary! Thank you. Goodnight Mise," Desti said quickly, then made her way as fast as she could to the cook's door. As she went she smoothed the skirt of her simple dress.

She was very relieved that she would not have to wear some ridiculous dress to this banquet unlike the last one. Upon greeting Treas he quickly led her down to the water's edge where tables had been set up and there were torches on poles driven into the ground to help light the area as the sun set. A wild boar on a spit was being turned over a fire, and villagers were all about talking and laughing, children were splashing in the water and there was even a man showing off his juggling! Somehow it all seemed so much more festive than the grand banquet at the manor. The food was simple in comparison to the meals she had been enjoying lately with Rage. But unlike those splendid meals everyone here really seemed to be happy despite the fact that they really did not have enough for everyone to have his fill. And everything paled in comparison with Eternity.

After the meal instead of getting up, everyone sat still as Nity began what street teachers do best - teach. Normally street teachers are men of high education who teach on the subject that they learned; in turn their listeners provide them with money and or food. Nity on the other hand, had never been to any kind of school but he taught about Eloi as no one ever had, he seemed to know and understand more than even the highly esteemed Garatin leaders did!

Desti was awestruck by the man! Never before had she really understood about Eloi, but the way Nity explained things made it all seem so much more real. He also spoke of peace and forgiveness- even for those who did not deserve it, could such things be!? At one point she looked over at Treas hoping to share a smile with him over the wondrous things being said. But Treas did not look awestruck, instead he looked uneasy and fidgeted a lot as if the things Nity said made him feel uncomfortable, why would that be?

After Nity was done everyone got up and began talking again as if at a family gathering. The children began to chase fireflies, but it had gotten quite dark and people began to leave. Desti found herself next to Treasure's friend, Est. He was a tall man and seemed quiet enough, but she had seen that he could more then hold his own in a debate!

"Tell me, how did you come to meet Treas?" she asked, not really sure what else to say.

Est looked down and chuckled, "Through a business transaction," he said as though it was a joke.

Desti did not understand; what kind of business!? She frowned.

He grew still again and studied her face then said, "There are many things in Treasure's past that he's not likely to tell you. But this I can tell you; he bears many scars, and not all are in his flesh," he said this with a deep seriousness.

Desti was terribly confused, what had he meant by "scars"!? But before she could ask, Treas came up.

"Are you ready to leave?" he asked her.

She noticed that Est looked away as if feeling guilty. Treas and Desti walked back to the manor in darkness, and they did not speak; somehow Desti could not make herself ask him about what Est had said. When they reached the manor Treas reminded her that he would be going with Nity further inland for a few days, and that he would not see her for a bit. She nodded, then wished him farewell. Slipping through a postern and across the court yard to a cook's door, she went through the manor as quietly as she could, it was late and she did not want to wake anyone.

"Where have you been?" her father's voice startled her and she spun round to face him. He was standing by an open window looking out into the darkness. Had he been waiting for her?

"I went to a banquet with Treas," she explained.

"Without consent!?" he turned to her. It sounded more like an accusation than a question. Desti had never seen him this angry before and it frightened her!

"I-I did not think that you would mind," her open honesty was impossible to doubt, and it seemed to soften his heart.

"It's late-" he said calmly as he closed the window pane. "-Go and sleep, we'll talk more of this on the morrow." He sounded tired.

She nodded, still confused as to why he had been so angry but she did as he asked.

Chapter 15

Sickness

Wilder heard a door slam shut and then running feet. He forced his eyes open and looked around his chamber; it was all in shadow. After his incident with Desti earlier he had found it hard to fall asleep. What time was it now? He decided that it must be very late indeed. Someone shouted down the hall, but the words were muffled and Wilder could not understand them. What was going on? Was there a fire in the stables!? Had Nity somehow learned that there was an assassin out for him? Had he and his rebels come to defend themselves?

Wilder felt a sudden spike of panic and he was wide awake. He jumped from his bed and ripped back the curtains from the window. The thick glass revealed nothing and he bent the latch as he tore open the pane. He stuck his head out- but the night was dark and silent. No, not a fire, but something was wrong none the less! He got dressed as fast as he could. With no idea of what he would find waiting for him in the darkness, he tucked a throwing knife into his belt. Whatever was out there would not find the assassin unarmed.

He decided against taking a torch - he worked better in the darkness. He slipped out into the wide hallway, the shadows told him nothing but his sixth sense told him that he was alone. He went down the hall staying close to the wall and brushing past the tapestries. A light appeared in front of him and he soon saw that it was a maid servant coming towards him carrying a lantern. But before she noticed him she turned down another hallway. Wilder quickened his pace and followed her down the hall. Something was not right.

Half way down the hall there was an open door and golden light spilled out of it. Wilder came to the door and looked in. All shouting had died away to hushed whispers. Loyal was kneeling before a bed with a wispy canopy, her long black hair was out and she still wore her bed clothes. Her face was filled with worry. There were several servants all busy about the room, one was pulling a rope to work an overhead fan, another was mixing some spices into a cup of water (the smell was almost overwhelming) and a manservant came in through a back door carrying a pot of steaming water. Rage stood at the foot of the bed. He turned and saw Wilder in the doorway, and he came to him. His short black hair was topsy-turvy and his face was lined with concern. Wilder had never seen him like this.

"What is it, Rage?" Wilder asked in a low voice.

"Its Mise..." his normally strong voice trailed off in uncertainty as he looked across the room at the bed. Wilder looked too, and he for the first time noticed her; she was sunken down in the bed, dark smudges were under her eyes and her face was colorless.

"Rage," Wilder's voice made Rage turn back to him as if he were in a trance. "She's dying," he whispered.

Wilder looked back at Mise. It was as though death cradled her, but he did not see her, instead he saw the face of Desti - this was how she had looked the night he had given her up for dead. But Eam had not given up so easily; she had said that there was still hope. Indeed a few days later it had been Eam who had taken her daughters place. Determination hardened his face as he asked, "What can I do?"

Rage looked at him for a moment; it was as though Wilder's voice had made him snap out of his shock. "There is an herb man south-west of here on the edge of the Cokhawk, in the town of Fornor-" Wilder wasted no time.

"I'll return in five days' time with him," he turned to go when Rage laid a hand on his shoulder.

"Wilder... she's my only child." With a nod from Wilder, Rage returned back into the room.

Desti appeared at her father's side like a ghost, her eyes were wide but she seemed calm. For this, Wilder was thankful.

"What is it? Daddy."

"Mise is very sick. I'm going to find an herb man, and I need you to stay with Loy- she will need strength before this is over," he spoke quietly. She nodded.

In five minutes Wilder was out in the stables. He took with him a cloak, and a few light weight weapons - there was no time for anything else! All he could hear was Promise's shallow wheezy breathing - that and the pounding of his own heart. No, Mise would not die! Not if he could stop it, and Eloi help any man who stood in his way!

Up in Mise's chamber, Desti watched helplessly as Loy wrung out a wet cloth and placed it on her daughter's forehead. And Rage paced like a bear in a cage.

"Mother?" Mise's voice came weak and shallow, "Why are you worried Mother?"

Loy smiled bravely at her, but could find no words to say.

Mise frowned as she looked around, "Where is my flower? I must take care of it…" her voice faded off.

Desti's heart throbbed! Mise did not understand - no, and how could she? Desti took in a little breath with the realization that Mise - was going to die.

"No, Eloi please…spare her," she whispered, it was something she had once thought Eloi would not listen to - but Nity had said that Eloi heard every plea. She looked out the half open windowpane and watched as her father rode away. "Hurry…" she whispered into the night.

Four agonizing days passed by as Rage, Loy and Desti waited for Wilder's return. Desti had been sitting on the window seat in Promise's chamber for most of the night; she had been able to convince Loy to catch a few hours of sleep a little while ago. For the past four days Mise had been delusional, begging her mother to bring her home and to not leave her alone again. Loy could only cry softly in response. Other times Mise would scold her father for forgetting to take her out riding, and would ask when he would keep his promise.

It was at times like that when Desti did not know how much more she could take and she would wish that Treas was with her - but he was far away with Nity now. She looked up as Rage entered the room; he went straight to his daughter's bedside and took Promise's hand in his own.

"My father said that he would return tomorrow," Desti spoke softly.

Rage looked up at her as though he had just noticed her, there were tears in his eyes and the best he could do was nod. It scared Desti to see this great, proud Tarven so broken; a deep weariness settled over her. She wanted to plead with Eloi for the life of Mise- but the words would not come, indeed why would Eloi listen to her? She had heard it said once that Eloi held all life in his hand; now she wondered if he did not also hold death in the same hand. Did he even care that a young girl was dying!? That could not be so! And yet he did nothing… Eloi must have turned a deaf ear to her plea.

Perhaps Eloi only listened to some people - like Nity - yes that must be it, Eloi would listen when Nity called. Desti's mind began to wander as she slipped off to sleep, slumped on the window seat.

She awoke with a start! The room was dark, and she was alone with Mise - no the room was not dark, the sun was rising. There was a soft commotion in the hall; it's what had woken her. Then she heard a voice - it was her father, he had come!

"Please, mother-" Mise murmured "take me home." Even in sleep she was tormented. Desti came to her side and took her hand.

"You'll be coming home very soon, Mise," she whispered to the girl.

Just then, Loy came into the room looking more hopeful than she had in five days. Behind her came a maid servant carrying a lantern, next came Rage, and following him was an old man. He was stooped with age, he had a long white beard that hung from a round face, and he shuffled more than walked into the room. His dirty clothes seemed to cling to him, his Namesake was Healer.

Desti decided at once that she did not much like herb men- but all their hope rested on this one. Wilder came to the door a moment later, Desti felt relief wash over her and she ran into his arms, feeling safe at last. Wilder had dark circles under his eyes and his unshaven face was sweaty and dirty, he looked exhausted as he leaned against the door frame and put his arm around her.

"Daddy, I think she's dying…" she whispered aloud her worst fear. His arm tightened around her and she gladly huddled against him.

Healer had gone straight to Promise's bedside. He had then bent over her and was silent as he listened to her breathing. He also opened up her eyes and looked into them. Mise slept through it all. Ler then turned to Rage and said, "There are a few things I can do," he paused and looked at Rage.

It took a moment for Desti to understand and when she did, her dislike for the man grew even more; he was waiting to be paid! It did not seem to bother Rage; he quickly pulled out a pouch of coins and handed it to Ler. This man has Rage wrapped around his finger Desti thought with disgust. After feeling its weight in his hand for a moment, Ler promptly tucked the pouch away in his cloak. He then went digging through a saddle bag that he had brought with him, and he pulled out three shallow wooden bowls, some green herbs and a glittering knife. He then explained that he would have to "bleed" Mise. Desti did not understand what that meant but it sounded terrible and she could not understand why Rage nodded his consent. Desti looked up at her father, but his face told nothing.

Ler had a servant fill one bowl with water and he crushed the herbs and dropped them in. It made a strong smell (it made Desti feel a little dizzy) and he put the two other bowls under Promise's wrists. He had two servants hold her arms in place; he then made a swift cut across both her wrists. Desti felt sick as the blood welled up in the cuts then dripped steadily into the bowls.

Mise stirred and mumbled, "Where…? Where is my flower?"

Desti looked at the bedside table where Promise's Cres`aren grew in its little pot; it had grown to five inches but still bore no bloom.

"I'm afraid that there is nothing more I can do," Ler informed Rage. The herb man had worked from dawn to high noon - but it felt more like midnight.

"What do you mean?" Rage asked not really sure he wanted to know.

"She's dying, and there is nothing more to be done," he said bluntly.

Loy began crying softly at the news, and Rage felt his entire world give way beneath him - the man in whom he had placed all his hope in, faded before his eyes: all that was left was just another man - as helpless as he. Promise would die. A sharp pain struck him, but Rage knew that it was not pain; it was heartache.

Ler packed up his things and left the room without even looking at the little girl whose wrists were bound in bandages, whose face was as pale as death. Loy held her child in her arms and wept uncontrollably - heedless to all else, beyond any and all comfort.

'Noooo!' her heart screamed, 'No...'

Chapter 16
The Unthinkable and Impossible

Rage felt he would go mad! Life without his little girl? Unthinkable! And yet, what more could be done? Death had already made its claim. He was feeling desperate (something foreign to him indeed!) Despite his daughter's condition, his spies had still kept watch on Nity. Rage knew vaguely that the rebel was back in town - but rebellions were the last thing on Rage's mind. All he knew was that Nity - could do the impossible. At first he was inclined to believe that the stories were nonsense, but now he was not quite so sure: there was the story of the village with the black plague, the poisoned well and more recently, there was an old man. In his youth he had been a thief; he had been caught and punished by having every bone in both his hands broken. He had since changed his ways but it was a sign of past crimes that he would carry the rest of his life or so everyone had thought. But one touch from Nity and the man's hands were healed! Nity continued to defy science, astound the world and pull rabbits from thin air. Rage was desperate.

"He went where!?" Wilder asked in astonishment.

"That's all he said, that he was going to Eternity and that he would return shortly," the servant girl explained.

Wilder could hardly believe what he was hearing! Rage gone to Nity? But for what propose? Had he snapped - had his military mind given way to madness!? Had he gone to arrest Nity, single handedly, without orders and without proof? Wilder would have gone after him in a moment if it had not been at that moment Desti cried out in desperation.

"Daddy..." her voice faltered.

Wilder spun on his heel and ran down the hall back to Promise's chamber. Desti stood at the door as if frozen, looking in with wide eyes; Loy was bent over Mise clutching her, tears streaming down her face. Wilder went to her but stopped at the sight of Mise, her eyes were empty and her breath caught as she whispered, "My flower... who will look after it?" Her eyes were open but she did not seem to be there. "It's going to-die…"

Desti came across the room and took hold of the bottom bed post, she felt like she was in a tunnel, all she could see was the pale, wane face of Mise, and the only sound was the thudding of her own heart. Promise's eyes fluttered shut like butterfly wings as she breathed her last, and death came to reap its harvest. Someone was crying; Desti realized that it was her.

Wilder only stood there, dazed- even numb, as though it was all beyond his understanding. He walked from the room and stumbled into a servant, "Go…" he said. "Go and find your master - tell him that… tell him." The servant disappeared to do his bidding.

Wilder leaned against the wall, he felt so utterly powerless, just like he had the night Dream had died and the nightmare had begun; so helpless that it frightened him! Back in Mise's chamber Loy sobbed uncontrollably and screamed at her servants to leave her be and not to touch her baby. Desti felt light headed, and her lungs burned for air. Life had never seemed so fragile to her before; how long she stood there weeping she did not know. At last she could take no more! She ran from the room and down the hall and past her father, blind to where she was going she ran into someone. For a moment she fought to get past until she heard her name.

"Desti!?"

She looked up and found that it was Treas who kept her from running; she did not question his presence, she did not care!

"She's dead!" she sobbed; Treas did not seem surprised and only put his arm around her. She was dimly aware that there was a group of men passing by them. Vaguely she recognized Est and one or two others, but someone ran on ahead of the rest; it was Rage.

He rushed down the hall and stopped at Promise's door; Desti looked up and was surprised to see that Nity was there also! Why? Treas gently lead her with the others to the door, she tried to resist; didn't they get it!? Mise was dead! There was nothing more to do but weep, she thought with bitterness, Eloi did not care…

Loy hardly noticed when her husband came up beside her and put his hand on her shoulder. Nity followed Rage into the room and the rest remained outside the door. Nity looked around at the servants and at Mise's nurse who was weeping quietly, he then ordered that all the servants leave. This aroused Loy and she looked up with fury at him.

"How dare you!?" she screeched at him! "Get out!"

Rage grabbed her arm, "Loyal no! He has come to cure Mise!"

"Promise is dead!" she sobbed at her husband as if it was his fault.

Nity spoke with a reassuring and calm voice, "She will wake," he said it with a note of sorrow but with confidence.

Loy looked at him as he was insane. "Oh yes!" she said with bitterness, "She's only asleep!"

"Loyal!" Rage pleaded, having no more strength left, she fell silent in his arms.

The servants all left when their master nodded at them, and Nity spoke.

"Est, Dien, Peare come, the rest of you remain outside."

No one questioned him this time. The door closed and Rage, Loy and the three who had been called in were alone with Nity. He bent down beside the bed and took Mise's hand in his own and brushed away a dark curl from her cold face. Loy stiffened in Rage's arms but said nothing, and to the astonishment of Rage, tears came to Nity's eyes! In the back of his mind, Rage wondered what it was that Nity would do. He had found Nity by the waterfront and begged the street teacher (actually begged!) to come and cure his sick daughter. Nity had not even hesitated, but as they crossed the court yard of the manor a servant came running to them with the news that Mise had died and yet Nity still came!

Again Rage wondered what he would do; he had painted himself into a corner, indeed what could he do? And yet Rage did not listen to reason this time, instead he believed that Nity could still do something-anything.

Nity bent close to the lifeless face of Mise and whispered firmly, "Promise, wake!"

Mise took a shuttering breath and her eyes fluttered open! Loy gasped in unbelief and Rage stood unable to move! Nity smiled faintly as

Mise lay there and gazed into his eyes as the color came back into her face.

"I need to water my flower," she whispered.

Outside the room Wilder, Desti, Treas and the others who had come with Nity all stood silent and solemn. They were all shocked to hear laughter and looked up at the door as if anxious to silence the disturbance. Desti pushed away from Treas and looked through a haze of tears at the closed door. She then heard the voice of a little girl and her breath caught, Treas jumped forward and caught Desti as she fell limp to the ground!

Chapter 17

Might Have Been

It was early, much too early to be as drunk as Ree was - but she did not care. She had been sitting at the "Cobble Stone" ale house for hours, just staring off into nowhere. Her dark hair made her face look even whiter than normal. She looked so cold and intimidating that no one would even walk near her; it was an effect that she had been perfecting for months. She was angry- angrier than she had been in a long time! There was a woman that she knew, Silver was her Namesake, she was a common prostitute and everyone knew it. A few months ago Sil had wanted to die - so ashamed of her life was she that death was a better option. Ree had all but wished her good riddance! But Sil had done something completely unexpected - she had gone to Nity.

In the eyes of the law Sil was beyond pardon, and in the eyes of Eloi she was forever guilty - that's just how it worked. But Nity had told her that her past was forever forgotten in the eyes of Eloi! He had told her to go and make for herself a new life. It had made Ree so angry! Why should Sil get another chance at life? She did not deserve it, she had chosen that life! If anyone deserved a new chance at life it was Ree! After all Ree had been tricked into the life she now led, and who did Nity think he was that he could speak for Eloi?! As if he had the right!

That had been three months ago, and Ree had comforted herself in the knowledge that Sil could not change her life - no matter what Nity said! But just that morning, Ree had seen Sil - she had gotten married to a well-respected man and Sil looked as much a lady as anyone ever did! That was the reason that brought Ree to the "Cobble Stone" so early in the day. Why should Sil be set free from her past and Ree be left behind? Why did freedom have to come from Nity!? Nity was everything that Ree despised - why should she crave acceptance from him!? Ah yes, the true reason for her anger.

But even still, even if Nity did the impossible, even if Ree was made innocent in Eloi's eyes, even if freedom was finally hers - the stain would still remain. No one could truly change that. Ree stood up (rather unsteadily), she had to go and sleep this off, that night there would be an important rebel meeting – Ree could not miss this one. She left a few coins on the table and stumbled out onto the street, and then slowly made her way to her inn.

'This is a strange dream'... Ree thought to herself, for she knew that she was dreaming - she had never been to such a place as this before; she stood in a desert, silent, still and alone. It was a black desert - the same color as her cloak. The sky over head was gray and colorless, and the sun did not seem to even be there. She began to wander about, waiting to wake up. Then she realized that she had been here before; this place was her life, cold, empty, and lonely, stretching out before her endlessly, hopeless and meaningless...

At last she came to what she thought must be a wall - a clear wall, reaching from horizon to horizon, but despite it appearing to be clear - she could not see through it. All she could see was the reflection of the black desert and her own reflection, a bleak sight it was. But she stared at it for what seemed a very long time, until at last, she began to see through it to the other side. What she saw took her breath away; it was a vast green land stretching away as far as the desert did - and further still, warm, peaceful and bursting with life. Presently a woman came out of the woods and began to walk with her back to Ree; it was a young woman and with her came a man. The young woman hung on his arm as they walked along together; they seemed so happy and obviously, so in love. Just than a child came out of the trees and ran towards the couple. Ree watched as one enchanted, as the man turned and picked up the child and swung him around. The woman bent and kissed the child and then with both of them taking a hand the three of them walked away swinging the boy between them. They were making their way up a little hill and on top of the hill rested a little cottage with a thatched roof. Out of the cottage came an older woman and she waved to the threesome and then greeted them with hugs and kisses. She embraced the young woman a moment longer than she did the rest and it was clear that they were mother and daughter.

It was such a happy family gathering, and Ree felt a sadness flood her as the younger women turned and for a moment met Ree's gaze. Tears stung her eyes as Ree recognized the woman – it was herself! The cold reality came over Ree hard and quick; what she looked upon - was what might have been.

Ree awoke and the first thing she noticed was that her face was wet with tears. Oh, how cruel these dreams were! She sat up with difficulty, her body feeling heavy; her cloak clung to her like cob webs. She looked about her room with contempt; it did look like a desert! Screaming she threw her pillow at the wall. She didn't want this! This guilt! After all it was not her fault, no; she did not choose this life - it was forced upon her! Gra had done this to her! She was sobbing now, for try as she might, the truth was still there.

Ree had a throbbing headache, but she went to the rebel meeting anyway. She stood at the back of the ale house where the meeting was being held (the ale house keeper was a supporter of the rebel movement). Despite her headache, Ree had not missed a word of what was said. The revolution would come. After sixty years of occupation, the Tarvens would be driven out! A death for a death; Garatin would at last have its revenge...

In a few months' time the oldest Garatin festival would come, it was a week-long event that had been celebrated every year since the days of old. The entire thing was centered on Eloi and every Garatin participated - indeed, it was the heritage and identity of every Garatin. It would be celebrated in even the smallest of fishing villages on the Nennor Sea's eastern shore, in every mountain hut on the north fringe of the country, and in the most isolated towns of Garatin's wild lands.

From far and wide Garatins would come to the city of Garason until it overflowed and still they would come. For there, in the center of the city, was an ancient fort of marble and stone, inside sitting on a dais was the Vase. Beautifully crafted and hand painted thousands of years ago, it was said that Eloi himself lived within the Vase.

As was tradition, the head of every family would come to the Vase and write down on a piece of parchment every evil that they and their family had done during the past year - anything that was contradictory to the laws of Eloi. Each thing (big or small) would be written down and in the days of old the parchment was taken before the vase as an apology to Eloi for doing such things. According to tradition Eloi would look into the family and determine if they were sincere; and if they were, the parchment would burst into flame and the family's past was forgotten in the eyes of Eloi. Now, under Tarven rule, the Garatin leaders would chose whose parchment to burn; despite who was sincere and who wasn't.

Ree had no interest in such things; she only saw it as the government's way to control the people. After all, if Eloi was as great as they said; how could he be kept inside a Vase? The only interest she had in it was that the festival was the perfect setting for a revolution! Everyone who was anyone would be in the city; every rebel leader across the country knew of the plans. They would even ask the infamous Nity to join the cause; after all, he was a rebel too. Ree cringed at the thought; she wanted nothing to do with Nity.

"You can feel it in the air…" Ree turned at the voice.

It was Receive, another rebel like herself, Eive looked about the room and smiled as if she could actually see the revolution happening! Ree nodded in agreement.

"I've heard of your skill with a bow." Eive commented.

Ree did not answer.

"You have not gone unnoticed by the council, they have seen your passion for the rebellion, and I think that you will play a big part in what is to come."

Ree looked at her - how did she know this? Could it be true that the council would ask her to do something - out of the ordinary?

Eive's confidence suddenly faded. "Do you think that the people will join us when it comes to it?" she asked, showing how unsure she was.

Ree took in a deep breath. "The fires of unrest have been kindled, and the people feel it…" Ree smiled, blood would spill. She was so ready for this - so ready for revenge against Tarva – revenge against the world. After all, the world had taken what might have been hers.

*   *   *

When Desti came to after her fainting spell in the hallway, she opened her eyes to find Treasure's anxious gaze and behind him her father's worried face. Her first question was, "Mise…?" She whispered fearing it was all a dream; a dream about hearing the dead girl's voice.

Her father nodded and took her hand, "She's alive," he had said.

Alive and not only that, but after looking up into Nity's face and declaring that she needed to water her flower, Nity had helped her out of bed and across the room so that she could do just that! At first Loy had tried to make Mise stay in bed, saying, "You need to recover your strength, you are not well!" But Mise would have none of it, and kept reassuring everyone that 'I feel fine!' But Loy would not leave her daughter's side, so convinced was she that Mise would have a relapse.

Nity left soon thereafter along with everyone else he had brought with him- except for Treas. He had stayed behind to see that Desti was all right, but he left as soon as he saw that Desti was indeed well. He had looked very bewildered and had asked Desti if Mise had truly been dead.

"Treas-" she had assured him, "She was dead - and had been dead for some time before you came with Nity…" she was as confused as anyone, but her respect and hero worship of Nity increased with every day!

It had been one week since the impossible had been done and still no one could believe that Mise was really going to live - except for Mise herself.

"Desti?-" Mise asked, "-Why do you keep looking at me like that?"

The two of them were in the enclosed garden of the manor, sitting on a stone bench. The day was typical of a Garatin early summer day. The sky was a perfect blue, and the scattered clouds were fluffy white. The breeze off the lake cooled the afternoon quite nicely. Desti smiled when Mise caught her looking at her.

"I'm sorry, Mise. It's just that…" she looked down and bit her lip.

142

"I was there when you stopped breathing! You were dead," she whispered looking up at her. After a moment of silence Desti's curiosity got the better of her. "What was it like?" she asked.

Mise frowned into her lap, "I don't really remember…" she closed her eyes. "It was dark- but warm, at least it was where I was… there was something evil nearby!" she said, her voice trembling with fear.

Desti looked at her, not sure of what to do.

"But… I was being protected," Mise said with wonder as she opened her eyes- all fear gone.

"Protected by what- Or by whom?" Desti asked confused.

"I don't know, I don't even know how long I was there for! Then I heard a voice," Mise whispered. "He called my Namesake, and told me to wake."

"How is it that you only heard Nity's voice? I mean - your mother was weeping uncontrollably!"

Mise shook her head, "I don't know - all I know is that I had to obey him, I felt him pulling me back - he called and I had to answer."

They were silent for a time as they both thought about different things.

"Desti? Who is Eternity? I asked my mother but she wouldn't tell me! Why wouldn't she tell me?"

Desti thought for a moment, what was she to say? Of course Rage and Loy frowned upon Nity because he was a Garatin and they were Tarvens - but didn't Mise have a right to know?

Mise spoke before she could finish thinking, "Is he a dishonored and banished prince of Garatin?" she sounded a little too excited about it.

"No!" Desti laughed at the thought of it; Nity of royal blood! "In fact he grew up in this area; I think his family's trade is building fishing boats or something."

Mise looked confused, "But? He must be someone special!" she said fervently.

"Why do you say that?"

"Well… he woke me," Mise said simply, her childish logic held truth none the less.

Desti sighed, "I don't know anything about banished princes, Mise. Some say that he's a rebel that needs to be stopped, and others think that he's just pure foolishness. But there are some who say that he is a man of peace and that he is the one that Eloi promised would set all of Garatin free," she said, repeating what she had been told by Treas.

Mise interrupted her, "You mean the one in the old Garatin stories!?"

"But how do you know of the old Garatin stories? I hardly know of them myself!"

Mise took on a mischievous look. "My nurse back in Garason has a daughter who is just my age, and she has a friend who is a Garatin! My nurse's daughter tells me all about the old Garatin story's - but don't tell, my mother and father would never approve!" she said solemnly. "The stories tell of a legend of a prince who will come and save the Garatin people! That's why I thought Nity might be a prince," she explained.

"I don't know of any legendary princes, Mise. But what I do know is that - Nity can do the impossible. You are proof of that," she said with a smile.

Mise smiled too, in her mind, Nity would always be a magical prince - who else could tell the dead to live again?

"-with Mise's curiosity of the man growing every day... what would you do if you were in my position?" Rage turned from the fire to face his friend as he asked the question.

"You forget; I am in your position," Wilder said with little enthusiasm.

The two of them were in Rage's private study.

Rage sighed, "I know... but my orders come straight from Ister! I've no doubt that he will have little sympathy for my situation, in fact I doubt that the man is even capable of sympathy!" he added under his breath, as he turned back to stare into the flames.

"Then you have not written him?"

"No!" Rage scoffed, "Nor am I likely too, at least not of this incident. If I did tell him of what happened Ister would doubtless arrest me for being a rebel sympathizer!"

Wilder gave him a level look. "Are you?" he asked quietly.

Rage returned his look, "No, old friend, I am not a rebel sympathizer. I will not let a rebellion happen, not if I can stop it!"

"But nor will you order the death of the man who saved your daughter," Wilder said aloud; giving voice to what Rage had not yet dared to admit.

Courage heaved a deep sigh.

"And Loyal? What does she think of all this?" Wilder asked at last.

"I have not told her of the reason we have come here, but I am sure that she has guessed it," Rage whispered. "I have crossed too many lines..." Rage leaned against the fireplace mantel and gazed into the flames once more.

Wilder looked away, it was not often that his proud friend admitted that he had no answers. Wilder instead looked about Courage's study from where he leaned against a wall, then his gaze drifted out the window. Instead of a pane, there was grill work over the window, and as he looked through it he noticed for the first time that his daughter and Mise were sitting in the garden just below the study. Just then Treasure came into view, he approached the two girls and began to talk to them, and Wilder could see Desti's face light up. Now that was another problem all together! What was he to do with his own daughter? What were the odds that after two and a half years two people would bump into another again? But now this lad was not just a street urchin but a rebel too! No good could come of it, of that Wilder was sure. Would this young man have the courage to ask for Desti's hand in marriage? Did Desti even know? Or was she completely oblivious to this young man's feelings for her?

"You should keep a closer rein on her."

Wilder turned to see that Rage had come to stand by him at the window. Rage looked tired but had wiped all weakness from his face, and seemed ready to put a hand to something that he could control. Wilder gave a short sigh, this was something else they disagreed on; Wilder did not want an argument now.

"She is my daughter - not my horse," he said simply.

"Oh yes, you did always have strange ideas about such things," Rage snorted.

Wilder said nothing, they had problems enough to spare without having an argument on child rearing.

Chapter 18

The Mines

It had been almost a month, and life had gone on rather simply for Treas. That day, in the garden, he had gone to tell Desti that he would be going with Nity on a bit of a roundabout trip. Nity wanted to travel around Quy Lake and teach in the many tiny villages and over the past month that's just what they had been doing. Nity had not done the impossible as often as usual, but it never ceased to amaze Treas, Est and the others, every time Nity did do something. Common sense simply said that these things could not be done! And yet Nity did them.

Treas had not given up arguing with himself daily but the argument was becoming weaker with every passing day. He didn't want to forget what the mines had taught him; that having a soft heart made you vulnerable to heartache. And yet, was having a heart of stone worth the sacrifice of not loving anyone? He wanted to believe it was, but he was having a hard time convincing himself. That was one of the reasons he had joined the trip, to get away from Desti so that he could think; some escape! Now he was with Nity, constantly listening to his teachings; it was like Nity was setting the standards of how one is to live, of how Eloi meant them to live. Day after day it became clearer that Treas did not measure up. The mines had made him a hard man - one who fought tooth and nail for the only cause he believed in; himself. He tried to tell himself that he had never been perfect, so why should it bother him now? But what surprised him was that it did bother him! But he did not want to measure up to Nity! He did not want to become devoted to his teachings - he did not want to rely on anyone; what if they failed him?

As if Treasure's life was not complicated enough, more complications were about to set in. It was a blustery day, and Nity and the others were on the east side of Quy Lake. Nity was teaching (as per normal) in the middle of a no-name village of fishing huts surrounded by trees (seeing as how they were close to the Quy Marsh).

"- see how the fishermen go through their nets and pick out all the bad fish, like the 'says ren' and the 'c`krak'-" Nity spoke to a small crowd of mostly women and children. They were all watching the men folk do their work; the men took a keen interest when Nity started using them as an example. Treas listened from the outskirts of the square, with arms crossed.

"-the fishermen keep only the good fish - for the bad have no use. Eloi will do the same when time runs out; Eloi will save only those who have remained true to him, for the others have no use. It will be terrible when time runs out, and only the blameless will escape!"

Treas winced as the fishermen picked up a barrel of the bad fish and dumped it before two big dogs, who devoured the fish quickly. Nity was speaking to the crowd, but he was talking straight to Treas. Treas knew that he was not blameless; he would not be saved when time ran out. He had lived a life far from blameless - and Nity knew it too. Treas looked away; he could not stand this anymore!

Just then the wind picked up and moved a willow tree that was off to the side of the square; Treas noticed a man chopping wood beside the tree. The man was dressed just like any of the other fishermen and Treas had not even noticed him before, but in that moment the man looked up at Nity with an intensity that could not be missed. Treas knew this man; it was Wilder. A shiver went up Treasure's spine and he had hard time breathing! Memories flashed through his mind at an alarming rate - everything came together at once! That dark and sinister thing that he could not remember about Desti's father came clear and vivid at last; a cold, wet day, a loud conversation between a group of Tarven soldiers about assassins.

The word whispered through his mind in an eerie way - just as it had that day so long ago, the day he learned that Desti's father was an assassin; Wilder had been in Garason to assassinate Liveran. The moment passed and the wind died down letting the long willow leafs to hang straight again and the assassin was invisible - once again.

Treas looked away at once, at last he remembered his past and it was far from pleasant! He understood all too well; Wilder was here to kill Nity! Treas looked back at Nity; did he have any idea of what was out there, just waiting? 'Great!' Treas thought to himself, just great! The father of the girl he loved was out to assassinate the man that Treas had sworn allegiance too! Could things get any more complicated?!

"So what have you to report? Is Nity meeting with the different rebel groups as we suspected?" Rage asked.

Wilder sighed; he had been gone for four weeks and only now had just returned. "No… no, all Nity has done this past month is teach, and on occasion do the impossible. I saw no sign of rebel activity at any time - night or day." Wilder was tired, he had hardly rested. He was intent on proving that Nity was a vicious rebel leader, so that he could justify the killing of a man who had saved the life a young girl - instead Wilder had only convinced himself that Nity did not fit that part at all.

"Rage, are you so certain that this man will lead a nationwide rebellion?" Wilder asked, showing his doubts in the matter.

Rage frowned. "He has the entire country wrapped around his finger." He began quietly, building up as he went. "Wilder, there are hundreds of rebel groups in the north of Garatin alone! On their own they could never succeed - but all that is needed to unite them is one man - Nity has that power behind him now!" He stopped to catch his breath.

Wilder was thoughtful. "Nity does not speak of bloodshed," he said softly. "Indeed he speaks of reform, but not of the country, but reform of the heart. If he was to start a rebellion it would be against the age old traditions that keep men away from Eloi. His acts of kindness and love go far beyond what hatred is capable of - you know of the things he does, they are not destructive - you are witness with your own eyes! Your daughter lives today because of him! What rebel would do such things for his enemy!?" Wilder finished calmly and boldly looking Rage in the eyes, and to his surprise, tears glistened there.

"What choice do I have, old friend?" Rage said trying hard to hold his voice steady. "With Ister breathing down my neck, and sending news that rebel groups in Garason are planning for revolution in just a few months? What choice do I have with the entire country waiting for Nity to say the word? I am left no back door out!"

"He saved your daughter," Wilder reminded him, knowing that that one thing alone tipped the scales dramatically.

Rage turned away as the tears choked him, weakness was so foreign to him!

*   *   *

Treas looked up and saw Desti making her way to him. He looked around; the last thing he wanted was to be found alone with Desti - it was a terrible thing to think! But it was obvious that Desti's father did not like him - only a fool could miss that! It was a wonder that Desti had not been forbidden to see Treas at all. But the town was silent and there was no one on the grassy lake shore, except Desti and him. Treas steeled himself as Desti came closer with a smile on her face. Now that he remembered the truth about Desti's father - how could he keep that secret from her?

The two of them walked along the lake and talked for a time, and Treas realized how much he had missed her over the past month- how could he consider never seeing her again?! Desti wanted to know about Nity (her curiosity had grown) but Nity was the last thing he wanted to discuss!

"Do you know if you will be returning to Garason for the festival next month?" he asked to change the subject.

"Oh, I don't know, doesn't seem likely that Rage would celebrate a Garatin festival does it? Will you and Nity be going?" she asked.

"No, I don't think so." It was too dangerous for Nity to return to Garason right now; there were too many people who wanted him dead. There fell a silence; finally Treas asked what had been eating at him. "Desti, do you know why your father is here? It just seems strange that he would visit a friend for so long," he added quickly looking out over the lake.

Desti looked away too as though uncomfortable. No, she did not really understand why they were here, or why her father had gone away for a month on 'business'. Nothing made sense, but then she did not want to understand. She shook her head.

*   *   *

"Where are we going?!" Treas asked in astonishment.

"To Garason, for the festival," Est explained with patience.

150

"Who is? When?!"

Est smiled, "All of us are going, in another week just like we have every year." An excited look came to his face as he said. "There will be many who will travel with Nity to the city - and with I, my brother Fin, Dien and his brother Peare, Mag, Sid, Chal, Vive, Cern, Rizon, Ave and Stor – we are all loyal to him no matter what, and there will be many from this village alone who will come with us!-"

Treas was confused, he knew all the men that Est had just mentioned and they were all close friends of Nity. But Treas did not understand what Est was talking about, he interrupted him. "What do you mean?"

Est looked around them as though afraid someone might be listening, "Nity hasn't said it yet, but we can all read between the lines. It's going to happen! Nity will claim the Garatin throne and take up sword against the Tarvens!"

"Claim the...? You mean a revolution!?" Treas was having a hard time keeping up.

"Yes; I do, Nity has enough men behind him now - anything is possible! Eloi meant for Nity to rule this Kingdom - and so it will be." "

The fire in Est's speech sent shivers down Treasure's back - but not for the reason that Est meant - all Treas could see was a dark figure hidden in the shadows... just waiting.

"Where is Nity now?" Treas asked anxiously.

Est frowned at his uneasiness but nodded to where Nity was. Treas hurried in that direction, they were in a tiny village that was a day's journey from the lake - and Rage's manor (they would be going back that way before long.) Treas crossed the tiny square and went around back one of the cottages. There, out in front of him was a flat level grassy place with a well off to one side. There were fires with wild boar roasting over some of them, and a small crowd was milling about. There was a flute player and a juggler, and there was even a man putting on a little puppet show for a handful of children. They all watched as if the simple handmade puppets were really alive - it looked like a happy family gathering. Treas tried to imagine them as a violent mob fighting for freedom in the streets- but he couldn't do it. He spotted Nity quickly; he was sitting down on a log tossing a ball back and forth with a young boy. Treas sat down beside Nity and tried to calm himself. Nity tossed the ball to him and Treas in turn tossed it back to the boy.

"Est says that you will be going to Garason soon," Treas said, trying to sound natural.

"We all will be going to Garason - I had hoped that you could join us," Nity said it like he really meant it.

Treas ignored the invitation. "I don't think you should go," he said quietly.

Nity turned to him and the boy started to play with someone else. "Why do you think I should stay here?"

"You have made enemies of very important men in Garason."

"Treas, those who do not swear allegiances to a king are against him - how can I but chose to make enemies of those who would stop me?"

It made Treas pause, was he against Nity? How could Nity just brush aside men like the Garatin leaders as if they were nothing?

"There are men out there who would rather see you dead," he spoke the warning in a low voice. It irritated him when Nity only looked at him like this was old news. "There are assassins out there watching you! Wilder is out there- I-I mean-" he stuttered "I mean they are out there just waiting for you to make a false move! If you go to Garason now - you'll die." His speech was passionate, but it seemed to have little effect on Nity.

He nodded sadly, "Yes, I will die."

This blew Treas right out of the water! Was Nity agreeing with him, that he should not go to Garason? Treas did not know how to respond and he frowned.

Nity sighed as though frustrated that Treas did not understand, he stood, Treas stood with him. Nity's face was grave as he looked at Treas, he put a hand on Treasure's shoulder.

"One day, Treas, you will understand," he squeezed his shoulder, offered a smile and then walked away.

It was two days later, and Treas had gone on ahead of Nity to Rage's manor- he wanted to see Desti. In a few days Nity would travel through on his way to Garason, that's when Treas would join his company - he wasn't about to leave him. After all, who knew what awaited them in Garason; a revolution or Nity's death.

He was with Desti by the lakeshore laying down in the grass while she sat against the tree. She was telling him a story of something that had happened over the past two years.

"-I and my father were so worried about Willow that we were ready to travel the three days to the north just to see if a man we knew could do anything for him. But father decided to wait until after we had finished plowing the field before leaving, so we had to use our old mule to do the rest of the plowing while Will limped around the corral. But do you know what happened the evening we finished the plowing?" Desti asked with a smile.

"What?" Treas asked.

"When we came to put the mule back in the stable, Will was prancing all about the corral; all sign of his limp was completely gone!" Desti laughed, Treas propped himself upon his elbows and looked over at Will in disbelief.

Desti continued through her laughter, "He had pretended to have a lame foot so that he wouldn't have to do any plowing!"

Treas joined her in laughing, Will, who was grazing a few feet away, only looked up at them and blinked. When the laughter died down they sat in silence for a bit, Desti bit her lip; it was time to go fishing for the truth.

"So, that's the last two years of my life in a nutshell…. What about you?" she asked hoping that it didn't sound too forced.

"Oh, as I said; not much to tell," he said as he sat up and looked over the high grass that lined the lake.

"How did you meet Est?" she asked, going a step further.

He shrugged, "Don't remember."

"He said that he met you through a 'business transaction'…"

He looked at her, "You asked him?"

153

She nodded, and when he did not comment she said, "Treas, I know something happened."

His mouth stayed tight shut, and she sighed and tried a different question. "How did you get that scar on your shoulder?"

This time he sighed, "You saw that did you?" he paused for a time, and Desti thought that he wasn't going to say anything more- but he did. "It happened a long time ago - it doesn't matter anymore."

"How long ago?"

Treas thought for a moment; how long had it been? Not even a year! For a moment the sky dimmed and he was back in the mines…

Desti's voice brought him back. "Treas?" she asked uncertainly, and then with frustration, "Why won't you tell me?"

He took a deep breath. "It was a few weeks after you had left, I was - traveling when by chance I came upon some slave dealers and they took me as another one of their slaves. That's how I got the scar; it's a brand. I was then taken to the Dinco Mountains to a silver mine. After a time I tried to escape, I didn't get too far though. It was then that Est and Fin bought me and then gave me my freedom," he said, in a detached voice, as if all of it had nothing to do with him.

"Oh, Treas… I didn't realize…" Desti whispered.

Treas put on a brave smile, "It's all in the past- It doesn't matter anymore!"

"How long were you there for?"

Despite what Treas had said… the past did matter. What Est had once said to Desti was true; Treas bore many scars, the worst one being what the mines had made him into; a brutal man. He thought of all the times he had done something less than honorable… there were more times than even he liked to think about! The face of the seventeen year old flashed before his eyes bruised and swollen, the result of his cruelness. He recalled how once he had woken up in the 'den' and realized that the slave next to him had died in his sleep and Treas had literally crawled over his body so he could go through the dead man's belongings.

"Two years…" he whispered Desti's answer.

She gasped softly. "Two years?!...Treas I– I didn't know," she said somewhere between shook and sympathy. "But!-" she said as she realized, "That means that you have only been free for just a few months!"

"Five and a half," Treas said before he realized it, he recovered quickly though. "But really, Desti! It's in the past!" he did not sound very believable, but she nodded anyway.

Now she understood; when they had run into each other in Garason some months ago, she had noticed how strong he looked and how grown up, he seemed so far from the street wise lad that she had known, and his eyes had looked so empty: he looked as though he had tasted the world and found it bitter. Those had been her exact thoughts and now she understood.

She sat silent as she tried to think it all through, but Treas could hardly bear the silence. He needed to change the subject!

He stood and stretched, then stood before her and pulled her to her feet. "Anyway, it would appear that Nity and the others will be going to Garason after all, I'll be going with them too."

Desti took in a breath as she tried to think. "Ah… yes, um- it seems Rage and the others will be going to Garason too, I and my father will be going along with them," she smiled, "You'll be able to show me all the wonders of the Garason festival after all!"

He smiled too, but somehow Desti knew that it was not genuine. But she did not say anything - she had enough to think about!

Chapter 19

Sunshine and Flowers

Desti walked through the extensive gardens that surrounded Courage's manor. Lush bushes and trailing vines surrounded her but she did not notice any of it, she was too deep in thought. She felt like the entire world was keeping secrets from her! She looked up as she rounded a corner in the garden and there in front of her was her father sitting on a stone bench. She smiled, anxious to forget all of her troubles with Treas - at least for a moment.

"Hello father," she greeted him.

He smiled as she came to sit down beside him, her shoes clicking on the stone path. "Where have you been?" he asked presently.

She remembered how he had reacted that time she had gone to the banquet with Treas, and she was inclined not to tell him - but she would not lie to him. "With Treas…"

He only nodded, and for that she was relieved.

"Have you recovered from your trip?" she asked politely.

He laughed, "I've never had such a tiring trip!"

It made her frown, he had not told her where he had gone, and perhaps it was because she felt like everyone was hiding things from her, that made her ask.

"Father where did you go?"

He grew quiet. Desti felt her resolve harden- she needed to know!

"Daddy, you once told me that I didn't need to know about your past, I agreed with you then only because I didn't really want to know - but you were wrong! I do need to know! Don't you think it's time that you told me?" she felt something change in the very air; instinctively she knew it would never be the same again.

Wilder looked out over the garden, only but a few moments ago it had been a safe and happy place - but now Wilder felt far removed from that world of sunshine and flowers. Somehow, deep in his heart, he had always known that someday his little copper haired girl would want, no, need

156

to know the truth.

"Before I meet your mother, I lived a dark life," he began in a faraway voice, "I was an assassin..."

Desti could not hold back a small intake of breath.

"Eam never approved, but it was not till after we married, when we embraced our Garatin heritage, and gave over to Eloi, that I gave it up. I promised Eam that I would never do it again, and then we left for the Byla Wilderness, far away from my former life."

Desti looked away as she tried to take it all in.

Wilder took a deep breath, and started talking to Desti - instead of himself. "Then, as you know, almost three years ago Rage came and found me."

"But what does Courage have to do with this?" she asked, almost protectively.

"He was my superior. I took orders from him and he is the captain of a group of highly trained soldiers. Trained as assassins."

Desti's heart began to beat faster and her breath came much too quickly, she felt the curtain that had protected her for so long being torn from her fingers, revealing the dark secret that her father had hidden for so long. Her stable, safe and predictable life was giving way to something unknown, wild and dangerous...

"What did Rage want from you?" There was no turning back now.

"There was someone who needed to be eliminated - a rebel who was causing trouble in the country, but he was arrested before the job could be done, much to my relief."

The truth was making it hard for Desti to breathe as she half asked half stated, "Liveran?!"

"Yes, Deliverance."

She nodded, somehow she knew that the worst to was yet to come. "And now? You're here for someone else?"

"Yes Desti, I am-" his voice broke. "I'm so sorry! I never wanted you to be involved!-" but before he could finish, Desti sobbed.

"You're here for Nity!?"

"Desti, I…"

She stood up, moved away from him, and looked at him like he was a stranger. "Daddy how could you?!" she accused him through her tears, "Nity is no rebel! How can you and Rage even consider such a thing - after what he did for Mise?!" she sucked in air.

"Desti…" Wilder pleaded, he had never meant for this! He half stood and reached for her hand - but she backed away from him and shook her head as though trying to understand him.

"Daddy…?"

Oblivious to the tears and pain, a butterfly flitted between them; Desti turned on her heel and fled back to the manor.

Wilder stood looking after her, a tear escaped his eye as he whispered, "Eam what would you have done…?" his voice faded off, and he bowed his head and wept.

So heartbroken was he that he did not hear a broken sob coming from somewhere in the garden. When he finally left the gardens, he did not notice the huddled form in the rose bushes. For it was amongst the sunshine and flowers that a young girl's world was destroyed in the innocent mistake of over hearing words that were not meant for her ears. In the blissful world of childhood, Mise had never even wondered what it was that her father did. But now, huddled among the roses - she knew the truth of it all. Mise gulped for air as the horrid thought came to mind of her father planning the death of the man who had awoken her from the dark sleep.

"Daddy?" she whimpered as she raised her face to the sunshine, "Why!?"

At last she jumped up and ran through the garden and into the manor. Heedless to all she ran down wide hallways and past startled servants. When at last she reached her chamber, she threw herself on her bed; her nurse came running in after her.

"Mistress! What is it?" she tried to touch Mise.

"Leave me alone!" Mise screamed at her.

The nurse, afraid Mise would cry herself into a relapse ran to find Loy. Upon seeing her daughter, Loy dismissed the nurse and sat next to her daughters hunched up body and pulled her into her embrace. For a time she just let Mise weep, feeling her daughters sobs tear at her breath, and then through her shuddering sobs Mise told of what she had overheard.

What is a mother to do? Loy had never been told what it was her husband did; there were secrets in their marriage - she had accepted that long ago, but she was not blind! Indeed, she had guessed Courage's work many years ago. She even knew why they were in Quy - who else could Rage and Wilder be here for, but Nity? It had always bothered her, but she would comfort herself in saying that, Rage did these things out of duty - he was not a blood thirsty killer!

Things had just gotten out of hand; it was hardly Courage's fault that the only man who could save Mise - was the man he meant to kill. All these things passed through Loy's mind as she tried to comfort her daughter, she looked about her at the room. It had always made her heart heavy knowing that her little girl would someday need to know the truth - but did it have to happen like this? In one brief moment the foundations of Promise's world had been shattered! Mise raised her head to look at her mother.

"Mother, why?" she implored, "Why must father assassinate Nity!?"

"Oh Mise! Try to understand! Nity may very well start a war."

Mise shook her head. "Mother, I don't understand! All I know is that Nity has more compassion and love than anyone has ever had, he has proved it time and again that his love knows no bounds, he has love enough for even the daughter of a Tarven - how can such a man start a war?!"

For a moment Mise waited for an answer with a tear streaked face - but Loy had no answers, not even for herself. At last Mise cried herself into an exhausted sleep, and Loy left her daughter and went out into the hall; she walked along feeling drained, until Wilder came around the corner.

"Loyal, have you seen Desti? She and...we-"

Loy interrupted. "I know."

He frowned, "Then you have seen her?"

"No, I have not. Promise overheard you two in the garden..."

His face changed as he realized what she must have overheard. Loy nodded. "She now knows the truth."

"Loyal- I'm sorry…"

She shook her head sadly, "This day was bound to come."

Not too far away in the shade of a healthy willow tree, more tears fell in earnest, for more than one foundation had been tested that day.

"I never meant for this to happen!" Desti said in a pleading tone, as though Treas could somehow make it all better, but she knew that he couldn't - no one could. "What am I to do? Father has always been there for me, my closest friend! Oh Treas! What am I to do?"

"I don't know," Treas said with open honesty. After he had told Desti about the mines he had stayed behind by the water's edge - completely lost in the pain of the past, and then Desti had come running to him in tears and had managed to tell him of what had happened. Treas had never before comforted someone in tears, and he felt quite helpless. The best he could do was awkwardly held her and pat her on the back.

"But Desti, you've made your decision!" he said at last. "You can't second guess yourself now! Why, wasn't it just a few days ago that Nity talked of this? He said some may have to choose between him and their family, he said that a soldier can't swear allegiance to two different kings, and nor can you be loyal to both Nity and your father." Treas could not believe that he had just said that! When Nity had said those words Treas had privately scoffed at them, he knew that if he had a family and if it came down to choosing between them and Nity, he would not choose Nity over his family- indeed who would? But Desti had.

Desti looked up at him with a tear-stained face and shook her head. "It's clear to me that Nity is the one who has been foretold since the days of old, clear to me as the light of day that Nity has been appointed by Eloi himself to restore freedom to Garatin! Why can't my father see that too? Every Garatin should be longing for the day when a Garatin rules this country - whether he is of royal blood or not! Yet my father wants to kill him!" Desti pulled back from Treas, her tears spent.

Treas could not help but feel relieved.

"How could my father keep this from me this whole time?" she asked out of frustration and pain.

Treas realized that the time had come; no more secrets, no more lies. He did not know what it was that motivated him, all he knew was that he could not keep silent any longer. He took her hand in his, and prepared himself for the worse.

"Desti…I knew about your father."

Desti frowned, "What do you mean?" she asked cautiously.

Treas remembered the last time he had held back the truth from her, she had forgiven him - then, but would she do so now?

"I knew beforehand what your father was."

"How…?"

He sighed, "After you had left three years ago, I happened to overhear some men talking about Rage and ever since then I have been putting the pieces together." He looked at her for a moment and squeezed her hand. "Can you forgive me for not saying anything?" he asked gravely.

She looked away as though wishing she was far away. "Yes Treas, I can forgive you," she looked back at him with pain, "But it will take a long time for me to trust you again."

He nodded; what else could he expect?

That night Nity and the others came earlier than expected, and Desti spent the night in their camp. She sent a message to inform her father of where she was, but she could not bear to see him so soon. She lay awake looking at the stars that night. 'What am I to do?' she asked herself. At long last she fell asleep. When morning came she knew what it was she had to do. She told Treas that she would return shortly, he asked to go with her but she told him to stay, with a frown he did as she asked. She then went to her father.

"I just need more time to think," she told him, looking down.

The two of them stood in the courtyard of Rage's manor. Wilder nodded, but his heart ached. "What will you do?" he asked.

"I'll journey with Nity and Treas to Garason for the festival, which will give me enough time to think." Her throat felt tight. "I'll go to Rage's manor to find you once there. I love you." She managed to say, she then went up on tip toe and kissed his cheek. She turned away quickly before he could see her tears.

Chapter 20

Dust

A few days later and the long line of villagers and peasants journeying to the city began to form; mostly it was a festive air, as family and neighbors met on the road. Nity and the others only had a few horses among them (including Willow) so the horses only carried food and other packs, while everyone walked. By the time they had left the Quy Lake region and entered into the grass lands, the road south was so crowded that Desti could no longer tell who was traveling with Nity and who wasn't! The grass was about shoulder length along both sides of the road here so it seemed very close on the road indeed. Desti craned her neck so she could see up ahead to where Treas had gone to talk with Est. When she caught sight of Treas she looked away, things were just too confusing! Will, showing his uncanny ability to read her thoughts snorted in agreement. Desti gently tugged on his reins as she walked in front of him, and tried to sort out her thoughts and troubled feelings.

First she finds out her father's secret about being an assassin and then she finds out that Treas helped to keep that secret! As if that was not enough she felt something growing in her heart about Treas - something sweet and unfamiliar... she pushed the thought aside without analyzing it. She looked up as Treas made his way towards her, she offered a thin smile but it faded when she saw the tension written on his face (was it new or had she just been too preoccupied to notice it before?)

"What's wrong?" she asked as he took up stride beside her.

He shook his head, "Nothing," he murmured.

"Really Treas, what's wrong?"

He sighed, "Its Nity."

This surprised her, "What about Nity? Treas you're not making any sense!"

He looked around as if Nity might be sneaking up behind them, "He's just...acting strange."

She frowned, "How so?"

163

"Desti, this is supposed to be it! This is his march of victory!"

"You think that he's going to claim the throne," she stated it more than asked.

"This is the perfect time! It's what everyone has been waiting for-" (it made Desti shiver, was her father waiting too?) "-but Nity's not acting like a king coming into his own city - but more like he's going to his execution!" He realized just how ridiculous it sounded as soon as he had said it.

"He's just nervous! That's all."

Treas nodded, but he did not look like he believed it.

It made Desti wonder; would next week bring about a new king and a free country? - Or would Nity disappoint them all? She looked up ahead again, and this time just glimpsed Nity walking up ahead of them. Yes the entire country would hold its breath this next week, and wait to see what he would do.

*   *   *

Wilder swayed in the saddle, his face was set in granite and his mind made up. A cloud of dust floated past him, then settled back down to the road, only to be stirred back up again by the wagon that Loy and Mise rode in. (Loy insisted that Mise ride in a wagon, less she fall sick again.) Rage had made certain that they were ahead of Nity and his company on the road; he also had a line of guards ahead of them and behind them on the road for privacy. The road was not so busy, there was only a group of wagons a little ways ahead of them - but Wilder knew that it would get more and more crowded the closer they got to Garason.

Wilder looked over at Rage, he was riding on his black stallion, and was dressed in the black and silver garb of a Tarven knight, he reminded Wilder of a wolf relentlessly hunting it's pray- bent on bringing it down, regardless of what it cost him! This hunt was destroying him, but Rage did not see it! The wind picked up, but only brought with it more dust to blow into the rider's faces. Wilder could taste it in his mouth, and the long high grass that now surrounded them bowed to the wind. Wilder noticed a lone rider up ahead that was approaching them at a trot. Wilder did a double take when he realized that it was a Tarven soldier! The soldier stopped and spoke to the guards ahead of them, then stood still as Wilder and Rage approached. They stopped their horses as they came in front of him.

He brought his right fist to his breastplate over his heart, and said, "Captain Courage?"

"I am he," Rage said as he coolly looked the young man up and down. "Who do you come from?"

"I bear a message from Ambassador Sinister," the soldier informed stiffly.

"And the message?" Rage asked, a little impatient.

The messenger glanced at Wilder, perhaps wondering if a Garatin could be trusted. He then reached into his saddle bag and produced a leather cylinder with a gold tassel hanging on the end, he handed it to Rage. Wilder watched his face as Rage pulled out the message that was inside, but his face gave away nothing as he read it. When Rage had finished the young man spoke again.

"The ambassador bids that you follow his orders at once to avoid further insurrection."

Rage nodded and brought his own fist to his heart, and the messenger added.

"I await further instructions." He then dipped his head to Rage, glanced at Wilder once more then turned and rode up to the guards to ride behind them.

Wilder and Rage nudged their horses back to a walk.

"And what urgent orders does Ister have?" asked Wilder, though he might have guessed already what they were.

Rage looked behind them to make sure that the wagons were too far away for anyone to hear what was being said, and then lowered his voice.

"Ister wants IT to be done before Nity enters the city; he will not risk Nity marching into the city like this! I suggest that you make the whole thing look like an accident, the less people talk about it the better-"

Wilder interrupted, "No."

Rage looked at him sharply; he was looking straight ahead.

"I can't do it."

Rage frowned, "What do you mean?" Their horse's stopped walking.

"I won't do it, Rage," Wilder returned Courage's gaze.

"The orders have been given-This man will cause a war," Rage said quietly.

"Perhaps a war is just what is needed!" Wilder gritted his teeth, "You don't see it, Rage, but Tarva is killing this country as surely as it's killing the rest of the world!"

"You are forgetting that you're a Tarven yourself," Rage said darkly.

Wilder answered without missing a heartbeat, "I'm not forgetting my ancestors! But nor have I lost sight of what I believe! Nity is not my enemy! It's cost me my own daughter to see that - what are you willing to put at risk, Courage?" It was a low blow; they both knew what Rage had put at risk- and should have lost.

It was the first time in a very long time that Wilder had ever lost his temper. Rage's face went cold; Wilder had dared to go somewhere that Rage never thought he would! Promise's pale face flashed before his eyes. A moment of silence followed...

"Are you refusing orders?" his tone was low, but never the less-threatening!

"Yes, I am," Wilder said almost with pride.

"You could be arrested for high treason Wilderness," Rage warned with a dark air.

"Only if you turn me in! Courage," Wilder spoke the Namesake as if it were a curse word.

The tension snapped between them!

"So be it," Rage said, his eyes spitting venom.

Wilder broke his horse into a gallop and flew past the guards; it was then that he realized that he was gripping his sword hilt. Would it really have come to that?! The wind cooled his face as he flexed his hand. He glanced over his shoulder back at Rage, and he felt something die within him. Had he really declared war against his old friend? Oh how far they had come since the days of old - their friendship had always been rocky, always there had been sharp edges, always there had been things that they did not discuss, but never- never had they been against each other. Wilder lifted his head as another cloud of dust rolled past, and he wondered if the dust between him and Rage would ever settle again.

Chapter 21

The Mob

Treasure and Destination had parted company with Nity and the others a day ago, when Nity had turned aside from the road to visit a friend. Treas had wanted to show Desti a bit of what the festival was like, so the two of them had rode on into Garason by themselves.

"The city sure is different..." Desti said trying to sound like she was enjoying herself, as she sat atop Will and took in the crowds around them.

Treas looked over his shoulder at her with a big smile, "Isn't it great!?"

Desti laughed, "Well that's not how I would put it."

He frowned, "What's wrong?"

"It's so...crowded! How you can stand it I'll never know!"

Treas took a deep breath as if he could inhale the city itself! "I love it! It's so easy to forget your own troubles, when surrounded like this..." he stopped as if he had given away something he had not intended to. "I love the city" he ended, hoping that she could not see through him.

She laughed, "If there is one thing I've learned it's that I much prefer the open wilderness to any town or city!"

Treas turned in the saddle to give her a strange look, "Really? Doesn't it get...mundane?"

"Oh at times, but there is always lots to do, you always know where you belong - what's expected of you, sometimes I feel trapped- but I feel even more trapped in the city!"

"Doesn't it get..." he looked away for a moment, "-lonely?"

She sighed, "Yes, at times, but father is always there..."

They were silent for a moment, then Will rounded a corner and from his back Desti saw a grand fort before her. It was shaped as a large square with stone walls reaching up at least three stories high. On each corner there was a square tower with peaked roofs, and fluttering in the wind at the top of each tower were long narrow white flags. Facing them

168

were mammoth sized double doors made from some kind of black wood that had become shiny over the years. The doors were reinforced with iron, and high on all four walls were a row of arched windows with colorful panes.

The fort looked as old as time, but still strong and durable. Upon seeing it Desti's breath stilled - what was this place!? Then as if a switch had been turned on Desti noticed the crowd that was filling the huge court yard surrounding the fort. There were merchants selling trinkets of all kinds and there were jugglers and violin players - it looked festive, but at second glance Desti saw different; this was a rushed pushy crowd. Desti also noticed that there were important looking men in rich robes, Desti guessed that they must be the Garatin leaders that she had heard so much about, and there were also armed Tarven soldiers.

"What is this place?" Desti said over the din as Treas steered Will through it all towards the fort.

"It's the 'Vase,'" he replied, but it made little sense to Desti.

"The what?" she asked.

"This is where the heart of every Garatin beats; Eloi dwells here."

Then Desti remembered Nity talking about this place, she looked around and saw that at some stands men were peddling parchment to burn, she looked back at the fort and felt a sense of awe. They stopped right in front of the huge doors and dismounted. Treas tossed a coin to a stable boy standing nearby along with Willow's reins, and then he took Desti's hand and they slipped inside the big doors.

Desti's breath came softly as she beheld the sight. Inside the big doors was a hallway with a high ceiling that went all the way around the inside of the fort and in front of Desti were slightly smaller black doors that were cracked open an inch but she could see little inside the inner chamber. Along the hallways were torches and grand tapestries that were richly embroidered. They told the history of Garatin in bright colors and strange pictures. Desti found herself standing in front of one that depicted a great battle, knights and soldiers were in fierce combat and amongst them astride a wild looking horse was a Garatin, man his face grim and set, he held his sword aloft. She stood as though entranced, why had her ancestors fought a hopeless battle- what had drove them to go on when all others would have given up?

Treas tugged on her arm and whispered, "This way." She tore herself away and followed him as he led her to the right along the hallway. The torches flickered as they went by. Around the corner there was a narrow staircase leading up. They climbed the stairs quickly. Up top, Desti found she was looking over a balcony at the inner chamber; it was at this level that the colorful arched windowpanes were located; their golden sunlight streamed through and tiny dust particles floated through the beams of light, by their light Desti could see the chamber below.

The floor in the chamber below was crafted out of a pink hued marble. Along the outside of the chamber there were marble pillars that rose up to support the balcony. There were torches on the pillars that flickered and mingled with the sunlight. In the center of the room was a dais and resting on it was a Vase. Desti could see even from the balcony that it was beautifully crafted; it was pale cream colored clay, and around its middle was a golden band - studded with jewels. Covering the vase were tiny figures painted in gold. It had an oval shape, sweeping up to a narrow mouth which then flared out to an elegant rim. Spilling out of the mouth was a white silk cloth, symbolizing Eloi's purity, and perhaps making sure that he stayed within. It was almost as tall as Desti herself!

"They say that Eloi dwells within the Vase its self," Treas said in a faraway voice.

Desti tore her eyes from the sight so as to look at Treasure's face; he looked sad, melancholy even!

"But Nity says-" he continued in a quiet voice, "-that the Garatin people have grown foolish in thinking that they can keep Eloi shut away. He says that Eloi is too big to be kept in one place and that despite their efforts, Eloi is not blind to the evil that they do, and that one day the Garatin leaders will pay for encouraging the common people to believe such things."

Desti looked below at the Garatin leaders who were entrusted with conveying Eloi's laws to the people, they looked so regal and why shouldn't they? They were educated and wise and closer to Eloi then any could ever get! - And yet Nity said that they were misleading the people, and did evil behind Eloi's back. Desti wondered briefly if Nity could be wrong… after all, what did he know of Eloi? He was just a common country lad, and for thousands of years the Garatin leaders had said that Eloi was in the Vase. But then- their logic was all wrong! They said that Eloi was great and powerful! – If so, then how could he be kept blind and powerless behind clay walls? Nity must be right! But if Eloi was not in the Vase- where was he? - Her thoughts were interrupted.

"Do you hear that?" Treas whispered. She looked at him; he was straining his ears, she did the same. Then she heard it; a noise from outside. They both turned to the windows but they were too high to see out of. Treas then lead her along the balcony to the corner, and there in the shadows was a wooden ladder going straight up (she wondered how he knew it was there.) He went up and then she followed.

The ladder led through a trap door out onto the roof, the noise had grown to a low roar, and she realized what it was; a riot! She followed Treas to the battlement and felt sick as she peered over, but whether it was from the height or the sight below she did not know. What she saw was the crowd below but it had grown (if possible) and was swelling like a sea full of waves.

Desti soon realized that it was not a riot but a procession! There were many waving narrow white silk ribbons, an age old symbol of Eloi, and many more were shouting and cheering.

"Look!" Treas shouted over the crowd and pointed. Desti looked to where he pointed; there were several men on horseback and it was for them that everyone was cheering. The group of men was being led by one man on a spirited dappled gray. The horses pranced and skidded along as the crowds pressed around them.

"It's Nity!" Treas shouted with excitement. "Desti, he's done IT!" he said grabbing her arm; his eyes wide like a child.

"Done what!?" Desti was confused.

"What we've all been waiting for! He's going to declare himself King! He has the people's approval, they are waving the symbol of Eloi; no one can stop him now! He's finally done it!"

Desti felt her stomach do a back flip, all her mixed up emotions collided at once; this was the man who was bringing freedom and the man her father meant to kill. This was the man who held all of life's answers, the answer as to why the Garatin people had fought so courageously- and why they would fight again, and in that moment, she felt as if she would follow him anywhere!

The crowd began to settle down, and waited for Nity to act. He dismounted, as well as did the others (Est, Fin and so forth.) Treas tugged at her sleeve.

"Come on, we should be with him in his hour of triumph!"

"Treas wait! What's happening?!"

Treas stopped at the alarm in her voice and came back to look, for the crowd had suddenly erupted into shouts and screams! There seemed to be a lot of movement around Nity, then Desti realized why; he had kicked over a peddlers stand knocking its contents onto the ground! And like wildfire the crowd closest him broke out into a mob! They kicked over stands and shouted things like 'down with the Garatin leaders and their lies!' Desti watched in a daze as she saw Tarven soldiers pour into the square with spears and drawn swords! Nity disappeared from sight, and Treas was pulling at her arm!

"Come on, Desti! We have to get out!"

     *   *   *

Ree had heard the noise, she had seen the procession, been a part of the crowd that had filled the streets. She had felt her heart quake. Nity…. The storm had broken, and there was no place to hide, not for this creature of darkness; this storm would destroy her! She had followed Nity through the streets until he had reached the Vase. She had wanted to run, and at the same time, she couldn't! Like a moth, beating its wings against a flame. She had told herself that the only reason she was there was because she was waiting to see if Nity would declare rebellion. But in all truth she couldn't stay away! At last she turned her back, Nity would not do anything, and so she would leave. But no sooner had she thought this than the crowd became a mob out of control!

Her heart took wing; Nity was a rebel after all, and it would begin today. But then he had disappeared- without a trace, and the mob was left leaderless. Tarven soldiers appeared and their very presences doused the mob in seconds! No one had a great wish to be arrested, and Ree was among the many that slipped from the square.

That had all been an hour ago. Ree now sat, silent and brooding, the rebels had called an emergency meeting after what had happened at the Vase. Ree was now considered one of the leaders and had been included in the meeting. She was slightly angry with the other leaders for not telling her the reason that they had such high hopes that Nity would join them. She now knew the reason; they had inside information. One of Nity's friends had contacted them several months ago, and said that he could persuade Nity to join the rebels, the man's Namesake was Concern, and he was with them now.

"I thought we had come to an agreement!?" the rebel leader who's Namesake was Devotion, said with a hot face to Cern.

Cern looked back coldly, "I said that I was not sure what Nity would do when he got to Garason, we all assumed that he would declare himself King-"

"You assumed that he wasn't a coward!" Devo interrupted him sharply.

Cern looked away, as if confused, "He was so close..." he whispered.

Ree just barely heard it, her liking of Cern grew even less- he was so weak! Just like Gra had been.

"I don't know why he didn't follow through with it; I had thought that the crowds' enthusiasm would spur him on," Cern said turning back to Devo.

Devo snorted as if he found it funny, but not enough to actually laugh.

"Then tell me Cern, of what further use are you to me? If you can't manipulate him to declare rebellion - What use are you?" he said, with a cold air in his voice, sounding even deeper than normal.

Cern's face hardened, "It would appear that it is I who doesn't need you, I can go elsewhere - I can't say the same for you." With a last look at everyone he then turned on his heel and marched for the door of the ale house; it slammed behind him.

Ree watched him go, and wondered if they had just missed out on the rebellion, if anyone was to lead it - it would be Nity. Cern was hoping to force Nity into rebellion - hoping that under the right circumstances Nity would snap. Cern was a rebel at heart - he wanted Nity to bring liberty so much. But now he had left. Ree looked at the others, they looked dazed, Devo looked as though he had just realized that Nity was their only hope - and he had just sent away the one man who whispered in Nity's ear. At last Devo looked around at the downcast faces (except for Ree's, she never showed emotion).

"Do not lose hope," he said to them, "Nity will yet declare rebellion, and when he does - we'll be there!"

Eternity's conduct had baffled more than one that day; Wilder stood leaning against the wall of a side street. He had arrived in Garason some time before the sun rose, and had watched the streets come alive. He was deeply troubled, not only had he lost the respect of his own daughter, but the friendship of a dear friend, and all because of Nity. And now it looked like Rage had been right after all! Nity was a rebel, he would not have started the riot if he had not been. But…he had left! Victory had been within his grasp, he could have proclaimed himself King in a heartbeat, the people would have fought to the death against the Tarvens if only they had a leader - but he had tossed it all to the wind, and disappeared. What manner of man was this?

Thankfully, only a few arrests had been made, the Garatin leaders had been anxious to assure the ambassador that nothing had really happened and that they had complete control over the people. There was no need to send in more Tarven soldiers - that was their fear; if Ambassador Ister thought that the Garatin leaders could no longer control the situation, then they would be 'relieved of duty'. In other words, stripped of ALL their power and authority in any matter! And, the government of Tarva would completely take charge of the country forever. Such was the fear that gripped all sensible folk. What if Nity (or anybody else for that matter) tried to start a rebellion- and failed? Then Garatin would truly be an occupied country.

Wilder could feel the entire city- nay, the entire country holding its breath and waiting for Nity's next move. Did he know that his actions would affect the whole country? Did he know of how many lives rested in his decisions? Wilder sighed heavily, if only that was the least of his worries. Where was Desti? She had said she would go to Courage's manor. But how could Wilder go there now? And would she not have disappeared with Nity after the riot? Was she safe? Could he make her understand his decision? Would she believe him when he told her that he had broken with Rage and would no longer seek Nity's death?

*   *   *

"Treas? What's going to happen?" Desti asked sounding scared and vulnerable.

Treas rubbed his forehead and without looking away from the window he stood at said quietly, "I don't know, Desti, I don't know."

It was afternoon, and the white fluffy clouds of the morning had turned into gray. It had taken the two of them a long time to get through the city after the 'incident' at the Vase but they had eventually made it to the inn that Nity and the others had agreed to meet at before they had parted company. But they were the only ones there. No one else had come, and they waited alone in an upstairs room. Treas had only opened up one of the shutters and he hid behind the other as if under siege.

"Do you think that Nity and the others were arrested?" she asked fearfully.

Treas sighed, but just as he opened his mouth to answer his face lit up, Nity and the others were making their way down the street towards them leading their horses.

"There they are!" Treas said with relief. All was well.

Chapter 22

The Web

'The quest of a life time.' That's what Nity had called it; it had been one day since the mob, and Nity had promptly gone out into the streets to teach - regardless of all the warnings that Est, Treas and the others gave him to stay out of sight. He insisted that no harm would befall him that day. Sitting on the steps that led up to an old statue in a square, Treas Desti and the others listened as Nity told a story of a young man who all his life dreamed of being knighted by the King, and finally his chance came! The King agreed to knight him, but only after he had proved his worth, he must go on a quest. The young man was willing to give up anything for the chance of knighthood, and he left at once.

But the road to success was not easily accomplished, many things he endured, many foes did he face, many a night did he wonder if he would survive - but he did, and the price was everything that he possessed. At last he returned to the King broken and half alive, but his quest was accomplished, and the King knighted him - as his just reward.

Nity then explained his story; the King was Eloi- and to be accepted by him, one must give up everything - for to be knighted by the King- was worth anything! It was indeed, a treasure worth any price…

Treas had jumped when Nity used his Namesake; his words seemed to pierce his very soul! More and more he began to see that if there was one thing that he longed for - it was to be 'knighted by the King'. He no longer cared if he got hurt by opening up his heart to people! How could others love him if he did not love them? Yes, being hurt was better than not being loved! Oh, how he longed to be different! To be honorable and trustworthy, to put aside the loneliness and pain, to become worthy of Desti's love! He longed to be like Nity; close to Eloi.

Yes, he desired to be what his Namesake implied. Treas turned away from Nity; he could bear it no longer, as much as he longed for these things - he knew that he could never achieve them. That's when he saw him, looked into his very eyes as he crossed the courtyard towards Desti and himself.

Treas stood to his feet as he felt an overwhelming impulse to land his fist across Wilder's jaw, perhaps it was because it was the only thing that he could control at that moment. Fortunately for him, Desti also saw the approach of her father, and must have sensed Treasure's hostility, for she placed a hand on his arm to restrain him. It was for her sake and her sake alone that he held his fist in check (even if the odds would not have been in his favor!). Wilder came up and stood before his daughter; he then turned his gray eyes on Treas.

"Would you mind if I had a few private words with my daughter?" he was polite but Treas did not miss how he said 'my daughter'. Treas looked at Desti almost hoping that she would say something like 'father please go away!' but instead she nodded at him; he gave one last look to Wilder then strode away down the steps.

"He's very protective of you," Wilder observed.

Desti looked at Treas as if she had not thought of it that way before. She looked back at her father. "I'm happy to see you again, father-" a lump came to her throat, and she could not go on, indeed all she wanted to do was fall into his arms! How could he be an assassin?!

"Desti there is something you must know."

"What is it?" she asked wearily.

"Orders came that Nity was to be taken care of at once."

Her eyes widened but he went on before she could say anything.

"I refused those orders."

Her face went blank; could she believe this - after all the lies?

"I've begun to see Nity, and what he does in a new light."

Still she could not speak.

"I have broken company with Rage... and I wish to know the man who will change this sad country".

A tear glistened in her eye.

"Desti, can you forgive this foolish man?" he asked at last.

Laughing and weeping she threw her arms around his neck! But in a moment the joy was gone and she pulled back. "What about Rage?"

He grew solemn, "He is as determined as ever to bring Nity down,

177

when I refused the order, he threatened to arrest me."

She gasped, "But! He wouldn't arrest you... would he?"

He did not reply to her, and instead asked, "Does Nity know of his danger?"

She nodded.

"And he is still out in the open?" he asked with a frown.

"He will not be detoured - but... he has spoken so much of death lately."

Wilder's frown only deepened, "It would seem that he has something planned..."

That night Wilder could not sleep - but he was not troubled, instead he felt so at peace, as though he had just won an argument, as though he had just been in a heated debate and finally...it was over! After his discussion with Desti, she had introduced him to Nity. A few weeks ago he would have said that he knew everything about this man- after all, he had been the man's shadow for many a month! But now he knew that he had only just touched the surface to a very deep pool! Yes, beyond a doubt this man would bring freedom! After meeting Nity and spending the rest of the day with him and his company Wilder and Desti had gone to an inn and taken a room for the night. Desti had fallen asleep almost instantly on the bed. Although comfortable on the floor, Wilder stayed up most the night- just thinking. Yes Wilder was at peace, even though all his troubles had just begun.

*　　　　　　*　　　　　　*

Mise peeked into her mother's chambers, her mother sat on a cushioned stool with many handmaidens dressing her dark hair. Mise entered the room to stand in front of her, and Loy took her daughters hand in her own and smiled. It had been two days since they had returned to Garason, two days since the riot at the Vase. Rage had ridden on ahead of them into the city promising to meet them at the manor, but after making their way through the crowds Loy and Mise had arrived at the manor devoid of Rage. He had come home late that night and then left only a few hours later. This routine was repeated the next day. After two days Mise had not even glimpsed her father and she could sense that things were not right.

"Mother?"

"Yes dear, what is it?"

"Where's father?" she asked sadly.

Loy chose to ignore it, "I don't know," she said airily looking away.

They both knew it to be a lie; Rage would be where ever Nity was.

"How is your flower?" she asked to change the subject, (Mise had taken special care of it ever since Nity had helped her to water it).

"There is a bud on it now…" Mise lacked enthusiasm.

"Oh isn't that exciting!?" Loy said as if to a young child.

Mise looked at her with a pout, "When will he come home, mother?"

Loy reached out to wipe away a tear that escaped her daughter's eye and slid down her face. "Sweetheart… soon everything will return to normal and everything will be all right!" she smiled bravely at her.

Mise nodded but wondered if things could ever go back to the way they use to be; had things gone too far to ever be all right again? Mise had a sudden urge to go and find Nity - if anyone could make things better - it was him! But it hurt too much to even think of Nity, if her father had his way… Nity would die.

*   *   *

The wind swept through the hot muggy streets, and touched the black stone figure that stood in a second story window with open shutters. At least many thought that she was made of stone - how else could she be so cold? It was on such days when the cold black silk turned into a furnace, and Ree felt like she would burn up. But today she hardly noticed the heat. Her arms crossed and her face dark, she had been standing at the window for the past twenty minutes - ever since she had returned from the latest rebel meeting.

Some might wonder what it was that she was thinking, but they would have been surprised to know just how vulnerable and insecure she felt. The past day had dragged by like a dying animal; the week of the festival was four days from being over and Nity had still not done a thing! The rebels felt anxious and uneasy - would Cern have talked against rebellion to Nity, just to spite them? What were they to do? Their one chance was slipping away!

Finally the rebel leader, Devo, could take no more, and he had gone to Nity and asked him to join in the fight. But of all the high and mighty, stuck up - Nity had declined! With all the manners of a duke! As if he was of royal blood, like he was too good for the low-life rebels. At least, that's what Ree wanted to believe, but in all truth it was as though he had something else planned - but what!?

Devo had then called a meeting, he had been very flabbergasted indeed, that Nity should have plans that did not include them was very insulting! It had been decided at the meeting that they could not wait another day (Ree agreed). IT must be done that night! The word had been sent all over the city - it would be a bloody morning, and the cries of freedom would be heard that night!

She took a deep breath... Perhaps tonight, after all her long imprisonment - after three years she would at last be free of the black silk, would at last prove her innocence and finally fulfill her Namesake. Her skill with the bow surpassed anyone else, and she had been given the honor of starting the rebellion! At midnight she would shoot a flaming arrow into the ambassador's residence, as the first signal, and the sparks of liberty would leap into life! Indeed it was not ideal; they should have done this sooner. Tomorrow would begin the burning of the parchment at the Vase, but there was no other way about it! They could not wait. There was even the high hope that Nity would still join them - how could he resist when the whole city rose up as one? Ree would catch a few hours' sleep before it all began. She turned from the window but her reflection in a tiny mirror that was pinned up on the wall caught her attention; a woman within a black cloak and a pale face stared back at her. Her breath caught, but not because of the coldness in her own eyes but because peeking out of the collar of the cloak was the stain. In the past three years the stain had never infected her neck or face, but now she could see that it was creeping up her neck, she quickly pulled her cloak close about her neck, and swallowed hard; was there no end to this black magic? She closed her eyes.

*   *   *

Loy stood at her window with the panes thrown wide, taking in the view - but truth be told, she did not see the city and its walls, nor even the green rolling hills beyond that seemed to shift under the veil of heat. She had been betrothed to Rage when she had been sixteen, and had left her home in Tarva to marry an unknown man in an unknown land. But she had admired him at once - he had everything that she lacked in life. He was so strong - while she was so weak. He knew what he wanted out of life and how to get it - she would just follow him. He was the husband and leader - while she was just the wife, and a poor one at that, she couldn't even give him a son!

He was the provider- while she raised their child. She did not interfere with him and his work, and he never asked for her advice - even if he did, how could she ever help him? She could only get in the way… He would find his own way out of life's troubles - that's what she had come to believe. Such was the role of a woman of Tarva.

"Mistress? You called for me?" Loy turned, one of her young handmaidens stood at the door.

"Yes, Gentle. You have a younger brother- do you not?"

The girl looked very confused, but said none the less, "Yes mistress I do and his Namesake is Challenge, and he's about eight, and my mum says that she did right by giving him that Namesake-" she was cut off.

"Yes Ntle, but tell me; would he be willing to do something for me?"

"What did you have in mind? (If you don't mind me asking)."

"I need this letter delivered." Loy held up a peace of folded parchment.

Ntle outright frowned this time, "He works down in the stables - don't you have messengers who will do that?"

If Loy had not have been so well brought up she would have rolled her eyes. "Will he do it for perhaps… a few coins?" Loy's offer made Ntle's eyes enlarge.

"Oh I'm sure he will! I'll go and get him now!"

Then Loy smiled her approval and the fifteen year old girl ran out of the room. Why did Loy prefer to use a young stable boy instead of any number of her husband's loyal messengers? Because at this point she did not know to whom they were loyal; to Rage and his family or to Tarva. Just then Mise entered the room slowly; she held the familiar little flower pot.

"Look mother," she held up the five inch plant; on one of its curled tips was a tiny, ivory, star shaped flower.

"Oh Mise! It bloomed!"

Mise only nodded.

"Promise, what's wrong?" she asked her daughter.

Mise looked up at her with a long face, "I just wish father was here," she whispered.

Loy took her daughter into her arms and said with determination, "He will be- if I can help it!" She tapped the letter on Promise's back.

*   *   *

Desti smiled as she watched Treas, he was standing with Est and Fin and he was showing them how to juggle. They had been talking about it like it was some sort of magic trick and so Treas had picked up three apples and began to show off. After a few moments he tossed the apples to Fin and laughed when Fin tried to juggle the apples himself. Fin's attempt at juggling only lasted a few seconds before they all dropped to the cobble stones. Treas then came to sit down beside Desti on some stone steps leading up to a city well; he picked up another apple that was sitting beside her.

It was late morning, and Nity had gone to a market square. But on the way huge crowds began to follow him, so they had all settled down for a giant picnic. After a few moments of silence where Treas was just tossing the apple up and down, Desti felt that she had to say it.

"You know Treas, you really should believe him," she looked at Treas full in the face.

"Who?" he asked carelessly.

"My father," she answered quietly, "He's really not trying to trick anyone."

182

"Who said that he was?"

"You think he is," she said boldly putting out her chin.

He tried to laugh it off. She shook her head; she felt heat rising in her face.

"You act like he's a no good thief!-" before she could finish a Tarven boy came up to stand in front of them.

"I was told you might know where Wilderness is," he stated. Desti took a deep breath as she calmed herself.

"Yes, I'll take you to him, this way." She got up and led the boy across the square.

Treas watched as Desti led the boy to her father, "You're wrong Desti," he whispered sadly. "I could never hope to be half the man your father is…"

Desti watched as the boy handed a letter to her father. And then without a word; he ran off.

"Wait! Stop!" Desti called out as he disappeared through the crowd. "Why do you suppose he did that?" Desti asked, but Wilder did not answer. Desti looked at him but he was already reading the letter. She then peeked over his elbow at the message, this is what it said.

To my husband's friend, Wilder.

I know that you and my husband had a falling out (Rage is not the easiest man to get along with), but I fear for my husband's life. The ambassador bid him to go to a meeting last night, and he has not come home. He took no one with him, and no one knows where he is. Please, he was not himself when he left; I fear that he may have done something rash.

For the sake of old friendship- find him.

Loyal

Desti looked up at her father, his face was dark.

"I know where he is," he said with determination.

She struggled, but it was no use; she was stuck in a black web of silk threads. She could not get out - no matter how much she struggled! She went limp in exhaustion, and then felt the web quiver; the spider was coming to claim its victim... 'I'm going to die.'

Ree awoke with a start and continued to struggle, but she was met with resistance! Strong hands held her!

"Get up!" a hard voice commanded.

She was pulled to her feet, she looked about her in bewilderment; two Tarven soldiers stood on either side of her and held her arms tightly, another stood before her. It was still light out - what had gone wrong?

"Are you Freedom?" the soldier in front of her demanded.

"Oh that's her all right!" her landlord volunteered. He stood by the open door, and he seemed to be enjoying himself. "And she ain't paid her rent yet!"

"I did not ask you!" the soldier shouted at him, "Come on move her out!"

She was led down the back stairs and to the door - that's when she saw what had gone wrong. Standing by the door was Receive!

"Yes that's the one I told you about, she's one of the lead rebels," she told the soldier as he came down. As he passed by her he dropped a bag of coins into her hand.

Ree felt anger rise up within her; she had been betrayed by a fellow rebel! She was then taken out onto the street - but as she passed Eive she glared at her and spat in her face.

Chapter 23

Emerald

"Where!?" Desti asked, after her father's exclamation.

Wilder looked up from the letter and over the busy square. "Here," he replied with confidence. Desti looked around too and wiped her forehead; the heat was oppressive in the crowded square.

"Here? Are you sure?" she asked with uncertainty, she found it hard to believe.

"Whatever happened last night - Rage will be here! He has been obsessed with Nity's whereabouts for the past four months and longer, if Nity is here - so too will Rage." He craned his neck looking out over the crowd with new eyes. "Look, Desti," he hesitated for a moment, "Will you help me look for him?"

"Of course, I'll ask Treas to help too."

She turned to go but Wilder grabbed her arm and said, "If you find him… don't approach him! This all may be a trap, come tell me as soon as you see him." She didn't really understand but she nodded anyway, and went to find Treas.

Wilder tucked Loy's letter inside his tunic, and made his way through the crowd, all the while going over all the possible dangers that he now faced; the letter could be a trap and Rage could be waiting with soldiers to arrest him for insubordination. But no, Wilder dismissed that possibility; Rage had too much pride to stoop that low. Wilder reached a wall and he put his back to it and scanned the crowd for any Tarven; but he could not see any. He walked to a different corner, but still he could not see him… perhaps he was wrong, perhaps Rage wasn't here - but then where was he?

It was then he saw him! At least it might have been him. The man he was looking at was the only Tarven in sight but his beard was over grown and did not resemble the close clipped one that Rage always wore. The man had dark circles under his eyes making it look more like he had been in a fight. He looked like something that the cat had at some point considered eating! But it was Rage none the less, and despite looking like he had not

185

taken care of himself in days he still wore his weapons but most importantly; he was alone. Or were there soldiers somewhere out of sight, waiting for a signal?

Wilder took a deep breath; trap or no, for the sake of old friendship a risk must be taken. "Courage?" he called out as he stepped forward.

Rage turned toward him and the two faced each other - like adversaries. "I was hoping to find you here," Rage spoke the first words.

Wilder's jaw tensed as he wondered what would happen next. "It seems that we were both hoping the same," he said at last. "Loy asked me to find you, she seemed afraid that something happened with the ambassador last night."

"Ister summoned me to a meeting…" Rage explained what had happened after he had left Loy. Feeling rather distraught (truth be told, she had good cause to be worried); he had wandered about for a long time that night with many questions that have no answers. How lost he had felt! He had not felt confident or strong - he felt scared. Somehow, everything that he believed no longer made sense: his whole world felt like it was crumbling about him. But as always, his strength and sense of purpose won out in the end. He knew what it was he had to do.

He went to the old council chambers that he knew so well and burst in on the meeting that was already underway. He stood before the men, but for the first time in his life - he felt no courage and he could not speak. A group of power heavy men sat around a large round table, and stared at him. There were Tarven captains on one side and Garatin leaders on the other side.

"So glad that you could join us," Ister said with no humor, he sat facing Rage on the other end of the chamber. "I have called you all together to discuss what is to be done about Nity. Despite complaints from some-" Ister glanced at the Garatin leaders, "- the man has done nothing against Tarva or its laws."

"But he HAS broken Garatin laws and traditions!" one of the stiff lipped Garatins said.

"I care very little about laws made by superstitious pale-faced

Garatins," Ister pronounced the word like it was distasteful.

The Garatin leaders went very pale indeed for a moment then turned very red in the face.

"You have a duty to uphold Garatin laws! And the man's crimes are punishable by death! We have no authority to carry out executions, so it is your duty to do so!" demanded the Garatin leaders.

"Tell me Rage-" Ister said with boredom, "How do you stop a cock from crowing?" Whether Ister was referring to Nity or the Garatin leaders was uncertain, but a few of the Tarvens smirked. Ister continued in a more business like tone. "This matter could have all been taken care of if you had better control of your men, Rage. You were foolish to have told your man Wilderness everything about the problem- you should have ordered him to take care of it at once; instead of letting him wander off in the middle of the night! But I'll give you another chance to prove yourself; I want you to take your men, Rage, and I want you to arrest Nity tomorrow night, if only to please the hen house. We have a man here by the Namesake of Concern, he will be able to tell us where Nity will be tomorrow night; he has agreed to help us." A Garatin man stepped forward from the shadows, he looked nervous. "I will decide what to do with Nity when the festival is done in two days' time," Ister finished.

Rage straightened his shoulders, "No," he said simply - but firmly.

There was a silence. The torch light flickered as the men- Tarven and Garatin alike- starred at him in a mixture of shock and awe.

"I refuse these orders." Rage explained what had happened the night before to Wilder who listened without comment. "I then left, before they could come up with a response."

"Why?" Wilder asked at last.

Rage was silent for a moment, "You once asked me why it was I always had to disagree with you. Well, now I agree with you; Nity is just what this country needs!"

For a moment they searched one anther; and both found an old friend.

Rage put his right hand on Wilder's left shoulder and Wilder did the same. They still had their differences - Rage was still a head-strong Tarven and Wilder was still a soft-spoken Garatin but they would forever be old friends.

"Wilder-" Rage grew serious again, "You know that the danger does not end here. Just because I won't, does not mean that someone else won't arrest him."

Wilder smiled in his confidence, "In this crowd? No, they would not dare upset the people - and what charges do they really have? He is above reproach!"

Rage was silent as he thought on this, and then he got a strange look in his eye. "Wilder? Will you introduce me to Nity? I would know the man I have pledged allegiance too." Wilder smiled.

"It seems as though Rage has had a change of heart…" Desti explained to Treas, "but father's still not sure that he can be trusted, and thinks the best way to know for sure - is to stay close to him, so he'll be returning to Courage's manor-"

"And you'll be going with him," Treas finished what she was saying.

She bit her lip but could not hold back a smile, "I think that everything will be all right now! Treas? Won't you come with us?" she asked hopefully.

He shook his head, "No I want to stay close to Nity."

Her brow furrowed, "Why?"

He shrugged, "I just don't want to leave him now, but I'll see you on the morrow when we all take our parchment to the Vase."

She smiled, "All right."

Then he did something completely unexpected; he leaned forward and kissed her on the cheek. She looked at him with wide eyes as he smiled and then turned away. She was flying so high that she couldn't remember much of the ride back to Rage's manor, nor even of the happy reunion between Rage and Loy, or the sheer joy on Promise's face when Rage told her of his change of heart.

Indeed Desti went to bed still floating.

A prisoner was sick in the Tarven barracks prison where Ree had been taken a few days past. The guards were afraid that it was contagious so they sent for an herb man. Ree looked up as the guards led him into the dark hallway. From the torch light she could see that the herb man had a stooped back and he shuffled more then walked - Ree caught her breath as she realized who it was; Healer...

Ler looked up into her eyes and stopped before her cell, she could not move - she could not speak; this was the one man who knew her secret... the stain.

"This prisoner isn't the one who is sick," the guard said when Ler stopped.

"Oh yes she is," Ler whispered then said aloud, "What is this prisoner sentenced to?" Ler asked.

"Tongue slitting," the guard said curtly.

"Well the ambassador should rethink that, I know this woman." With surprising quickness he reached in between the bars and grabbed Ree's right wrist, he then pulled off her black glove. "She is a murderess, and I have no doubt a sorcerer who has been caught in her own black magic; even death would be too kind," he said as the guards stepped back in shock and disgust.

Her entire arm was a sickly black and her skin looked thin, revealing red veins; even her nails had turned a shade of ebony! Ree pulled back her hand and jumped back from the prison bars as she hid her hand in the folds of her cloak - but the damage had been done.

"A witch..." breathed one of the guards as he took another step.

"I will tell the ambassador of this - disturbing news," the other guard said with a swallow.

Ler gave a wicked smile as he threw back her glove and walked away. Ree watched them go, and she felt a prison door close on her fate...

*   *   *

Desti could not sleep that night and finally gave up around midnight; she wandered the halls of Rage's manor hoping to exhaust herself.

189

Soon she found that she was thirsty and thought that the easiest way to a well would be through the kitchen. Approaching the door she heard a voice- it was Treasure's! She peeked into the kitchen and took in the sight; the cook stood at the back door. She was wearing her night cap and her eyes looked heavy. She was holding a candle and she was indeed fit to be tied!

"Go away!" she hissed through the half open door. On the other side of the door stood Treas, his eyes were wide and his face flushed. He was breathing hard as he looked up and saw her.

"Treas!?" she exclaimed.

"It's Nity!" he gasped, "He's been arrested!!!"

Earlier that night, Nity had taken Est, Fin, Treas and the others to the gardens of Jes'reel. They had wandered about the gardens with their spirits high, they joked and laughed as they savored the thought of putting Nity on the throne. It was only then they realized that Cern was nowhere to be found, but no sooner had they realized this than Cern appeared - leading a group of Garatin soldiers. Cern then identified Nity and the soldiers arrested him. Est had flung himself at one of the guards and had almost gotten himself killed, Fin had pulled him away and everyone scattered, and Treas found himself fleeing along with the others for dear life; he had not known where to go so he went to Desti.

Desti had at once gotten dressed and awoken her father who in turn had awoken Rage, and when they heard the news, Wilder and Treas went to the Garatin prison where Nity would be kept overnight (Rage thought it best that he stayed behind). Treas and Wilder had returned empty handed many hours later. They hadn't even been able to see Nity; nothing could be done till the morrow.

"Destination! Wake up, Desti!"

Desti felt someone jumping on her, and she had that strange sensation one gets when rudely awakened. Her eyes opened and the world came into focus, an unwelcome sight to be sure. She sat up as Mise continued to pull at her; she had been lying on a day bed in Courage's chambers with tapestries on the walls and a massive fireplace. The night before came back in vivid images; Treas at the cooks door with the horrid news of Nity's arrest. She remembered what had followed next but could not recall when she had fallen asleep. She looked around; the sun was shining through the thick windowpanes.

"Mise where is everyone?" she asked in her disorientated state.

"They've all gone to Nity's trial," Mise answered.

"His trial!? Why did they not take me?"

"Because there is nothing to do - but wait," Loy informed, as she glided into the room with poise and dignity, her shoes clicking on the stone floor. "Besides, there is nothing they can do to him, Nity has broken no laws. I heard that at daybreak this morning the Garatin leaders brought him before Ister and tried to accuse him of starting a rebellion. Ister found no truth in the claims and not knowing what to do he sent Nity to the Garatin King, Ordained, since he was in the city, but Dain wanted nothing to do with him and sent him back to Ister. He is, as we speak, having a public trial for Nity, and we all know that the people have nothing against him, so the inevitable is that they must release him."

"How do the Garatin leaders wish Nity to be punished?" Desti asked wanting to know the worst.

Loy hesitated, "They hope to have him executed," she said softly.

Desti gasped.

"But, we need not fear that, there is nothing they can do," Loy assured, "Now, if you will excuse me." She then left the room.

Desti sat still, trying to take it all in.

"Desti?" Mise spoke up, "I'm scared, what if my mother is wrong? I think something terrible is going to happen to Nity!"

Desti felt sick in the pit of her stomach, "Mise, where is the trial?"

"At the coliseum, a tournament is being held there today so there are lots of people there already."

Desti felt panicked, "When is the trial?"

"Soon…"

Desti's heart sunk, "Then there is no way to get there in time…"

she said out loud in despair.

Promise's eyes snapped with mischief, "There is a way..." she whispered.

Mise lead Desti out into the courtyard and towards a large barn - but it wasn't the stables. Mise looked about then slipped into a side door and Desti followed. It was dark inside and the smell of hay was strong. Desti stood still waiting for her eyes to adjust to the darkness.

"Mise? Where are you?" she called out.

"Over here."

Promise's voice came from a ways away and it was muffled. Desti wondered how big the barn was! It seemed to be all open, with only one oversized stall, and that's where Mise's voice had come from. She then heard a squeaking noise, like the hinges on a big door, and then a huge shadow came swiftly out of the stall - but there was no noise.

"Mise?" she asked uncertainly.

"Desti, I'd like you to meet my father's pet, Emerald!"

Mise hauled on a rope and a latch released; a panel slid way from the roof and a shaft of light shot down on a giant beast. Desti gasped and jumped back in fear. The beast had a regal head with a curved beak. From the crown of its head several green feathers stood erect, and it was metallic blue from its neck all the way to its belly. Its stout legs ended with clawed talons, the wings were wide and strong and flecked with green and purple feathers. Its tail was long and rested on the floor, it was made up of long green feathers that were narrow at the base and wide at the end, each one ended with blue and purple circles; its back came up to Desti's waist.

She could hardly believe her eyes, Treas had once described them to her but she never thought they were so big! What she looked upon was a Cokhawk. The great bird looked down at her with one violet, curious eye, it then snapped its beak and arched its wings, and Desti felt for sure that this was the end! Then the beast shook its feathers from its metallic neck to its curled tail, until every last feather laid flat.

"We call her Em," Mise said as she came forward with a strange looking saddle.

"We're going to ride IT to the coliseum!!?" Desti asked horrified.

"Oh yes!" Mise nodded vigorously, "It's the only way to get there in time, and you needn't be afraid of her; we've had her for years!"

Hesitantly Desti helped Mise put the saddle high up on the birds back close to its neck. Sewed into the saddle were several brass rings and tied to them were leather straps, used for tying oneself into the saddle. Desti then gave Mise a leg up onto Em's back and gingerly climbed up behind her. Mise then showed her how to tie herself into the saddle.

"Just a precaution," Mise said, sounding very grown up.

Desti didn't feel reassured, "So you've ridden her before," she stated more then asked.

Mise took her literally though, "Well...I've seen my father do it."

'What!!!??' Desti almost screamed but it was too late, Mise had tapped Em's neck and the Cokhawk stretched out her wings. Desti became familiar with a new terror and she pulled the strap around her waist tight as it would go and then she wrapped her arms around Mise for dear life and squeezed her eyes tight shut.

Emerald beat her wings against the barn floor, sending hay everywhere, and causing the girls' copper and black hair to become tangled together. Desti opened her eyes just in time to see Em emerge through the opening in the roof, perch for a moment on the ridgepole and gave out a lonesome cry and then take off! Desti was amazed at the grace and ease of which a bird of that size could fly, and she watched as Rage's manor turned into a child's play house! And then she looked beyond it to the city walls - and further still to the green rolling hills.

Mise tapped Em's neck again and she turned westward towards the hills of Dumah - but the sky seemed to go on forever! Desti noticed that the blue metallic feathers on Em's neck that met the wings turned into scale like plates and that was where Mise was tapping to steer. The metallic feathers shone like jewels when the sun caught them, and Desti had to look away as it was so brilliant! She looked down as they passed over the city walls and to her surprise she could see their shadow beneath them, just a tiny black dot. Then she looked up and with a start realized how close they were to the clouds! She relaxed her hold on Mise, and stretched out her hand into the wind and let it move her entire arm as if she herself were flying! The wind whipped her breath away but she didn't mind, beneath them the hills of Dumah rolled away to the horizon, dotted all about them were large stones and she wondered what they were. The hills looked like sleeping giants as they soared over them, and then she saw it, nestled within the hills like a huge gray snail; it was the coliseum.

Chapter 24

The Stone

Ree stood blinking in a golden hall with carved wooden pillars, many lords and their ladies were silently standing by - just watching, and on his throne sat the King. He had a noble face, and she knew at once that he could do no injustice. One after the other people came forward presenting their case against her, some she knew, and others were complete strangers, there was a child that she had grown up with, people that she had once known, her land lord, Sil, her mother and then… Gra.

Each one had a firm case against her - she could not deny a single word! Finally the king had heard every witness, and he said, 'I have heard the evidence against you and I find them all to be true, your sentence… is death.'

Ree awoke with a shuddering breath. The shackles on her wrists clinked and she realized that she was no longer in the Tarven prison - then she remembered, she had been transferred to the coliseum. Why, she did not know, for as she had dreamed, her sentence was death - it had already been decided - so why be brought here? She looked around the dark cold and dirty cell - it would all be over soon.

Boots scraped outside her cell door, the lock clicked and the door swung open. A guard dragged her to her feet by her arm and then escorted her out into a torch lit hallway. She looked at his face but it told nothing; this is it, she thought, I'm going to die. The guard turned sharply and climbed a flight of steps. She found herself out in the open on a balcony. She stumbled but the guard held her up, she felt like she was in a trance. The sunlight made her blink, and the creature of darkness - had nowhere to run.

Somewhere within the stone walls below, Nity waited for his fate to be decided. A thought came to Desti as she looked below at the coliseum; only a week ago the people of Garason had lined the streets to declare him King and now they came to condemn him. Desti tried to shake the thought, after all; the people did not want his death - why would they? Desti momentarily lost her stomach as Em plummeted down to the 'giant snail', the wind rushing in her face brought tears to her eyes and pulled at her hair.

A few terrifying moments later and both Desti and Mise were disentangling themselves from the saddle, and then they slid off Em's back. Mise called over a stable boy and gave him a few coins to watch Em. No sooner had they turned towards the sheer walls of the coliseum then they heard, "Desti!?" They turned.

"Treas!-" and so it was, he was coming towards them, Desti looked beyond him but saw no one.

"Where is my father?" she asked.

"I don't know - I came alone." He was a little out of breath, and Desti knew that things were serious when he only glanced at the Cokhawk. "Come on, Nity's trial will be starting soon," Treas said as he led them through the small crowd of people who were just mulling about. He led them under a dark archway and into the coliseum.

Treas and the girls came out on the inside of the coliseum. Desti looked about with wide eyes; she had never seen a structure so big before! All along the inside were stone benches that seemed to stretch up to the sky. They were filled with people and the din was overwhelming. At one end was a balcony high up on the sheer wall, at the base of this wall was a large archway, the means by which to enter the dirt ring in the middle; a tournament was being set up.

Desti hardly had time to really look before Treas was leading them up a long flight of stairs through the benches, until he found an empty one; they all sat down and caught their breath. Nothing seemed to be happening at that moment so Desti took the opportunity to ask Treas about the night before.

"Treas, what happened when you and my father went to the prison last night?"

"They wouldn't let us see Nity," he began out of breath. "So we waited to see what would happen and then I saw Est! He was there too, but when I called to him..." he frowned.

"What? What happened?" Desti prompted.

"He just looked at me like - like I was a stranger! He then said that he didn't know me!" Treas said looking at her like the whole thing horrified him. "Then he ran away!"

"Maybe he couldn't see who you were," Desti suggested.

He shook his head, "There were torches everywhere - no Desti, he was afraid of being arrested himself…."

Desti found it hard to believe that Est could ever betray Nity like that!

"And where is my father now?" she asked.

He shrugged his shoulders, "I left last night after you fell asleep to see if I could find Fin or any of the others-" he stopped; something was happening.

The crowd was hushed as criers came to stand among them, out on the balcony a figure appeared, Desti squinted as she tried to see him better; he wore a billowing red cape.

"That's Ister!" Mise said as they all looked on.

Two figures, escorted by guards came out; one on each side of Ister: the one on his left was robed in shiny black. Above him, on the balcony, hung a red banner symbolizing Tarva. The one on his right was Nity. Above him was a white banner for Garatin. Desti could see him clearly; he wore the same white tunic with billowed sleeves as when she last saw him. Trumpeters stepped out onto a higher balcony and lifted up long golden trumpets with red banners hanging from them, they blew in harmony and everyone fell silent. Ister seemed to be saying something but, from where Desti and the others sat, they could not hear; she was just about to say something to Treas when the criers began to call out.

"People of Garatin, I, Tarven Ambassador Sinister, regret to disturb your festivities, but it is custom that I release to you a prisoner of your own choice this week of festivity."

Treas breathed a sigh of relief, "He wants to release Nity!" he said with a smile.

The criers continued, "Under the red banner is a woman who is suspected of wielding black magic, is a known rebel and she has also been found guilty of murder- but under the white banner is a man that you all know; he is Eternity! Despite his arrest, the charges against him are all false, this man has committed no crime; he is innocent! Shall I then release him?!"

Desti's heart took flight, all would be fine! But the next moment her heart went down into her toes… For the crowd was not cheering, in fact a pin could have been heard if one had been dropped! Desti sat in shock, and then beside her Treas jumped to his feet.

"Release him!" he cried out as loud as he could! Desti could not find her voice, she heard a few other voices crying the same thing, but she doubted if Ister could even hear them!

Then the criers began again, "Would you rather Ree be released - a murderess?"

The cries of 'no' were lost in the cheering as the crowd at last found a voice, Desti could hardly believe it! She and Mise joined Treas in screaming 'No' until their voices went hoarse, but it was no use. The trumpets were blown and again the crowd fell silent.

Ister seemed to be trying to convince the crowd that they were wrong, "And what shall I do with Nity - an innocent man?"

The response was deafening but very clear, "THE STONE! THE STONE!" the crowd cried as one.

Desti fell back against the bench.

"What use have we for rebel leaders who can't start a rebellion?" a man behind Desti called out. She looked back at him like he was a wild animal but he did not even care! She felt totally defeated and helpless, Nity would die…

High up on the balcony, Ree stood in stunned silence… Ister stood tall as he looked out over the people who were crying for the 'stone', he muttered something underneath his breath.

"Guards, you are my witness; I had nothing to do with this innocent man's death," he said out loud.

Ree slowly looked past Ister at the man of whom she had feared so long. He stood erect and yet somehow broken, but he did not look like a man who had just been sentenced to death - a death he did not deserve - one that she deserved.

"Take this man back to Garason and prepare him for execution, I want it over with before nightfall."

Ister turned and for a moment he looked into Nity's face; then turned to go. Then, as an afterthought, said without turning back, "And give this woman her release papers."

Ree couldn't breathe, and the noise of the crowd sounded like it was coming through a tunnel, she was being led back down the steps and through a few dark echoing halls. She looked up and could see a white, blinding light; it was from outside! They stopped a few paces from an archway, and the guard produced a key. He unlocked her shackles and they fell from her wrists to the ground with an unearthly clatter that echoed through the silence. The guard shoved some papers into her gloved hand; it was her freedom... She was released: Nity took her place.

It did not make any sense! She was guilty, Nity wasn't! Why should he die the death that she deserved? She walked to the archway that led out into the open and stood in the light of the sun, but its warmth did not penetrate - nothing ever would. Never before had her cloak felt so heavy- No... she was not free.

The crowd became excited as the tournament began and it took some time for Treas, Desti and Mise to exit the coliseum. Once out, all three of them climbed onto Em and she took off. Between the three of them not a word had been spoken; what was there to say? Treas felt numb as the wind blew in his face, the trial kept on playing over and over in his mind, how could this be happening? Em flew lower to the ground and with less ease - but Treas did not know this; indeed he hardly noticed that they were even flying!

They were fast approaching the city; he looked behind them at the coliseum and saw that there were dark storm clouds to the west. After a terrifying decent into the barn, Mise had a stable boy tend to Em. Then

Desti insisted that Mise go back inside; with reluctance she obeyed. Treas could see that the girl was so frantic that she didn't fully understand what was happening. Then again, did he? He and Desti took to the streets at a run. They had to find Est or Fin or anyone for that matter; they had to do something! They searched frantically for an hour, but they couldn't find anyone. At last they had to stop and catch their breath. Desti practically fell against a wall in exhaustion, she was close to tears!

Treas would have been ashamed to admit just how close to tears he was. Instead he ran a shaking hand through his hair, and tried to gather his thoughts – they had been to just about every place he could think of that the others would be, but they hadn't found anyone. They couldn't keep running around like this; it was pointless!

"Come on," he said at last, and turned to start running again.

"Where?" Desti called after him.

"To the Tarven barracks! That's where they will have Nity!" he called over his shoulder.

Desti picked up her skirts and followed him. It was not long before they arrived. There was a large crowd gathered in the street around the closed gate - but they were as silent as the grave. Treas pushed until he came within sight of the gate; Desti managed to stay on his heels. Now there was nothing to do but wait.

Treas looked around them breathlessly and wondered how many of this silent crowd had, like him come in the hopes of rescuing Nity - and how many of them had come only for entertainment... Treas jumped slightly as the gate was raised from the inside, and the crowd stirred. Tarven soldiers came out in full armor and drawn swords; they were expecting trouble. The soldiers began to clear a path through the agitated crowd.

The snap of a whip was heard, and a terrible grinding noise began from inside the barracks. A figure emerged from the courtyard, he was doubled over and there were ropes slung over his shoulders. The ropes were pulled tight by a large stone double his own size that he dragged behind him; the crowd began to shout and push but the soldiers held them back. The stone grated against the cobblestones and sent pebbles shooting out from under it. The man's tunic was torn and bloody, and there was an entire sleeve missing. His back was torn and bloody beyond repair, and his face was cut and swelling with unformed bruises, one would hardly recognize this man as Nity.

Treas turned away, physically sick, he gagged once and shut his eyes trying to forget- but he could still hear the whip whistle through the air, ripping through the flesh on his back - again and again. Just how many times he did not know; - and still it continued! Treas opened his eyes; he was no longer in Jarg - but in Garason. And it was not his back that was torn- it was Nity's...

Just then Nity looked up directly into Treasures eyes; he knew! Treas knew the agony that Nity was in, the scars on his own back burned with remembrance. Nity looked away but Treas could not forget the pain on his face.

Desti clutched his arm.

"Treas! There must be something that we can do!"

"It's too late, Desti! It's too late!" he shouted at her, angry that he could do nothing.

"What do you mean?!" she shouted back with fear.

Treas pointed to Nity's back, "I told you before! The whips are coated with poison! It's too late to do anything - he's already dying!"

Desti looked at Nity's back, it was hard to see beyond the blood but there were bright red streaks shooting from his wounds. The nightmare had just begun...

Wilder and Rage rode their horses hard from the so called 'trial' back into Garason, and they all but abandoned the horses in an alley, and joined the crowds who surrounded Nity and the stone. They were separated as Wilder fought his way deeper through the crowd until he was pressed against a Tarven soldier. He watched in shock as the man he had planned to assassinate inched by at a snail's pace. He felt an uncontrollable frenzy take him and he pushed past the soldier and grabbed the captain by his tunic.

"On what charges has this man been arrested?!" he demanded

feverishly.

"High treason against his Majesty Ordained and violation of Garatin laws, is that not good enough for you? Garatin," he sneered and pushed Wilder away.

Wilder felt his face go hot and he would have done more than just push the Tarven but a commotion broke out and averted the fight. Nity had slipped and lay face down as he groaned, one of the soldiers was kicking him and shouting at him to get up. As Wilder looked he was shoved from behind by the captain.

"You! Pick up the ropes and drag it for him! I want this over with before the storm comes." As if to speed up the process, a roll of thunder was heard.

The ropes were ripped from Nity's shoulders and he was then flung atop the stone. Wilder was pushed into position; he looped the ropes around his chest and leaned into them. From the crowd, Rage watched as his friend started to drag the stone along. In the back of his mind he wondered what the solders would have done if they had known that the man who now dragged the stone was actually a citizen of Tarva. Soon sweat formed on Wilder's brow and his boots slipped once or twice on the cobblestones, he could feel the ropes digging into his shoulders. He didn't stop to think about what he was doing; dragging a man's tomb stone to his funeral! Nor did he worry about his own fate. He looked up and from where he was he could already see the city's western gate and the storm clouds on the horizon.

Ree shook uncontrollably as she stood in a narrow, deserted alleyway; if any had seen her they would have thought her crazed! She could hear the crowds approaching and she shook all the more. She drew in a shuddering breath as the sound of stone dragging against stone came to her ears. She should be the one dragging that stone! She should be the one slowly dying! She was the guilty one - and at last she admitted it! She killed Gra! She had… she wore the black cloak of guilt! It should have been her back torn to shreds! She looked up in time to see the stone being dragged by - but it was not Nity but a stranger who pulled it, then she saw a broken heap of bloody flesh on top of the stone - it was Nity.

She stumbled out into the street not really aware that she had, the crowd seemed to be moving fast - too fast and she tried hard to keep up. They passed by a stand of fruit and some of the crowd started to throw the fruit - but whether at Nity or the guards, it was not plain. Ree felt weak in the legs and she stumbled into a young woman with copper hair, but neither seemed to notice. Ree stumbled on in a daze, when she came to her senses - they were in the hills of Dumah…

Mise sat on the edge of her bed twisting her handkerchief over and over. If things had been right, Loy would have been very angry with her for disappearing like she had, but as it was, she only held her tight at the news of Nity's trial. Now both of them were in Promise's chamber, Loy was pacing back and forth, as she tried to keep her head. Mise bit her lip; oh, what was happening!? A curl hung over her face as she looked up; oh where was her father? What was happening to Nity? She tried to steady her breathing, just then she looked up at her flower and paused…

She would never forget how Nity had helped water her flower after waking her. She stood up and walked over to where it sat on a bedside table. All else was forgotten, for now, before her eyes the little ivory star flower was shriveling up! She picked up the tiny pot and held to up to her face, it shriveled and curled over before her eyes until it was nothing but a bit of brown dried-up leaf! A tiny breath escaped her lips, and she knew in her heart; Nity was dead.

Chapter 25

Set Free

Ree stood like a figure in stone as the long grass blew against her cloak. The stranger had dragged the stone out into the hills of Dumah. The ropes had been cut from the stone (the stranger just stood and watched) and the soldiers had started to dig the pit where they would fling Nity's body as soon as he died. The swift approaching storm clouds soon sent the crowds away, some would sadly shake their heads and turn away while others would mutter something about how he 'had it coming'. Ree was one of a few who stayed behind, but unlike the others she did not weep, all she could do was stand there in horrified shock. Indeed she hardly noticed the other people; she took a step toward the stone. The guards were too busy digging to take notice of her. Nity was stretched out on his torn back on top of the stone, one of his arms hung over the side towards Ree. He turned his head ever so slightly, and through swollen eyes looked at her. Her lip quivered as she beheld him, then he arched his back and tried to cry out, but the poison prevented him from taking a deep enough breath - it would all be over soon. In that moment her heart of stone shattered.

On the horizon the dark storm clouds stretched out like long black fingers - as if over-anxious to grasp all of Garason in its fist. Lightning flashed and was followed by an answer of thunder, the hills became misty with the coming rain, and the guards ran for the cover of a closed wagon.

But Ree no longer saw all this. Instead, she saw in her mind's eye all the horrors that had haunted her nights for the past three years; they all flashed before her eyes - merging into one another without definition. She was running, but it was in vain; the darkness was even closer. 'You're not who I thought you were...' the voice of Gra seemed to come from nowhere. She must hide! At last she found refuge in the darkness, it would keep her safe, and it would hide her as she prepared to cut Gra as deep as he had cut her.

She looked up as something disturbed her blackness; it was a tiny pinpoint of light in the darkness above her. The point of light seemed to gently beckon her to come closer, but if she did, then what she had done would be made known to everyone! No, she must stay away… A delicate black moth beat its wings against a deadly flame, afraid to go closer and yet too afraid to live without this light.

'You've turned cold, Ree-'no! It hurt, she fell back desperate to get away, she went deeper in to the darkness leaving the flame behind. But she began to stumble, and breathing became a struggle. Would she suffocate? Lightening flashed, and the creature of darkness fled from the coming storm, but there was nowhere to hide! She was in a black desert; lost. Then she saw - what might have been. Thunder rolled and the storm broke forth, but she could not flee! She was caught in a web - a black silk web, and struggle as she might it was no use, she was then brought before the King, and the evidence against her was overwhelming! She was guilty.

Lightning flashed again, lighting up her face in an eerie glow. She was thrust back into reality, and she was breathlessly standing before the stone, all alone. She looked up - and Nity's last breath escaped him - to come no more. Ree dropped to her knees and buried her face in her gloved hands, tears began to flow and for the first time in her life, Ree shed unselfish tears for another. Her sobs were so intense that they stole what little breath she had left. Her right hand fell away as she tried to bring in new air. The unjustness of it all made her weep all the harder; how could this happen? That the innocent die, and a murderer live?

How could Eloi let this happen? Nity had spoken in his name, and this was his reward!? Was Eloi not watching? Did he not know - was this beyond his power? Nity had been perfect and pure, and his love had known no bounds. Ree's head was bent and she did not see the drop of blood, it ran down Nity's lifeless arm that was hanging over the side of the stone, the drop hung for a moment on the tip of his finger, then it dropped onto Ree's black cloak - over her heart.

Out of the corner of her eye she glimpsed the blood soaking into her cloak, and she paused; a tiny hole appeared over her heart, and slowly the black silk began to peel away! She stood to her feet with tears still wet on her face as she watched her cloak peel and curl away from her in earnest and it began to fall away in large flakes! She held up her hand as the black leather dried up and blew away in the wind as fine dust!

She looked at her hand in astonishment; the stain… was gone. Her cloak lay about her in flakes and her pale skin was as plain as life. Her old, stiff clothes clung to her as the wind whipped past. Her mouth gaped open as she searched her arms but there was no mistaking it; the stain was forever gone! Her eyes lifted to Nity's dead body. Why?? Why had he done the impossible one last time - and for her of all people!? Why should he?

The rain came suddenly and drenched her. But Ree did not notice it as she looked on the still face of Nity. Somehow she knew that Eloi no longer looked upon her with judgment, no longer was she stained by Gra's death, Nity had taken her place… Why? Why had Nity done it?! Why should she gain from his death? For this she had no answer, but beyond all shadow of a doubt - this she knew; that by his death, Nity had set her free!

*   *   *

Far away in the fort of the Vase, the Garatin leaders carried on as if they had not just killed an innocent man. They carried on with the festival, and burned parchment like they had every year. High on its dais, in silence, sat the Vase as it had for many ages. Without warning, the stillness was broken as the Vase shattered, sending the shards flying throughout the room and deflecting off of the marble pillars! The Garatin leaders threw up their hands to protect themselves, as the white cloth that had spilled out of the Vase for a century fell to the ground. It seemed to fall forever, and those who peeked through their hands saw it happen; it hit the ground sending ripples all through it - but it had turned black… Nothing was left of the Vase but shards of clay and a black silk cloth.

Eloi could not be kept behind clay walls…

206

Chapter 26

Day of Darkness

It had been horrid for Desti to watch (on top of everything else) her father drag the stone for Nity. After he had dragged it out into the hills, he had joined her and Treas along with Rage. They had all fled back into the city when the storm broke forth. Treas had gone to where he and Est and the others had been staying in the hopes that they would show up, while the other three had returned to Rage's manor. The storm had raged all the rest of the day and continued to send torrents of rain all through the night and well into the next day.

Even at dusk a light rain spattered on Desti's face as she sat by her opened window. That's all she had done that day, she felt as though something important had died within her - leavening an empty gash. Without Nity, nothing seemed to matter anymore. Without Nity she was just wandering about without a plan or purpose - and without a destination. She watched as the night came in bringing with it a thick fog that swirled around in the night as hopeless as she felt. A soft knock came at her door and Wilder slipped in, he walked up behind her and rubbed her shoulders. Feeling numb inside, she leaned against him.

"I think it's time…. that we went home," he said at last.

She looked over her shoulder at him - but she really wasn't surprised. All that day she had been overwhelmed with homesickness. Yes, it was time to go home - and perhaps forget all that had happened here! She regretted the thought at once; how could she even think of forgetting Nity?

"We'll leave in a few days - after all this madness is over," Wilder added.

Yes that would give her enough time to wish farewell to Treas - but the thought only made her feel worse. With one last pat to her shoulder Wilder left the room.

After leaving Desti's chambers, Wilder began to wander the darkened hallways aimlessly and looked at the many tapestries without actually seeing them, he heaved a great sigh, yes it was time to go home, the past six (or was it just five?) months had been a nightmare best forgotten.

Nity was dead…

Wilder soon found that he had wandered through the whole upper half of the manor, and he now stood at the top of the sweeping staircase that led to the front doors. As Wilder looked down at the doors a great pounding began upon them, he watched as a servant skittered across the floor to answer the demanding knock. Time seemed to slow down as Wilder watched; he felt an unease take him - and then something snapped to attention within him!

"Don't answer that door!" he shouted the order down the stairs.

The poor servant girl jumped to a stop and stared wide eyed up at him.

"Don't answer that door," he repeated as the pounding continued with a vengeance. "Go and bring Rage," he told her at last as his face hardened. The girl rushed to do his bidding. For a long moment Wilder stood with a dark face listening to the pounding. Like a phantom Rage appeared at his side.

"They've come for you," Wilder said in a low voice, they both knew who he meant.

"I knew it was foolish to stay!" Rage whispered. "They've come to arrest me for insubordination," he said out loud, and for a moment nothing more was said. "Wilder, do something for me - for old time sake?" Rage asked, sounding surprisingly desperate.

"Ask it," Wilder said without hesitation.

"Get Loy and Mise out!" he whispered fiercely, "Get them safe away from this place!"

"Where would you have me take them?"

"Anywhere! The wife and daughter of a Tarven traitor are not safe in this city; you and I both know that they will accuse me of supporting the rebel movement."

Wilder shook his head, "I'll get them out but you'll come with us!" he said with determination.

Rage smiled sadly, "We'd never make outside the city gates, without me there is a chance. Get them out."

"I swear to you; they will be safe," Wilder vowed. Rage turned and began down the stairs but Wilder laid his hand on Rage's shoulder

"Farewell old friend… May Eloi never leave you." For a moment they looked at each other.

"Go," Rage whispered.

The door to Desti room burst open, and she jumped to her feet, Wilder came in without ceremony.

"What is it?" she asked at once.

"There are soldiers at the door arresting Rage," he said evenly. She only stared at him. "We must get Loy and Mise out tonight! We only have a few minutes before they search the manor for them."

Desti sprang into action without another word. Wilder left and she slipped on a riding dress with a wide skirt and stuffed another into her saddle bag. She also swung a hooded cloak over her shoulders; she looked about the room for a moment then hurried down to Promise's chambers.

When she got there she was pleased to see that Loy was already there helping Mise shove a few dresses into the small trunk that they would share. Mise had put her dead flower into a tiny trunk (Desti did not have the heart to tell her to leave the dead plant behind.) in two more minutes all four of them were standing in the hall looking at each other with a nervous excitement.

Wilder nodded when he saw that both Loy and Mise wore very simple riding dresses and cloaks, he heaved their trunk onto his shoulder and said after a moment, "We'll go down the servants' staircase and through the kitchen to get out into the court yard."

"What about the servants?" Loy asked with a touch of concern.

"The soldiers won't harm them. Come."

"Wait!" Loy exclaimed. "There is a secret passage from Courage's chambers that leads down to the servants quarters- it's faster."

Wilder nodded. "Lead the way," he said.

Loy then led them to Rage's chambers. She went straight to an oversized trunk, lifted the lid, and emptied the contents. Wilder noticed that her hands were shaking. When the trunk was empty, Loy reached down and lifted up a leather tie. The bottom of the trunk came up with it to reveal a narrow steep stair way leading down. Loy looked down uncertainly; she had never been in there and had only known of it because Rage had once told her. Mise peered down with wide eyes. Wilder caught Desti's eye and nodded to her, she nodded back and stepped down into the large trunk. Loy and Mise followed. Wilder grabbed a lit candle from its stand and went down last, closing the trunk as he went. Going down the steps he very nearly hit his head, the stairs were so steep. Clamped to the wall there was a torch. He took it from its rusty holdings and lit it with the candle. From its light he could see the three wide eyed faces of Loy, Mise and his daughter. He slipped past them and led the way through the winding passage. Dust and cobwebs were thick, but the way was always clear. After descending a circular stair, they came to a wooden door. Wilder paused for a moment and looked behind him to make sure that everyone was ready. He then pushed on the door; it was stiff but opened none the less. They found themselves in a cold room full of barrels; exiting through another door they came out into a hallway. Wilder led the way through the hall, mostly guessing the way. Desti brought up the rear as they rushed along. At last they reached the pantry, Wilder hastily grabbed provisions that they must have - but they all paused when they heard a loud crash from inside. Loy jumped but she managed to hold back a cry.

"They've began the search," Wilder whispered. With that he poked his head out into the dark courtyard; the fog was thick and deceiving, perfect for disappearing into, but dangerous none the less. As far as he could see there was no one on their side of the court yard, the stables were somewhere ahead - invisible in the fog, but Wilder knew that they were straight ahead.

Looking behind him he said quietly, "Go to the stables - and make no sound."

Desti took hold of Mise's trembling hand and led the way into the fog boldly. This time Wilder brought up the rear. As they crossed the courtyard they could hear the soldiers out front and could even see the glow of their torches from around the corner. Wilder stopped in mid stride when he noticed that Loy had paused and was looking towards the glow of the firelight. He put his hand on her shoulder and whispered.

"Loy, if we don't leave now - we may never get away, Rage wanted you and Mise kept safe."

She swallowed hard and her eyes misted, but she nodded and followed Wilder to the stables. Soon four horses were saddled and ready. Wilder looked at everyone; Desti's face was hard and showed no emotion while Loy tried to hide her flowing tears. Little Mise stood by her horse's head, nervously stroked its nose. He had watched her carefully tuck her flower-trunk away into her saddle bag.

"Is everyone ready? He asked, and they all nodded. He then led the way out of the stables then through the dark courtyard and to a side gate. They slipped out one by one, and then mounted up. Desti looked up at the sky, the moon was hidden and the stars did not shine through the fog, a night without the moon followed the day without sun…

Rage stood still with a stone face as the guards bound his hands behind his back; he was then led towards a steel wagon with bars. None of the soldiers dared to look him in the face, for many had served under him. One of these was the captain, his Namesake was Provider. Rage had known him for a long time. Vide watched Rage as he was led away; Vide had secretly loathed Rage and had resented taking orders from him, and now seemed to relish arresting him.

"I'll see that you and your family are punished for supporting rebels," he said coldly as Rage was led past him. A soldier marched up to him from the manor and made his report.

"We have searched the entire manor - and the wife and child are nowhere to be found."

Rage bent his head as he went into the wagon, he smiled.

"There must be something that we can do!" Loy said in a pleading tone. "If they've accused him of supporting Rebel activity - he'll be executed on the morrow!"

Wilder knew what she said to be true, and it made his heart quake at the thought. "Loyal, there is nothing we can do," he said slowly, "I must get you and Mise out of the city - tonight; there is no safe place for us here."

They had ridden out of the Tarven district but were still a long way off from the city gates - that was another problem all together; getting past the closed gates - but Wilder would find a way. They were now sheltered from the heavy fog in a damp alley.

"Can't you break him out while we go on out of the city?" she suggested hopefully.

He shook his head. "There is the curfew, if you three were caught breaking it, then you all would be put in prison for the night. It would not take them long to find out who you are, then there is Mise..." he paused, and Loy knew what he meant without saying it, she hung her head as hope faded. "I must go with you," he ended sadly.

"Mother?" Mise called softly from further back in the alley. Loy led her horse back to her daughter, while Desti came up beside her father.

Just then the sound of horses was heard on the street! Wilder thrust his hand back to signal for silence. They held their breath as a group of soldiers passed by on the street. None of them looked in the alley and Wilder breathed a sigh of relief. After a moment, Desti spoke softly.

"Daddy? I could not help but overhear, IS it so necessary that we get out tonight? Couldn't we hide somewhere - and then you could rescue Rage!" Wilder looked at her gravely.

"We must get out tonight."

"Why?" she asked.

"Desti-" he said in a low voice, "They are searching for us as we speak! Who would hide us? No Tarven would dare anger Ister, and every Garatin would turn their nose up. If Loy and Mise were caught - Desti if anyone found out about what happened between Mise and Nity - they would believe her to be a witch and burn her at the stake. They must be gotten out tonight."

"Then Rage will die," Desti said realizing it at last.

Wilder heaved a heavy sigh that could only have come from his very soul; he bowed his head and said with a catch in his voice, "Yes…he will."

They were silent for a moment.

"Daddy-" Desti said slowly, "What if - I were to break Rage out?"

Wilder looked at her; what was she up too? "What do you mean?" he asked carefully.

She looked at him with growing determination," What if Treas and I were to do it?"

"Treas?" he asked doubtfully.

"I know he'd do it! You get Loy and Mise out, and Treas and I will break Rage free, and we'll meet you outside of the city later tonight."

Wilder shook his head, "Desti, it's no simple thing to break a man out of a Tarven barracks. I can't let you take that risk."

"Daddy, if we don't try - Rage will die."

Treas sat still, gazing out into the night. After the execution he had gone back to the inn. No one had been there, but just as he was about to leave some of the others straggled in. Now on that dark and foggy night everyone was there - except for Cern.

Treas heaved a sigh as he thought over the dark news that had come that morning; Cern had been found dead… hanging from a tree - he had hung himself. Obviously he had never thought that it would go so far, maybe he had hoped to spur Nity into action by bringing soldiers to him- but now Nity was dead and Cern along with him.

Treas took a deep breath; it had been a trying day. Est, Fin and the others had been so paranoid that none had set foot outside the inn! And paranoid for good reason; the soldiers could very well come and arrest them too! They were even beginning to wonder if the inn-keeper could be trusted. They had been taking shifts watching the street, ready to flee if even one soldier should happen by. So far, there had been two false alarms and Treas did not know how much more he could take!

Even now as he watched the street, he could just glimpse Vive whose turn it was to watch; he was hidden in an alley and was ready to whistle the warning at any given time. Although late in the night - no one slept, in fact Treas was the only one upstairs; everyone else was down below by the back door, ready to run- or fight. Treas thought about Est; he was miserable! Est blamed himself for what had happened, said that if he had only stayed by Nity's side when the soldiers came instead of running away with the others, then Nity would somehow still be alive.

Treas did not see how that would have made a difference - no matter how bravely Est might have fought, he would have only been killed for his bravery and Nity would have died just the same. But Est could not be reasoned with, Treas was even afraid that Est might do something rash - like Cern had.

Tomorrow the festival would be over (how could anyone still be celebrating?) and they would be able to leave the city in the crowds unnoticed - but Treas had no idea of what he would do, Quy Lake was not his home. Then there was Desti; recently he had been doing a lot of thinking about her. It all came down to this; he did not deserve her. Just then a shrill whistle was sounded from below - it was the warning! Someone was approaching.

Treas tensed, he slid his hand down to his boot where he kept his dagger (a small comfort against Tarven soldiers.) He hardly moved and every muscle in his body was tighter then a violin string. A lone figure walked through the fog down the street towards the back door. Silence prevailed… A soft knock came at his door, but in the silence it sounded like a battering ram. He opened it with caution; Fin stood on the other side.

"What is it?" Treas asked preparing himself for the worst.

"There is someone asking for you," Fin replied (he seemed to have aged ten years in the past two days.)

Treas paused, "Is he alone?"

A strange look came into Fin's eyes, "Yes- she's alone."

Treas started; he had not been ready for this! He went quickly past Fin and took the stairs two at a time. At the bottom he looked up, the front of the ale house was filled with empty chairs and tables; the entire room was dark with only one lit torch by the back door. Est and the others all either sat or stood about the back door. They looked very somber and tense indeed; all their attention was fixed on the back door. Someone stood deep in the shadows; it was a slender figure that was hooded and cloaked, the hood was deep and completely hid the face.

Fin came up behind Treas from the stairs, Treas then noticed that a copper lock of hair had escaped the hood of the stranger; he stepped up close, and peered under the hood.

"Desti?" he whispered. A pair of green eyes looked up at him. "Desti what are you doing here!?" he whispered fiercely.

She pulled back her hood ever so slightly, "Treas, it's important!" she whispered.

Treas looked up and felt everyone's eyes on them, the tension had eased when they saw that he seemed to know this stranger, but they all continued to watch. He pulled her aside to a corner, hoping that they would get the message that this was a private meeting. His heart beat a little faster as he whispered.

"What is it- what's happened?"

"It's Rage! He's been arrested!"

Treas straightened and felt himself grow defensive; Rage belonged to Tarva, and Tarva had killed Nity. Desti followed his thoughts.

"Treas-" she began fervently, "I know I have no right to come here - of all places, now - of all times and ask you to help a Tarven - of all people. But Nity did not feel prejudice when he looked on the pale face of Promise - nor did he hesitate when Rage asked for help… so why should you? Please Treas! In memory of Nity and what he stood for – please," Her voice shuddered and tears glistened in her eyes.

Treas could not turn a deaf ear to what he knew in his heart to be true.

"What is it you need me to do?" he asked in a business like tone, relief flooded into Desti's face.

"He has been arrested for disobeying orders concerning Nity's arrest, and will be executed at dawn for insubordination and supporting rebel activity - Treas; he must be broken out of prison tonight!" Desti went on to explain about Loy and Mise; she saw doubt on his face and ended with a last plea. "Treas, do this - for my sake."

Treas nodded with determination then walked over to Est. He looked up as Treas approached and tried to show interest. Est was just a shell of the man he had been and it broke Treasures heart to see him thus, but even more so when he realized that he would never see him again...

"Est, I- I must do something, I won't tell you what- it's just safer that way, and by the time it's all done - you and the others will have left for Quy... so- this is it," he shrugged his shoulders.

Est nodded, "Then it is farewell Treasure, take care of yourself." They took each other by the forearm and looked at each other for a moment. Then Treas turned to go, but stopped.

"Quest-" he hesitated for a moment, "there wasn't anything that you could have done." Est knew what he meant and looked away as a haze came over his eyes. "I vowed that I would never leave him," he said in a faraway voice. "But when his need was greatest; I fled."

"You aren't to blame for what happened..." Treas said gently.

Est swallowed and nodded sadly, and then he frowned and asked, "Then who is?"

∗   ∗   ∗

After a bit of thinking Treas had come up with a plan of how to get into the barracks. He had worked it out with an old acquaintance (Consider was his Namesake.) Sid was to drive by the barracks with his hay wagon and he would undoubtedly be taken in for breaking curfew. His cart would be left in the barracks courtyard. That's how Desti and he were to get in; they would be hiding in the hay - getting out of the barracks was another matter altogether. The two of them sat across from each other in an alley waiting for Sid to come by in his cart.

"Treas? Where was Nity buried," Desti asked the sudden question softly.

Treas felt reluctant to tell her, but did it any ways.

"He wasn't buried, his body was dropped into a pit, out in the hills of Dumah and the stone was put over top of him. That's why these hills have all those strange stones, they are gravestones. Those hills are a mass graveyard for criminals, hence the name Dumah - meaning 'silent and still'". Treas hated even thinking about it; that was the last resting place of Eternity.

The mist swirled about them, as they sat there in silence, then Desti spoke again. "I just can't believe he's gone… I thought- I suppose I thought that he was invincible," she said sadly.

"Me too…" Treas whispered.

"When I was around him I felt like I was needed - like my life was going somewhere, like I had-"

"A destination?" Treas added, and she nodded.

"But now… everything is just going wrong, I'll be returning to the Byla - and I'll forget everything that's happened - I don't want to live on as if nothing happened! I don't want to forget." She bit her lip. "I don't want to forget you."

"Desti, no matter what happens - I could never forget you," Treas said, and continued with what he had been longing to say, "I love you."

A gentle smile touched her face as if to say "I know", but the smile faded quickly.

"Come with us," she whispered, "Come with us Treas! I can't bear to leave you behind again."

Treas felt his heart break for reasons that he could not explain; how could he tell her that it would never work?

"There is nothing that I would rather do," he said softly.

Chapter 27

Night of Shadows

Desti did not feel sure of anything, her heart seemed as though it would burst from beating too fast; for in that moment she was sure that Treas was going to kiss her! The rumbling of a wagon coming down the street jolted them back to reality, Treas jumped to his feet and took a deep breath as though to reacquaint himself with air. He clenched his fists as he tried to pull himself back to the present, he did not dare look at Desti. Sid pulled up in his hay wagon and Treas signaled for Desti to stay put as he stepped out onto the street.

"Thank you for coming," Treas whispered up at Sid, "Now, you understand what you've got to do?"

"Sure I do!" Sid slurred and Treas got a blast of his breath and he realized; Sid was drunk. When he had gone to see him a half hour ago he had been sober - so much for that. Treas nodded, he would just have to hope for the best. He then waved Desti over and helped her up into the back of the wagon. He then jumped up after her and they covered themselves with the hay as best they could. Even before they had finished Sid cracked his whip at his horse and the wagon lurched forward. The plan was simple enough - but would it work? What if Sid in his drunkenness announced to the soldiers in a frolicsome air that there were two people hiding in his wagon? If that happened then; goodbye escape plan! The wagon lumbered over the cobble stones and Treas knew that they must be close to the barracks - the same one where Nity had been flogged to death two days before.

"HALT! You halt!" a voice called out.

Treas nearly jumped out of his skin! The cart lurched to a stop and Sid began to swear and curse.

"What right do you have to be out past midnight?" the voice demanded.

Sid only cursed some more, and then from the sound of it he was dragged from the wagon seat while the soldier recited a well-rehearsed line about how he was being arrested for breaking curfew. Another soldier climbed up onto the cart and began driving it, Treas could hear the portcullis being raised; and he reached out in the hay until he found Desti's hand, he squeezed it. There was no going back now.

The wagon was stopped and the soldiers hauled Sid away. The portcullis was lowered again and Treas heard a door close - there followed a long silence that engulfed the court yard. Treas sat up in the hay and looked around, the poor beast that had the misfortune of being Sid's horse neighed softly but there was no other sound. Treas took in his surroundings, the court yard was surrounded by buildings but all the doors were tight shut. There were a few torches here and there but for the most part the yard was in shadow. High up on the ramparts sentries patrolled back and forth, Treas waited until the nearest turned his back and started walking the other way.

"Desti," he breathed.

She sat up in the hay and looked around; then with a fair bit of rustling they jumped from the wagon and crouched in its shadow.

"Where will he be?" Desti whispered.

Treas shook his head as he looked from door to door.

"There?" Desti asked pointing to a door.

"No, that's just where they keep the overnight prisoners," he answered.

"How do you know?"

Treas smiled, "I've broken curfew a few times myself!" and before Desti could comment he pointed to a door that lay across the yard. "He'll be in there. That's where they keep prisoners soon to be executed."

They scooted across the yard while their good fortune lasted, they then pressed themselves against the wall and looked about; no one had seen them.

Treas then creaked open the door and froze; just inside sitting at a table was a soldier! But before Desti even saw, a loud snore emanated from his mouth, and Treas breathed again. He managed to force his heart back into his chest as he realized how close it had been. He turned to Desti and told her to stay put; he then tried to slip in through the door when he realized that he held Desti's hand in a death grip. After letting go of her hand, he slipped in and looked at the fast asleep guard. Then he took a dagger from the table and clubbed him on the back of the neck with the hilt. The guard grunted then went limp; Treas sincerely hoped that he had hit him hard enough to keep him out for a few minutes.

"Desti," he called softly, she slipped in silently and looked at the guard gingerly. Treas then grabbed a ring of keys off the table and walked to the inner door. He tried a few keys before he found the right one; he hoped that Desti didn't see how badly he was shaking.

The door swung open revealing a dirt floored hallway with cells on either side. But it was pitch black, and it occurred to Treas that if there were any other prisoners then they would put up a racket if they weren't released as well - that risk would have to be taken. He motioned for Desti to bring a torch from the wall. She came close and the light flooded down the hall; all four cells - were empty!

Desti made a small noise that could have been a question mark, but before he could answer a deep voice sent Treasure's nerves through the roof!

"Destination?" a shadow stepped into the light from the cell on their left.

Desti rushed forward, "Courage!" she breathed.

Rage grabbed hold of the bars and Treas stepped up and began trying the many keys in the lock, Desti held up the torch so that he could see.

"Where are Loy and Mise?" Rage asked at once.

"Safe; my father will have them out of the city by now," Desti answered trying to keep her voice down.

Treas was trying to stop his hands from shaking, when he noticed Rage was looking at him.

"You came back for me?" it was not clear to whom Rage asked this, Treas looked up into his dark eyes, and felt a resentment rising up within him. But looking at Rage he did not find the enemy that he had expected. The key that he held slid into the lock and he turned it with a click. He never took his eyes from Rage as if to say 'stupid idea, huh?' and the door swung open. They nodded to each other and went back out to the other room where the guard still sat unconscious. Desti was about to return the torch into its holder on the wall, and Treas was just laying the ring of keys back on the table with a clink - when footsteps were heard outside!

Treas froze in a panic and his mind went blank as the door was slowly opened from the outside. Rage grabbed him from behind and pulled him back behind the second door. Rage pressed him against the wall and closed the door just in time! Desti, who was right behind the door, likewise pressed herself against the wall. Rage who was next to her silently took the torch from her trembling hand, and they waited…

It sounded as though there were two guards, and they talked loudly for a moment then fell silent in mid-sentence; they had realized that their comrade was unconscious! One of the guards took a sharp breath; and then they both ran to the inner door. The guards burst through the door almost crushing Desti behind it. The next few moments happened almost too fast for Treas to know what happened!

As the second guard rushed in after the first, Rage reached out like lightning and drew the guards own sword from its sheath. At the same time he knocked him over the head with the torch; the guard crumpled in mid stride. The first guard spun round and would have attacked Rage but Treas broke his trance-like state, and brought his foot up from the shadows and kicked the soldier hard in the stomach. The guard doubled over and Rage finished him off. All three of them jumped from the room and Rage shut and bolted the door behind them. It all happened in less than five seconds.

Treas stood there looking at Desti with wide eyes; Rage put the torch back in its holder and then took the unconscious man's sword and held it out to Treas, hilt first.

"Can you use it?" he asked, his breathing was surprisingly even.

Treas shook his head; he wouldn't know where to begin! With a sigh of impatience Rage looked at Desti as if to say, why couldn't you bring someone useful?, and then he pressed it into Treasure's hands and said. "Try your hardest then." The way he said it, made Treas want to try hard.

They then slipped from the building, and stood in its shadow, all was silent for a moment as they gathered their strength.

"Desti-" Treas whispered knowing that he must tell her now- soon it would be too late. "There is something that you must know about me." She looked at him. "When we first met I was a street thief - I stole to stay alive, today I am little better," he said it looking straight ahead.

"Treas?" she whispered uncertainly.

Ignoring her, Treas pointed to the hay cart and Rage nodded, (they had more need of it then Sid.) He then led the way across the court yard. Rage grabbed Desti's arm and said as they ran, "Turn the horse and cart back around to the gate."

She rushed ahead to do this while Treas and Rage went to the wheel of the lowered gate - just then shouting was heard from behind them; the guards from inside must have come to. Treas reached the wheel first and he grabbed hold of it. The iron muscles that the mines had given him tightened and strained as he single handedly turned the wheel. Rage was at his side in a moment and together they had the portcullis raised in no time. Treas looked up and saw a group of guards rushing towards them from across the yard! Desti ran up leading the horse and cart behind her. Rage locked the wheel in place and jumped up to the driver's seat. Treas gave Desti a leg up into the hay; she turned about and looked into his face. Treas would never forget those gray green eyes...

"Go," he whispered.

"Treas?" she grabbed his hand, "Come with us!" she grew frantic.

"I could only bring you grief," he whispered the truth that he had to come know, "I said GO!" he shouted.

Time seemed to stand still as Rage looked back at them and then to the soldiers behind them - fast approaching. Treas ran up to the front of the cart and gave the horse a whack on its rump; the horse screamed and broke into a gallop through the open gate. Treas stood still and watched as Desti rushed by.

"Treas!" she cried out and then the cart disappeared into the night.

Treas turned back to the charging soldiers, his nerves had turned to steel. He walked with confidence toward them - one, against eight. He then turned aside to the wheel and began to hack at the thick rope with his sword, blood pumped in his ears as the solders closed in. Just then the rope snapped and he grabbed hold of it with both hands, it carried him up the wall as the gate fell shut; ensuring Rage and Desti's escape.

Treas climbed over the battlement and looked at the guards below, he then felt that he was not alone - he spun round; a sentry stood there with his spear ready. Treas looked down at his hand - but he had dropped his sword when he grabbed hold of the rope! Without even looking up he spun round and made a break, running along the wall. He could hear the sentry following and shouting as he went, but Treas who had made a living of running from soldiers, out distanced him in a few seconds! He looked up just in time to see another sentry standing in his way; this one didn't seem to know what was happening and only stood there squinting into the darkness. By the time he saw Treas it was too late; Treas ran straight up to him and at the last moment grabbed hold of his spear high up and pole-vaulted bringing his feet up and kicking the soldier in the face. Treas landed behind him in a crouch, he glanced behind him and saw the first sentry coming up fast.

Treas thought for a split second then he wedged the spear across the walkway. He looked up then ran on. Treas turned in time to see his pursuer run into the spear and flip over it. Treas allowed himself a grin before he ran on. Glancing over the outside of the wall he noticed a pile of old hay; without a pause he hopped over the wall and landed in it. Jumping out of the hay he darted down a street, and did what a street thief does best; disappeared into the night of shadows.

Chapter 28

Doubtless

Wilder looked up and watched a hay cart drive through the long grass and then stop in front of him. The night was dark but he knew the driver. Rage jumped down from the cart, he looked tired but unhurt. But Wilder felt no relief; where was Desti? His heart pounded hard, something must have gone wrong. Rage looked beyond Wilder to where Loy and Mise were standing. Under a tree with a huge spreading canopy they had lit a small fire. Rage looked back at Wilder with gratitude.

"Where's Desti?" Wilder asked at once. Rage nodded to the back of the cart in answer. Wilder turned to go there but Rage put his hand out to stop him.

"She asked Treasure to come with us-" he said quietly. Wilder had expected as much. "-but he remained behind so that we could get safe away." Rage glanced at the back of the cart. "There's more to it than I know of."

Wilder nodded and Rage went to his wife and daughter, while Wilder walked to the back of the wagon. Desti lay in the hay like she had just been dropped there, but she sat up as he approached and wrapped her arms around him. He was a little surprised when he noticed that she was crying softly. He pulled back and looked at her; she didn't say anything and only fell back into his arms, leaving him to wonder what it was that Treas had said to her. He looked up at Garason to the west, glittering with many torches, off in the distance.

The early morning dusk spread over the hills of Dumah as the sun made itself ready for a new day. Treas wondered how the sun could rise at all after such a day of darkness. He had wanted to get as far away from Desti as possible, and it had seemed appropriate to come here - to this place of death. While Nity was alive there was a chance that he could change. Nity could do the impossible by just saying it; so it only stood to reason that if Treas hung about him long enough that he would change. Change into a man worthy of Desti - but now all those hopes were dashed; Nity was dead.

Looking up he saw a stone bench under a tree with spreading branches. He sat down, and looked about; there were flowers all about opening up to the promised warmth of the sun. But Treas did not see any of this beauty; instead he looked up into the branches of the tree. Cern had found life too much to handle too - he had hung himself…

Before the thought had formed in his mind a voice interrupted, "Beautiful morning."

Treas looked down at a Garatin man who was walking towards him; Treas looked around as though he had not noticed that it was even morning!

"I suppose so," he mumbled.

The man came to stand in front of him, "May I?" he gestured to the bench.

Treas wished that the man would just go away but he nodded none the less. The man groaned as he lowered himself down onto the bench beside him, Treas looked at him; he was in rough shape! The man's face was covered in bruises and cuts which made it difficult to tell the man's age. 'It must have been some fight', Treas thought to himself. They sat in silence, and Treas forgot that the man was even there; the longer he sat the more miserable he got.

"You look like you've had a rough life!" the stranger commented.

"Yeah, a rough life!" Treas laughed - but there was no joy.

"Why don't you tell me?" the man said in a fatherly fashion.

"It's sort of a long story."

"The sun is yet rising, and the day is young, I have no plans. What about your family?" he prompted.

"There is none," Treas began bitterly; "I grew up alone on the streets, earning what I could, and stealing what I had too."

"Living alone… it does things to people," the man said softly.

"Then three years ago I was taken as a slave to the silver mines of the Dinco Mountains, I was there for two and a half years… I should have died there," he said, sounding almost as though he wished it was so. He was silent as though lost once again in the mines. "Then two men came out of nowhere and bought me - and then gave me my freedom! I owe Est my life…" he whispered the last part to himself. "They brought me back to Garason and introduced me to-to… a man who could do the impossible!"

"Who was this man?"

"His Namesake was Eternity."

"Oh yes, I've heard of him," the man said softly.

"He was going to set free the entire country - and drive away the Tarvens forever! He introduced a new way of living… I wanted to be like him. But no matter how hard I tried, I could not break the habits I had picked up in the mines; I was heartless and- and cold, I didn't care about anyone."

The man only nodded.

Treas went on, no longer thinking about what he was saying, "And then I found Desti again, if there is anyone that I want to care about, it's her."

"You love this maiden?" the man asked knowingly.

Treas nodded, "A gentler soul you will never find," he said softly. "But it would never work - I could never make her happy, so I let her go. Then Nity died- needlessly - and I'll never be able to change, I'll always repeat my past." Treas finished and realized just how hopeless his life was.

The man spoke up, "What if this man did NOT die in vain - what if Nity's death was not as pointless as you think?" Treas could have laughed in his face!

"He's dead. And he didn't even die for his cause - he died as a criminal! Nothing was accomplished by it!"

"Can you be so sure of that?"

Treas frowned; what was this man trying to say?

"Yes, Nity died the death of a criminal - perhaps the death… that you deserved."

"What do you mean?"

"Nity could do the impossible - could he not?"

Treas didn't even nod.

"You have done things that deserve punishment - have you not? Nity took your punishment and your past with him," he stated.

Treasure shook his head, "I carry my past and my mistakes as surely as I carry the scars on my own back," he said darkly.

"What scars?" the man asked simply.

Treas would have liked to believe that Nity had done this impossible thing - but he saw no way for it to be true, so he pulled his tunic back over his shoulder to show him the scars.

"These," he said flatly.

"Where?"

This time Treas almost did laugh in his face! How could anyone miss the scars made by a whip?! He glanced over his shoulder - and paused; they weren't there! No...no- the light was playing tricks with his eyes! He reached for his right shoulder and the man smiled and said. "It's not there anymore."

Treas froze, "What's not there?" he asked with a guarded tone.

"The brand; it's gone too."

Treas narrowed his eyes; how did this stranger know of the brand? He almost ripped his sleeve as he looked for the scorching brand of slavery; but it was there no longer... He placed his cold hand on his smooth, unmarred shoulder in disbelief; he then looked back at the man with wide eyes.

"Nity has taken your place in his death, in Eloi's eyes - you are blameless, Treasure."

Treas jumped! "How do you know my Namesake!?" he whispered in astonishment.

The man got up and stood before Treas; he laid a hand on his shoulder and looked at him like a father might at his son - or the way someone would at his dear friend. Treas felt like this man could see right through him- as if he knew him inside out.

"Go-" the man said, "And become what your Namesake implies, become who Eloi meant you to be. Nity has made a way for you - this is something that you cannot earn, nor can you steal, it is a gift - accept it Treasure."

"Who are you?" Treas breathed.

The man smiled and then turned and began to walk away. As he went, the sun rose up before him and outlined him in crimson flame. Treas had to look away it was so brilliant. When he looked back, the man had disappeared behind the hills. Treas stood with no doubt in his mind as to who this man was; even if it was... impossible.

A whole new world opened up before him- free of guilt, lies, and scars. A treasure had been truly found. He felt his heart take flight.

*   *   *

Desti looked up as Will neighed; he was grazing just beyond the tree where Desti sat. It was late afternoon, and a gorgeous day; a huge contrast to how everyone was feeling. The five of them had done nothing but sit around the fire all day long. Desti still could not find it in her to tell her father what had happened the night before - she did not want to start crying again.

Wilder and Rage had tried to discuss what they were to do now, but they could not seem to focus, everything seemed to be going wrong; Nity was dead, Treas was gone, and neither Rage or Wilder could ever show their faces' in Garason again!

The wind touched Desti as she looked up, and there, approaching them was a man. Her father and Rage tensed and reached for their weapons as he neared.

"May I join you?" he gestured to the fire.

He was a Garatin and was most certainly alone, Rage and Wilder relaxed. A few minutes later and the stranger was sitting by the fire along with Wilder, Rage and Loy. While Desti and Mise sat together leaning against the great tree trunk; they all sipped from tin cups, tea that Loy had only just made (thanks to Wilder's traveling gear). The man introduced himself as 'Favour' and said that he had 'business' in the Corfin Forest. Both Rage and Wilder had found that odd but they said nothing.

"Have you heard the news?" Fav asked conversationally.

Rage stood and poured himself more tea, "Yes we know of Eternity's death," he said hoping that this man would just leave it be.

"That's old news!" Fav said with a loud laugh, "No, I'm talking about what happened this morning in Garason."

Everyone looked at him wearily.

"There are rumors that the companions of Nity stole his body in the night and are claiming that he's alive! As if a dead man could live!" he laughed. Desti and Mise looked up at each other ironically; no one joined in with Fav's laughter. He looked around at everyone still chuckling stopping when he realized that no one found it funny.

"Well it's just nonsense really," he ended with false dignity.

Around him, the others all exchanged looks; could they believe this strange news? Fav left soon thereafter (realizing that he really wasn't welcome), and left the others to their thoughts. The rest of the day past without incident, even Sid didn't come to pick up his horse and cart. The evening twilight was just settling in as Mise stood by the cart. She was watching someone approach from the city, it was a single figure and on foot. She knew that she should be afraid but somehow - she wasn't. Instead she watched as though enchanted; something was familiar about this man - perhaps it was the way he walked...

"Desti?" she called softly.

Desti came up beside her, "What is-" she cut her self off sharply, as she saw the man approaching. She gathered up her skirts and broke out running towards him, the long grass brushed past as she ran and copper hair few behind her.

"Treas!" she squealed out in delight!

He caught her up in his arms and swung her around, and then he held her tight.

"You came back!" she whispered.

"Eloi forgive me if I ever leave you again," he then bent his head and kissed her gently.

"Desti can you forgive me for what I didn't tell you for so long? It's why I made you leave without me - I knew that I could never make you happy - can you forgive me?" he asked anxiously.

She smiled, "Treas I knew that you were a thief even before you told me."

"You did? When?"

"Probably the first day we met," she almost laughed, "I had hoped that you would tell me yourself - and now you have. But tell me what made you come back?"

"I don't know if you will believe what happened this morning. Desti, Nity took my punishment for me, my past is now forgotten."

She frowned, "I don't understand - how do you know this?"

He hesitated only a moment, "Nity himself told me - I spoke with him!"

Her frown deepened, "We heard that his body had gone missing-"

"Desti, he is alive! I spoke with him! There is no way that I could doubt it! He said that my past mistakes are forgotten, because he paid for them."

She shook her head, "That's impossible," she stated.

"Yes…" he admitted, "It is."

Her eyes widened as she grasped what he meant, just then they heard Mise shouting behind them at the camp.

"It's Treas! Mother, father! It's Treas!"

Putting aside what Treas had said for the moment, Desti pulled Treas back to the camp, and what a reunion it was! Mise danced around as Rage and Wilder pounded Treas on the back and Loy clasped her hands together happily.

Desti could not have been happier, even if her mind was still spinning with the news that Treas had brought. Then Treas shared the wondrous news of Nity with everyone else, but even after showing them where his brand once was and assuring them several times over, he could still see that they had doubts - and he didn't blame them! Would he have believed it himself? It was quite some time before they all calmed down again, and it was an hour later when Treas finally worked up his nerve to ask Wilder. He went up to him while he was seeing to the horses.

"Sir?" Treas began, trying to be brave. Wilder turned to him with an up-raised brow and a stern face.

"I know it's forward of me – but - but I wish to travel with you and your companions-" Wilder's stern face broke and he gave Treas a hearty pat on the back, Treas stared at him in bewilderment as he said.

"I wouldn't have it any other way! Besides Desti's been miserable without you." Treas was thankful that the darkness hid his red face.

Wilder then led him with his arm around his shoulders back to fire where everyone else was sitting. He then announced that Treas would be returning with them to the Byla. "And I say it again Rage-" he continued, "the three of you should come with us- if only till you decide where you will go."

Rage had been unsure all that day of what it was they should do. Loyal who was gracefully sitting with her skirts spread about her spoke up, "Yes Rage let's do that!" Rage looked at her surprised that she would speak on the matter. Loy blushed- though no one could see it in the firelight, she was feeling strangely brave. "I know it's not my place- but where else are we to go?"

Rage smiled faintly and said, "Very well then, we shall journey with you." Wilder smiled.

"Oh good!" Squealed Mise, "Now we shall all be together!" Everyone laughed in relief as they realized that everything would be just fine. Desti then handed out bowls of stew that Wilder had cooked up. There was some discussion, and it was decided that they would continue on their way to the Byla on the morrow-the sooner they left these lands the better. Before long they all lapsed into silence. One way or another, their thoughts all turned to the news of Nity; while Treas wondered if they would ever really believe him.

After a time Wilder became restless and began to poke at the fire. Loy decided to make up some more tea while Mise wandered over to where her things were.

"What's your father's horse's Namesake?" Treas asked Desti out of nothing else better to say.

"Hmm? Oh, it's Bulrushes, we call him Rush." Desti thought about how Treas was going to travel with them, he would have to go into Hirfly to buy a horse. Treas interrupted her thoughts. "I thought that he'd be named after a tree like Will."

She turned to him, "But Willow isn't his Namesake," she said.

He frowned, "Then what is?"

She giggled, "Pussy Willow!"

Treas looked over at Will and stared at him in disbelief, "I see why you call him Will," he said with a grin. But their laughter was cut short when Mise came up to the ring of firelight and exclaimed.

"Look!" everyone did; she held out her tiny trunk that held her dead Cres`aren - but beside the dried up flower was a new shoot that was already three inches high! With eyes sparkling Mise looked up at everyone. "It died when Nity did - and now it's growing again; Nity must live!" she said it with unshakable certainty.

As Rage, Loy, Wilder and Desti saw for themselves, any and all doubt fled from their hearts; Nity lived!

Chapter 29

Free

The lonely cry of a Cokhawk could be heard as Ree made her way through the morning light. It was a little late for Cokhawks to still be hunting but Ree did not notice - so absorbed was she as she walked down the pine needle path that she remembered so well from her childhood. It had taken her a week to travel from Garason to the Cokhawk Forest - a week since Nity had set her free by his death - free from guilt, shame and the black silk - after three years, free from the stain!

Her eyes stung with tears even now as she thought of his last breath - but would her mother be able to forgive her the way Nity had?

Just then she turned a corner in the path and saw before her the little cottage of her childhood, and on her hands and knees in her garden; was Feren...

She looked older, and care-worn, why would that be? Ree wondered, what hardships could her mother have possibly gone through? Feren stood to her feet and wiped off her hands on her apron, then she looked up and her hand flew to her mouth as she saw Ree.

Ree froze on the pine needle littered path; what would her mother do? Ree was prepared to do anything to prove to her how she had changed in the past week - yes she had changed! More than anything she wanted to be loved - and to love once again - but what would her mother do?

Just then Feren called out in a broken cry, "Freedom!" She broke out into a run towards Ree with open arms; Ree felt her heart jump within her as she ran to her mother's embrace; for at last - she was truly Free.

to be continued...

Heart of Lead – Namesake Chronicles-Book 2

*   *   *

About the Author

Rachel Lang lives in Orillia, Ontario, Canada. *Heart of Stone* is her first book. Rachel also designs and sews unique animal themed handbags as well as fashion doll clothing. She enjoys painting with both acrylic and watercolor. She enjoys the many beautiful natural parks in Ontario as a camper and hiker.

Look for the author, Rachel Marie Lang, on the Facebook Page - "Namesake Chronicles".

www.ingramcontent.com/pod-product-compliance
Lightning Source LLC
Chambersburg PA
CBHW021235130626
46554CB00004B/1497